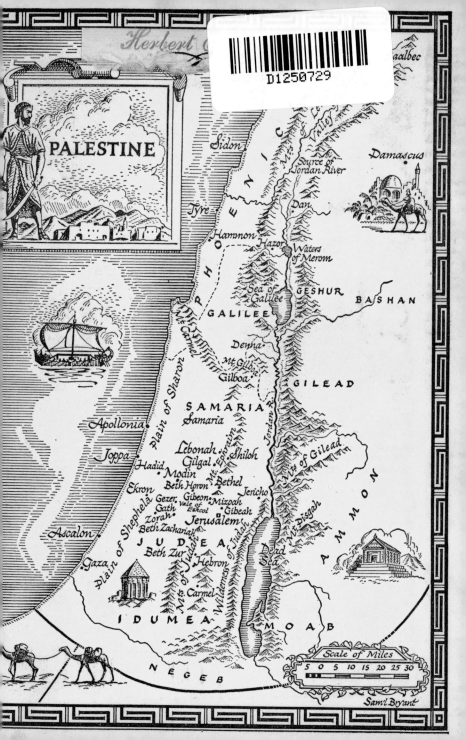

PALESTINE

Baalbec

Sidon

Damascus

Tyre

Hammon
Hazor
Waters
of Merom

Source of
Jordan River

Dan

PHOENICIA

Mts. of Lebanon Valley

Sea of
Galilee

GESHUR

BASHAN

GALILEE

Mt. Carmel

Plain of Sharon

Denba
Mt. Gilboa
Gilboa

GILEAD

SAMARIA
Samaria

Mts. of Gilead

Apollonia

Joppa

Lebonah
Gilgal
Shiloh

Hadid
Modin
Ekron   Beth Horon   Bethel
Gezer Gibeon   Jericho
Zorah Gath Vale of Mizpah
Beth Zachariah Eshcol Gibeah
Jerusalem

Mt. of Ephraim

Jordan R.

Ammon

Mt. Pisgah

Ascalon

Shephelah

JUDEA
Beth Zur
Hebron

Gaza

Plain of Judah

Mts. of Judah

Wilderness of Judah

Dead
Sea

IDUMEA

MOAB

Carmel

NEGEB

Scale of Miles
5 0 5 10 15 20 25 30

Sam'l Bryant

BY HOWARD FAST

Novels

PLACE IN THE CITY

CONCEIVED IN LIBERTY

THE LAST FRONTIER

THE UNVANQUISHED

CITIZEN TOM PAINE

FREEDOM ROAD

THE AMERICAN

THE CHILDREN

CLARKTON

MY GLORIOUS BROTHERS

Stories

PATRICK HENRY AND THE FRIGATE'S KEEL

Biography

HAYM SALOMON

GOETHALS AND THE PANAMA CANAL

History

ROMANCE OF A PEOPLE
(A History of the Jews)

Juvenile

TALL HUNTER

Edited by Howard Fast

THE SELECTED WORKS OF TOM PAINE

THE SELECTED SHORT STORIES OF THEODORE DREISER

MY GLORIOUS BROTHERS

Mʏ Gʟᴏʀɪᴏᴜs Bʀᴏᴛʜᴇʀs

HOWARD FAST

Little, Brown and Company · Boston · 1948

*Published simultaneously
in Canada by McClelland and Stewart Limited*

PRINTED IN THE UNITED STATES OF AMERICA

To all men, Jew and Gentile,
who have laid down their lives
in that ancient and unfinished struggle
for human freedom and dignity

A little more than a century and a half before the birth of Christ, a handful of Jewish farmers in Palestine rose against the Syrian-Greek conquerors who had occupied their land.

For three decades, they carried on a struggle which, in terms of resistance and liberation, has almost no parallel in human history. In a sense, it was the first modern struggle for freedom, and it laid a pattern for many movements that followed.

This tale, which is still celebrated by Jews all over the world as *Chanaka,* or the Feast of the Lights, I have tried to retell here, considering that in these troubled and bitter times there is both a need for and a value in recalling the ancient consistency of mankind.

Whatever is good in the telling, I owe to the people who march through these pages, those wonderful people of old who, out of their religion, their way of life, and their love for their land, forged that splendid maxim — that resistance to tyranny is the truest obedience to God.

A PROLOGUE

Wherein I, Simon, Sit in Judgment

O<small>N AN AFTERNOON IN THE MONTH OF</small> Nisan, which is the sweetest time of the year, the bells were sounded; and I, Simon, the least, the most unworthy of all my glorious brothers, sat down for judgment. I shall tell you of that, even as I write it here, for judgment is compounded out of justice — or so they say — and I can still hear the voice of my father, the Adon, saying:

"On three things life rests: on right, which is set forth in the Law; on truth, which is set forth in the world; and on the love of one man for another, which is set forth in your heart."

But that is a long time ago, as men think, and my father, the old man, the Adon, is dead, and all my glorious brothers are dead too, and what was plain then is far from plain now. So if I write down here all that took place — or almost all, since a man's thoughts are loosely woven and not like the hide of a beast — it is for myself to know and to understand, if there is any such thing as knowing and understanding. Judas knew, but Judas never sat, as I sit, over the whole land with the land in peace, the roads open north and south and east and west, the land tilled for the harvest, the children playing in the fields and laughing as they play. Judas never saw the vines so heavy they could not support their load, the barley breaking out like pearls, the grain cribs cracking under their fullness; and Judas never heard the song of women in joy and no terror.

Nor did there ever come to Judas a legate from Rome, as he came to me this day, making the whole long journey, as he put it — and you can decide for yourself when a Roman speaks the truth or when he lies — for one reason: to speak with a man and to grasp his hand.

"And are there no men in Rome?" I said to him, after I had given him bread and wine and fruit, and seen that he was provided with a bath and a room to rest in.

"There are men in Rome," he smiled, the movement of his thin, shaven upper lip as deliberate as all his other movements, "but there are no Maccabees. So the Senate gave me a writ and ordered me to go to the land where the Maccabee rules and seek him out . . ." He hesitated here for long enough to count to five; the smile went away and his dark face became almost sullen. " . . . And give him my hand, which is Rome's hand, if he offers his."

"I don't rule," I said. "A Jew has no ruler, no king."

"Yet you are the Maccabee?"

"That's right."

"And you lead these people?"

"I judge them — now. When they have to be led, it may be that I will lead them and it may be that someone else will. That makes no difference. They'll find themselves a leader, as they found them before."

"Yet you *had* kings, as I recall," the Roman said meditatively.

"We had them, and they were like a poison to us. We destroyed them or they destroyed us. Whether the King is Jew or Greek or — "

"Or Roman," the legate said, that slow, deliberate smile returning.

"Or Roman."

The silence lasted after that, the Roman and I looking at each other, and I could guess something of what went on in his head. Finally, he said, with a great and deceptive calm:

"There was a man in Carthage who talked like that. You might say had all the characteristics of a — Jew. And Carthage is sown over with salt, so that even a blade of grass will not grow there again. There was a Greek — Well, Athens is a slave market, where we sell the slaves. And about thirty years ago, as you may recall, Antiochus invaded Egypt with his Macedonians. That was not a war that pleased the Senate, so they sent Popilius Laenas with a writ; not with troops, but with a simple expression of the Senate's displeasure. Antiochus asked for twenty-four hours to consider the matter, and Popilius answered that he could spare twenty-four minutes. I believe that in eighteen minutes Antiochus made up his mind."

"We are not Greeks and we are not Egyptians," I said to the Roman. "We are Jews. If you come in peace, you can have my hand in peace. Save your threats for a time when you come in war."

"You are the Maccabee," the Roman nodded, and smiled and took my hand, and in the afternoon of the same day he sat and listened and watched while I judged for the people.

It was, as I said, in the month of Nisan — in the first part of that month, when the whole land is covered over with flowers and when the scent of the blossoms can be felt on the Mediterranean ten and twenty miles from land. And on the hills and the mountain sides, the evergreens shake loose from the frost and snow, washing themselves with their own fragrant oil; the cedars are tipped with bright green, and the delicate birch trees dance like girls at a wedding. The bees come to make their honey, and the people sing a song of gladness, for in the whole world — and how many travelers have not said it? — there is no land like ours, no land so sweet, no land so fragrant, no land so good for giving.

I, Simon, sat in my chamber; and it was told that "The Maccabee sits and judges." And among those who came was a tanner with a Bedouin slave, a boy of fourteen or fifteen years. At the side of the room, the Roman sat, dark and short and heavily built, his bare legs covered with black hair, his broad face jutting to a great beaked nose, a strange, foreign figure among our own people, who are long of limb and red or chestnut-brown in their beards. Like the Gentiles around us, the Roman wore no beard; clean-shaven, he sat with his knees crossed, his chin on his fist, watching and listening, always on his lips a cynical twist of a smile, the long arm of *pax Romana* touching for an instant the hard fist of *pax Judea* and finding it crude and uncivilized, and wondering, perhaps, when the legions would taste it and soften it. . . . But I wander. I said there was a Bedouin boy, and his master was a tanner of goatskin. A hard man, his master, as tanners are, with the hemlock stain beat into him and the cool look of a partisan in his eye.

He said to me, "Peace, Simon, and what will you do with a desert rat who runs away?"

Glancing at the Roman, I became conscious suddenly that I was a Jew and that this tanner was a Jew, and I was Simon who was Maccabee and Ethnarch of all the people; and the tanner was a citizen and no more, and that in all the world only a Jew could understand why he spoke to me as he did.

"Why does he run away?" I asked, looking at the brown boy, who was slim and lovely as a gazelle, dark and clean-limbed, the way the Bedouins are, with a great shock of black hair and a smooth skin, unmarred by beard or razor.

"Five times," the tanner said. "Twice I brought him back myself. Twice he was picked up by caravans, and I paid hard cash for him, and now my son found him in the desert, half dead. He had two years to serve, and now with what he cost me, he has nine years to serve."

"And that's justice in full," I said. "What do you want of me?"

"I want to brand him, Simon."

The Roman was smiling now and the boy was trembling with fear. I called him forward and he knelt. "Stand up!" the tanner said harshly. "Is that what I've taught you — to kneel to a man because he's the Maccabee? Kneel to God, if you must kneel!"

"Why do you run away?" I asked the boy.

"To go home," the boy whimpered.

"And where is his home?" the tanner demanded. "He was ten years old when I bought him from an Egyptian. Has a Bedouin a home? They blow like tumbling weed, here today, there tomorrow. I teach him a trade and make him ready for freedom; and he'd give it away for a lousy goatskin tent!"

"Why do you want to go home?" I asked the boy, old now, the years scraping through me like a comb, wondering, as I had wondered so often of late, why it should be I alone of all my glorious brothers.

"To be free," he whimpered. "To be free . . ."

I sat silent then, looking at the press of people across the back of the chamber, all of them waiting to be judged, and who was I to judge and with what and for what?

"He'll go free in two years," I said, "even as the law says; and don't brand him."

"And the money I paid the caravan?"

"Charge it to your own freedom, tanner."

"Simon ben Mattathias — " he began, his face blackening with rage.

But I broke in on him, roaring, "I've judged you, tanner! How long ago was it that *you* slept in a lousy goatskin tent? How short is your memory? Is freedom something you can put on or take off, like a coat?"

"The Law says — "

"I know what the Law says, tanner! The Law says that if you beat him, he can claim his freedom! Well, he can claim it from me here — do you understand me, boy?"

So it was that I judged and lost my temper, an old man, roaring at ghosts, I, Simon; and that evening, when the rites at the Temple were finished, I wrapped myself in my shawl and said the prayer for the dead and felt the tears in my eyes, the senile, lonely tears of an old and tired Jew. And then I went to my dinner table, where the Roman legate sat — he, the dealer in nations, the master of twenty tongues, the same cynical smile on his thin and knowing lips.

"You found it amusing?" I asked him.

"Life is amusing, Simon the Maccabee."

"For a Roman."

"For a Roman — and it may be that someday we will teach that to the Jews."

"The Greeks tried to teach us how amusing life can be, and before them the Persians; and before them the Chaldeans, and before them the Assyrians; and there was a time, as our legends have it, that the Egyptians taught us their own peculiar type of amusement."

"And you remain a somber man! It's hard to like a Jew — but a Roman can admire certain qualities."

"We don't ask for liking, only respect."

"Even as Rome does. Let me ask you, Simon, do all your slaves go free?"

"After seven years."

"With no payment to the owner?"

"With no payment."

"So you impoverish yourselves. And is it true that on the seventh day you do no work and on the seventh year your fields lie fallow?"

"That is our law."

"And is it true," the Roman went on, "that in your Temple, here on the hill, there is no God that a man can see?"

"That's true."

"And what do you worship?"

The Roman was not smiling now; he was asking a question which I could not answer, not so he would understand — any more than he could comprehend why we rest on the seventh day or why the fields lie fallow or why — of all the people in all the world — we must free all men, Jew or Gentile, in seven years. Yet, even the thought of that, inside of me, was hollow, and all I could see were the staring eyes of the Bedouin boy who wanted to go home to a lousy goatskin tent on the hot, drifting desert sand. . . .

"What do you worship, Simon Maccabeus, what do you respect?" the Roman prodded. "In all the world, are there no other men of worth than the Jews?"

"All men are of worth," I murmured. "Of equal worth."

"Yet you are the chosen people, as you put it so frequently. What are you chosen for, Simon? And if men are of equal worth, how can you be chosen? Or did no Jew ever ask that before, Simon?"

I shook my head somberly.

"Do I trouble you, Simon Maccabeus?" the Roman said. "You are too proud, I think. We are a proud people, too, but we do not scorn what others make. We do not scorn what others are or do. You hate slavery, Simon, yet your people hold slaves. How then? Why so ready to say good or bad, as if this tiny land were the center of the whole universe?"

I had no answers. He was the dealer in nations, and I was Ethnarch of a tiny land and a small people; and like a heavy sickness inside of me came the realization that I moved on currents beyond me, beyond my knowing.

So I sit tonight, writing down this account of my glorious brothers, writing it for all men to read, Jew or Roman or Greek or Persian — writing it in the hope that out of my own memory will come some understanding of whence we came and where we go, we who are Jews and like no other people, we who meet all the adversity and hurt of life with that strange and holy phrase:

"Once we were slaves in the land of Egypt."

PART ONE

The Old Man, the Adon

E VEN OF THE OLD MAN, MY FATHER, THE
Adon, I cannot tell you without speaking first of Judas. I
was three years older than Judas, but in all my memories
of my childhood, there is no memory without Judas. My
older brother, John, was gentle and sweet and good, but
not somebody to lead the four hellions that we were; so
out of the five of us, the old man held me, Simon, responsible
and always to the accounting. It was never a case with me
of "Am I my brother's keeper?" For I was that; and to me,
always, the bill was presented. Yet it was Judas who did
the leading, and like the others, I turned to him.

How shall I describe Judas, who was the first of us they
called the Maccabee, there coming to him what was his by
right, and to us only what fell from his shoulders? Yet the
curious part of it is that other things are more clear, it is so
long now: Eleazar, built like a great bull, with his big
grinning face; Jonathan, small, wiry, girl-like in his grace,
yet as brilliant and as calculating as Eleazar was honest and
simple — even Ruth as she was then, so tall and lissom, with
her high cheekbones and her great shock of red hair, yet
not red as I put it here, but lit through with sunlight. Judas
is not like that; there is no memory without Judas and no
memory completely of him, and about that I once talked

to an old, old man, a Rabbi who knew many things, but not his own age, which was lost somewhere in the past; and he said that people, the human flesh and blood, are compounded out of evil, so that when the good shines through it is like a blinding flash of God Himself; about that, I don't know and would have something to say before I agreed with him, but certainly it would be easier to paint Judas for you if Judas were like other men.

Judas was not like other men. Tall and straight, taller than any of us except myself, he had that tawny hair and beard that crops up so often in our line, which is the Kohanim — though more of us are red, as I am and as Ruth was; yet there were other Kohanim who were tall and blue-eyed and as straight and as handsome as Judas was; but other men are compounded out of weakness, even as the Rabbi said, and it is the weakness that makes a man knowable, as you will see.

Then we lived at Modin, a little village on the road from the city to the sea, not on the main road, which runs from south to north and is older than the memory of man, but on one of those little cart tracks that twists down through the hills, out of the wind-bent cedar and hemlock, across the valley, and back into the broad belt of forest that grows along the seashore. The village was a day's walk from the city, and all told some four hundred souls lived there — in the low 'dobe houses. Nothing unusual about Modin; there are a thousand villages like it, up and down the land, some larger, some smaller, but all of them pretty much the same.

We are a village people, except for this city where I sit and write; and in that, as in a hundred things more, we are different from all other folk. For among other people in other lands, there are two stages and two stages only, master and slave. The masters, with those slaves they need to serve them, live in walled cities; the slaves, in mud and wattled huts, scarcely more noticeable than anthills. When the masters make war, they hire great armies of mercenaries, and then it may or may not be that the slaves in the mud huts in the countryside will have new masters; it makes little difference, for outside of the cities men are like beasts and less than beasts, half naked, scratching at the earth so that the masters may be fed, neither reading nor writing, not dreaming and not hoping, dying and giving birth. . . . I say this not with pride because we are different, because we alone of all people do not live in walled cities; not with pride — how could I have pride and say the benediction, "We were slaves in Egypt"? Not with pride, but to make you who read and are not Jews understand how it is with us who are Jews — and even then there is so much I cannot explain!

I can only tell the tale of my glorious brothers and hope that something will come out of the telling. I can tell you that in Modin, then, there were two lines of 'dobe houses, and the street ran between them, from the house at one end of Ruben, the smith — though precious little iron to work came his way — to the house of Melek, the Mohel, the father of nine children which was at the other end. And in between were twenty odd houses on either side of the street, all sunny and old and venerable in the wintertime, but in spring and summer covered over with a wonder of honeysuckle and roses, with hot bread steaming on the sills and fresh-made cheeses hanging by the doors, and then, in the fall, the houses were festooned with garlands of dried fruits, like maidens in necklaces going to dance. The streets were full of chickens and goats and children, too —

but that changed, as you will see — and the nursing mothers would sit on the doorsteps, gossiping, while their bread cooled and while their men were out in the fields.

We were farmers in Modin, as we are farmers in a thousand other villages up and down the land, and our village lay like a nugget in the center of our vineyards, our wheat fields, our fig trees, and our barley patches.

In all the world there is no other land as rich as ours, but in all the world there are no other people who till their fields as free men. Whereupon, it is not strange that, talking of many things in Modin, we talked mostly of freedom.

My father was Mattathias ben John ben Simon, the Adon; always he had been the Adon. In some villages, one man is the Adon one year, and the next year another. But as long as people cared to recall, my father had been Adon. Even when he spent much of the year at the city, serving the Temple — for as I said we are Kohanim, out of the tribe of Levi and the blood of Aaron — he was still Adon at Modin.

We knew that. He was our father, but he was the Adon; and when our mother died, when I was twelve years old, he became less our father and more and more the Adon. It was not long after that, I remember, that he made one of his journeys to the Temple, taking the five of us with him for the first time. I have no memory of the Temple or of the city or of the city people before that; yet somehow I remember every detail of that trip — yes, and of the last trip the six of us made to the Temple some years later.

He woke us while it was yet dark, before the dawn, rooting us out of our pallets while we whimpered and protested and begged for more sleep — a tall, unsmiling, somber-eyed man, his red beard shot through with gray and here and there a streak of pure white, his arms frightening in their massive strength. He was fully dressed, in his long white trousers, his white waistcoat and his beautiful pale blue jacket, belted in with a silk girdle, his wide sleeves folded back. His great shock of hair fell behind almost to his waist, and his beard, uncropped, swept across his bosom like a splendid fan. Never in my life have I known or seen a man like my father, Mattathias; my earliest pictures of God substituted him. Mattathias was Adon, God was Adonai; I grouped them together; and sometimes, may He forgive me, I still do.

Sleepy, excited and terrified with the prospect of our trip, we crawled into our clothes, went out into the cold to wash, came back and gulped the hot gruel John had prepared, combed our hair, wrapped ourselves in our long, striped woolen cloaks even as the Adon did with his, five stunted figures striped in black and one giant, and followed him out. The village was just waking when the Adon marched majestically by, and one by one we followed him, John first, then I, Simon; then Judas, then Eleazar, and finally the small, already gasping figure of Jonathan — only eight years old.

And that way, for thirteen long, cruel, bitter miles, up hill and down dale, I and my brothers kept pace with the Adon to the gates of the holy city, the one city we call our own — Jerusalem.

To a Jew, there is a time when he first sees Jerusalem — and how shall I explain that? Other peoples live in cities and look down on the countryside, but from the country-side we look at our city. Then, even then, you understand, we were a conquered people — not conquered the way we were later, not on the basis that Jew and all that Jew means must be wiped from the face of the earth forever, but under the heel of the Macedonian, subject and abject, allowed to live in peace as long as we did not mar the peace. They didn't want us for slaves; there is a saying among the Gentiles, "Take a Jew for a slave and he'll be your master yet," but they wanted our wealth, the glass we make in our furnaces on the shores of the Dead Sea, our Lebanon suède, soft as butter yet enduring, our cedarwood, so fragrant and red, our great cisterns of olive oil, our dyes, our paper and our parchment, our finely woven linen, and the endless crops, so fruitful that, even on the seventh year when all the land lies fallow, no one hungers. So they taxed us and milked us and robbed us, but left us, at least for the time being, an illusion of tranquillity and liberty.

That in the villages. In the city it was something else, and that time, still a boy, walking with my brothers behind the Adon, I saw the first evidence of what men call Hellenization. The city was like a white jewel — or so it seems now, so long after — proud and high and lovely, its streets flushed by water from the great aqueducts that had brought water to our Temple from a time before any Roman dreamed of such a thing, its towers high and proud, its Temple the grand crown of the rest. But its people were a new thing, clean-shaven, bare-legged, as the Greeks go, many of them naked to the waist, watching us, sneering at us.

"Are they Jews?" I asked my father.

"They *were* Jews," he said, his voice ringing loud enough for anyone within a score of paces to hear. "They are scum today!"

And then we strode on, the Adon with the same, steady measured pace he had kept from Modin, but we children ready to drop with weariness, climbing higher and higher, past the lovely white buildings of the city — past the Greek stadium where naked Jews threw the discus and ran races; past the cafés, the restaurants, the hasheesh houses; through the exciting, bewildering turmoil of painted women with one breast hanging bare, Bedouin merchants, pimps and prostitutes, desert Arabs, Greeks, Syrians, Egyptians, Phoenicians; and everywhere, of course, the arrogant, swaggering mercenaries, the Macedonian troops — all colors, all races, these mercenaries, united only by the one and simple fact that their business was murder, for which they were paid and armored and fed.

To us children, it was one gorgeous tapestry; only later the parts sorted out. To us, there was only one recognizable factor, the mercenaries. Those we knew and understood. The rest was the bewildering complex of what had happened, over a generation, to Jews who wanted to be Greeks and who turned their sacred city into a whorehouse.

And finally, climbing on and on, we came to the Temple, and there we paused while the Adon said the blessings. Levites in white robes, bearded as the Adon was bearded, bowed to him and drew back the mighty wooden doors.

"And thou shalt love the Lord thy God," the Adon said, in his deep, ringing voice; "for we were slaves in Egypt, and He brought us out of slavery to build a Temple to His everlasting glory."

It is not of childhood that I desire to tell you, dipping back as I do into the past, here and there, almost aimlessly, so that I may have enough eventually for me to understand — and perhaps you too — why a Jew is a Jew, blessed or cursed, as you look at it, but a Jew; not of childhood, which is forever without a sense of time or the passing of time, but of the brief manhood of my glorious brothers, so terribly brief. But the one fathers the other, as we say. I went

to the Temple as a child, and I went again and again —
and finally, the last time, as a man.

If there's a mark of manhood, it's the end of illusion.
Then the city was a whore, and no magic pile of white stone.
Then the Temple was a building and no more, and none
too well built at that. Then the Levites, in their white robes,
were dirty, cowardly scum and not the anointed messengers of God. You pay a price for manhood; you give up
a world and get another, and then you have to weigh what
it's worth — article by article, measure by measure.

It was only Ruth that remained untouched. What I felt
for her and about her when I was twelve I felt when I
was eighteen and when I was twenty-eight. I said we went
to the Temple again and again, and finally a last time, but
there were things that happened in between. We grew; we
changed; the juice ran in us; we killed a man, we boys; and
there was Ruth. She was the daughter of Moses ben Aaron
ben Simon, a small, plain hard-working Jew who lived next
door to us and who was a vintner, with nineteen rows
of vines on the hillside. But he was a philosopher of sorts, as
all vintners are; and in a way we are a nation of vintners,
the people of the *sorek*, as the Egyptians call us out of
their own, slave-infested ignorance, envying what they
have not. The *sorek* is a black grape as big as a plum, fleshy
and bursting with juice. In the spring, it gives us *tirosh*, in
the summer the heady *yayin*, and through the winter *shikar*,
the deep red brew that makes an old man young and a
foolish man wise. A Roman or a Greek will say "wine," but
what do they know of the precious Keruhim, liquid gold, or
Phrygia, as red as blood, or rose-colored Sharon, or *yayin*
Kushi, clear and sweet as water, or *aluntit* or *inomilin* or
roglit? There were thirty-two brews that Moses ben Aaron
made in our little village of Modin, in his two deep stone

cisterns, and when it was specially good, he would send
Ruth with a beaker for the Adon. She would stand there by
the table, her mouth open, her blue eyes anxious and
troubled as the Adon poured himself the first cupful.

We shared her anxiety, the five of us; we would stand
still and quiet, watching her and watching the Adon. Wine
is the second blood of Israel, as we say often enough, a
sacred drink whether you taste it at the *seder* or bathe in it,
as Lebel the weaver was wont to do. The Adon never spared
ceremony if ceremony was indicated.

"From your father, Moses ben Aaron ben Simon ben
Enoch?" He prided himself on having at least seven generations of everyone in Modin at his fingertips.

Ruth would nod; later, many years later, she told me
what terror and awe the Adon inspired in her.

"A new vintage?"

If it happened to be a blend or a spicing or a honey
mixture or a souring, Ruth would wince with shame and
regret.

"For the Adon's judgment and pleasure," she would usually say, forcing each word, casting furtive glances at the
door, but beautiful, how beautiful, with her red hair and
her wonderful coppery skin, pulling the heart out of me
and making me think and dream of the day when I would
defy the Adon and do her honor and her will.

Then the Adon would wash his crystal cup, which had
belonged to his grandfather and his grandfather's grandfather. He would pour a measure. He would scan it in the
light. He would say the blessing, ". . . *boray pri hagofin!*"
Then he would drain it down. Then he would render the
verdict.

"My felicitations to Moses ben Aaron ben Simon ben
Enoch ben Levi" — an extra generation if it pleased him

particularly. "A noble wine, a gracious wine. You may tell your father that the table of the blessed King David ben Jesse served no better." And then Ruth would flee.

But she was ours. She wept with our hurts. She suffered with our sorrows. When they overcame their fear of the Adon, she and her mother cooked for us and cleaned for us and sewed for us — even as other women in Modin did. But we are a people blessed with fruitfulness; only Moses ben Aaron was cursed with a single child and that a girl, so for Ruth's mother the five sons of Mattathias became a recompense. But on my part, it was no curse, not of that sort. I loved her, and I never loved another woman.

So we lived in the endlessness of our childhood under the iron grip, the iron hand, and the unbending dignity of the old man, the Adon, our father — until suddenly childhood ended and was no more. When we did wrong, we were punished, as no other children in the village were. And, believe me, the Adon knew how to punish. There was a time when Judas was nine years old — already possessed of that unbelievable beauty and dignity that stayed with him all his life, already so different from me, Simon, already adored when he walked through the village, already offered the choicest of tidbits, sweets, cakes — and that time he was playing with my father's crystal wineglass, which he dropped and smashed.

Only he and I were in the house when it happened; the Adon was out, plowing with John; Jonathan and Eleazar were somewhere else, I don't remember where — and on the hearthstone were the slivers of that wonderful and ancient glass, brought back from Babylon when our people returned from the exile there. Never will I forget the abysmal terror on the face Judas turned up to me.

"Simon — Simon," he said. "Simon, he'll kill me! Simon, what will I do — what will I do?"

"Stop crying!"

He couldn't stop crying; he wept as if his heart would break, and when the Adon came, I told him, calmly enough, that I had done it. Just once, the Adon struck me, and then for the first time I realized the mighty force in the arm of the old man, the blow hurling me across the room and against the wall. And Judas, who had to let it out of him somehow, told Ruth — who came to me as I lay in the sun in the courtyard behind the house, bent over me and kissed me and whispered, "Oh, good, good Simon ben Mattathias, oh, good and sweet Simon — " I don't know why I write of that, for Judas was a child and I was already a man, as we reckon manhood, although close enough to Judas in age; and in any case, our childhood was not made of such things, but of a slower and sweeter pace.

We lay on the hillsides, watching the goats and counting the fleecy clouds in the sky; we fished in the cold streams; we once hiked to the great trunk road that passed north to south, and lay there in the underbrush as twenty thousand Macedonian mercenaries marched by, a proud show in their shining armor, on their way to fight the Egyptians; and we crouched on overhanging cliffs and pelted them with stones as they slunk back, turned away by the quiet word of Rome. And once, for a whole morning, we five of us traveled westward until from a high rock we saw the endless, shining expanse of the sea, the blue and gentle Mediterranean, with one white sail to mar its fine surface. It was Jonathan who said then:

"I'll go that way, westward, someday — "

"How?"

"With a ship," he said.

"Have you ever heard of a Jewish ship?"

"The Phoenicians have ships," Jonathan said thoughtfully, "and so have the Greeks. We can take them."

Three of us laughed, but Judas didn't laugh. He stood there staring at the sea, the first fair shadow of a beard on his clean-cut face, something in his eyes that I had never seen there before.

Jonathan was smaller than the rest of us, even when he reached his full growth, wiry and fast as a gazelle. He ran down a wild pig once, threw it nimbly and cut its throat. Judas, in a rage, struck his arm a blow that paralyzed it, so that his knife fell to the ground. When Jonathan would have leaped at Judas, I caught them both and hurled them apart.

"He kills for the sake of killing!" Judas cried. "Even when the meat is unclean and no good to anyone."

"You don't strike your brother," I said slowly and deliberately.

But I tear these things out of a past that was like a golden time. We were five of us always together, the five sons of Mattathias the Adon, growing like pups first, then together working, building, playing, laughing, weeping sometimes, browning under the golden sun of the land.

And then a man was slain by our hand and it was over — that long sun-drenched childhood in the old, old land of Israel, the land of milk and honey, of vineyards and fig trees, of wheat fields and barley fields, the land where our plows turn up ever and again the bones of another Jew, the land of valleys where the topsoil has no bottom, and of terraced hillsides that make it a more wonderful garden than ever the famous hanging gardens of Babylon were. Our play was over, our running wild and thoughtless, our games in the village street, our hours lying in the sweet grass, our sullen times with Lebel the teacher, his growling, "Would you be like heathen, so that the holy word of God drummed on your ears, but you could never see it with your two eyes?" We were done with our wandering in the pine forests, our caves in the snow, our traps for the wild partridge.

We shed blood and it was over, that time that has no beginning, and the brief, glorious manhood of my brothers began. Yet that is what I set out to tell, to put down here, to make both a tale and an answer to the riddle of my people, so that even a Roman may understand us, who of all the world's folks live without walls to guard us, without mercenaries to fight for us, and with no God that man can lay eyes on.

There was a warden of all the hill country from Modin to Bethel to Jericho, and three hundred and twenty villages were his to bleed and suck and squeeze. His name was Pericles, and he had a little Greek in him as well as other things. Those are the worst Hellenes, those who have just a trace of it or none at all, for it becomes a passion with them to become more Greek than the Greeks. Along with other things, Pericles had a little Jew in him, and for that reason, to purge himself over and over, his hand was more heavy than it had to be — which was, indeed, heavy enough.

That was still before the time when they decided that ours would be a better land in a better world with no Jews at all, and Pericles's work was to squeeze us. From three hundred and twenty-one villages, his contract was to deliver to Antiochus Epiphanes — the King of Kings, as he liked to style himself — one hundred talents of silver a year. A lot of money from a tiny district of a tiny land, but as much as it was, Pericles was determined to make one talent for himself where he delivered two to the king. That took squeezing, and Pericles squeezed, and each of the four hundred mongrel mercenaries who worked for him squeezed on their own.

He was a huge, fat, powerful man, Pericles, the pink flesh hanging in folds from his round, clean-shaven face, and while he was not much of a man, he was a good deal of a woman. When Reuben ben Gad's four-year-old boy, Asher, was found in the cedar copse with half of his entrails torn out, justly or not word went around that Pericles did it; he did other things that we knew about, in any case, and there was a story Jonathan told that was not good to remember.

At this time too it was Jonathan whose scream we heard, Judas and I, climbing to the little valley where he pastured our goats.

We broke into a run, and a few minutes later reached the lip of the valley. The goats were milling around and in the center of them, Jonathan struggled in the grasp of Pericles. Two Syrian mercenaries grinned as they watched, sprawled out on the grass, their weapons thrown about carelessly.

It happened quickly then. Pericles let go of Jonathan as he saw us, took a step back, and then Judas, knife drawn, was on him. The Greek wore a brass breastplate, but Judas cut under it, two sharp blows, and I remember how astonished I was at the gush of red blood. The mercenaries seemed to move with amazing slowness; the first was not yet on his feet when I caught him in the jaw with a rock the size of his head. The second scrambled for his spear, tripped, clawed to his feet and began to run — and at that moment Eleazar appeared, took in the scene at a glance, and leaped at the mercenary. In ten paces Eleazar caught him, swung him into the air, one hand about his neck, one gouging the underedge of his breastplate, spun him, and then tossed him like a ball. Eleazar was only sixteen then, yet already taller and stronger than any man in Modin. The Syrian fell with a sickening thud, and picking up his spear, Eleazar stood over him. But it was finished. The other mercenary's head was crushed in, the gray brains oozing onto the ground, and Pericles lay still in a pool of blood.

There were three dead men, and we had slain them; our childhood was over and finished.

We found the Adon and my brother John terracing. This way, from time immemorial, the land came into being. We build a wall on a hillside and then fill it in with baskets of soil from the bottom lands. At one end we build a cistern and an apron for the rainfall, and out of a piece of land so wrought will come five crops a year. The old man and my brother John labored there in the sun, their long linen trousers rolled up to the knee and dirt-stained, their bare backs glistening sweat, the Adon with his heavy stone hammer which with a shrewd blow here or there shaped the rocks for the wall — straightening then, the hammer hanging from his gnarled arm as he watched us approach.

Jonathan still wept. Judas was white as a sheet, and Eleazar had become a boy again, a frightened boy who has slain his first man, the unforgivable and absolute sin of murder. I told the Adon what had happened. "You're sure they were dead?" he said quietly, rubbing the hammer in the heel of his palm, his great red beard glistening on his bare chest.

"They were dead."

"Jonathan ben Mattathias," he said, and Jonathan looked at him. "Dry your eyes," the Adon said. "Are you a girl that you anoint yourself this way? A dog is dead — is that reason to weep? Where are the bodies?"

"Where they fell," I said.

"You left them there! Simon, you fool — you fool!"

"A Kohan — " I only started to speak of the law that forbids a Kohan to touch the dead, but the Adon had already started off. We followed him to the little valley, and there, without another word, he swung Pericles onto his shoulders. We took the other two bodies and followed him back to where they had been terracing. With his own hands, the Adon stripped the Greek and the mercenaries of their armor and weapons.

"Go back and watch the goats," he told Jonathan. "Dry your eyes." Suddenly, he threw his arms around Jonathan and held him close, rocked him back and forth for a moment, and then kissed his brow. Jonathan began to cry again, and the Adon said, harsh suddenly:

"Never cry again — No more. No more."

Still we were unseen, and unseen we rolled the three bodies against the inner side of the new wall, covered them over with dirt and then worked all the rest of that day until the terrace was completed. When we threw in the last basketful of dirt, the Adon said:

"Sleep forever, sleep deep. May the Lord God forgive a Jew who shed blood and a Kohan who touched the dead; may he tear out of your heart the lust that brought you to our land — and may he cleanse the land of all the filth like you." And turning to us, "Say you Amen!"

"Amen," we repeated.

"Amen," the Adon said.

We put on our tunics. Jonathan came with the goats, and with him we walked back to Modin, Judas carrying the armor and weapons, all wrapped in leaves and grass.

That night, after dinner, we sat at the table with a single lamp burning, and the Adon spoke to us. With a deep, old-fashioned formality he spoke, addressing us each in turn, and giving us each four generations, as:

"To you, my sons, to you John ben Mattathias ben John ben Simon, to you Simon ben Mattathias ben John ben Simon, to you Judas ben Mattathias ben John ben Simon, to you Eleazar ben Mattathias ben John ben Simon, to you Jonathan ben Mattathias ben John ben Simon — to you my five sons who have borne me up in my sorrow and my loneliness, who have comforted me in my old age, who have felt the weight of my hand and the bite of my anger — to you I speak as a man among you, for there is no turning back for them who have broken God's commandment. We who were holy are holy no longer. It is said, thou shalt not kill, and we have slain. We have exacted the price of freedom, which is always counted in blood, even as Moses did and Joshua, and Gideon too. From here on, we will not ask for forgiveness, only for strength — for strength."

He stopped then, and suddenly his age was apparent, the wrinkles deep on his face, his pale gray eyes clouded over with sorrow, an old Jew who had desired only what other Jews desired, gentle and peaceful years into the soil where his fathers lay. From face to face, he looked, anxiously, uncertainly, and I wonder what he saw there — the long, bony, sad face of John, the eldest; my own plain, almost ugly features; Judas, tall and beautiful, clean brown skin running into a curling brown beard; Eleazar, broad-faced, childlike, good-natured, wanting only to do my bidding or Judas's or Jonathan's, all the strength of a Samson with even more simplicity — and Jonathan, so small in contrast with the rest of us, yet like a knife-edge, pent-up, restless, a boundless desire for some unknown abiding all through him; five sons, five brothers . . .

"Put your hands on mine!" he said suddenly, laying his

big, fleshless hands palms up on the table, and we laid our hands in his, leaning toward each other — and how will I forget that, my brothers' faces almost touching mine, their breath mingling with my breath? "Make a covenant with me," he went on, almost pleadingly. "Since Cain slew Abel, there has been hatred and jealousy and bitterness among brothers. Make a covenant with me that your hands will be one — and you shall lay down your lives for each other!"

"Amen — so be it," we whispered.

"So be it," the Adon said.

My brother John married. I remember because it was the last day of grace, the day before Apelles came to take over the wardenship left empty by the death of Pericles. He married a sweet and simple girl, Sarah, the daughter of Melek ben Aaron, who performed circumcisions and who raised the sweetest, largest figs in Modin. "A fruit of her father's tree," they said of Sarah — and the pride of Modin was such that eight of the twelve slaves in the village were given their freedom, well in advance of the sabbatical, when they could have claimed it. That day, Modin was packed with our kinfolk — from as far as Jericho, for when you come down to it, who is there in Judea who cannot claim kin with someone else? Forty lambs were slaughtered and set to cooking. *Zalah* filled the whole valley with its smell, and pots of that savory sauce, *merkahah*, bubbled on every hearth. A veritable flock of chickens were killed and plucked, stuffed with bread, meat, and three kinds of old wine, and set to roasting in the common oven. I call it to mind because it was the end of something, the end of a whole life. There was a horn of plenty, flowing with grapes and figs and apples, cucumbers, melons, cabbages, turnips. The fresh baked bread, round, golden loaves, like the discus the

Greeks throw, was stacked in pillars, then broken all through the day, dipped in savory olive oil, and then eaten. Four times during the day, the Levites danced, and the girls still unmarried played the reeds, singing, "When will I have a fair young man? When will I have a suitor bold?" And then, in the common meadow at the end of the village, they joined hands and danced the marriage dance, a circle of laughing, swirling girls, while the men stamped their feet and clapped their hands to time.

I found Ruth after the dance. I was two years younger than John, and I knew what I would tell her. I found her in the courtyard of her house, in the arms of Judas.

It seems I hunger to search for and seek out fault in Judas — whom no man ever found fault with; but the fault and the uncertainty and the confusion, fear, and terror were in me, not in Judas. I, Simon, long of arm, broad and ugly of face, balding already at twenty, slow of movement and almost as slow of thought — I, Simon, accepted and considered only how we laid our hands one on the other. Neither of them knew. Yet for all that — may God forgive me — I was filled with such hatred that I went out of Modin, away from the dancing and drinking and singing, walking for hours, even after night set in. I had the thought, and for that surely I will not be forgiven, that I could have slain my own flesh and blood — and at last, when half the night had passed away, I came back. Before the house of Mattathias, the old man, the Adon, stood, and he said to me,

"Where were you, Simon?"

"Walking."

"And when a Jew walks alone on a night like this, there's no peace in his heart."

"There's none in mine, Mattathias," I said bitterly, calling him by his name for the first time in my life. But he did not react. He stood there in the moonlight, the venerable and ancient bearded Jew, wrapped from head to foot in his white cloak, the black stripes making an awesome pattern as they fell first lengthwise from where his head was covered, and then girdling him round and round until finally the earth rooted him, beyond passion and beyond hatred.

"And so you're no longer a boy but a man to stand up to your father," he said.

"I don't know if I'm a man. I have my doubts."

"I have no doubts, Simon," he said.

I started to go past him into the house, but he stopped me with an arm that was like iron. "Don't go in there with hatred," he said quietly.

"What do you know about my hatred?"

"I know you, Simon. I saw you come into the world. I saw you suckled at your mother's breast. I know you — and I know the others."

"The others be damned!"

There was a long moment of silence; and then, in a voice that almost shook with grief, the Adon said, "And ask me now if you are your brother's keeper."

I couldn't speak. For a while I stood there helplessly, everything gone out of me and empty inside, and then the Adon clasped me in his arms. He held me for an instant, and then I went inside and left him standing there in the moonlight.

Much can be explained, and then nothing; for the more I tell in this tale of my glorious brothers, the less it seems I understand; and the only thing that remains unchanged, unmarred, unblurred, is the picture of the old man, the

Adon, my father, standing in the moonlight in our ancient, ancient land. I see him as I saw him then, this old man, this Jew, in his great shawl that covered him from head to foot, the singular among peoples and nations, only able to say in affirmation, "We were slaves in Egypt — and we will never forget that we were slaves in Egypt." So it must have been then, in the long ago, when our people, twelve tribes of them, sick with wandering and longing for rest, came out of the desert and saw the wooded hills and the fertile valleys of Palestine.

Pericles was dead, and they sent us Apelles. Pericles was a wolf; Apelles was a wolf and a pig in one. Pericles had a little Greek in him, and Apelles had none at all.

You must understand about Greeks — you who read this when I am dead, and my children, and their children too. This is not a people, this thing we call Greek, not a culture, not Athens — not a golden dream, lingering somewhere in our memory, of the glory that was once made by Greeks. In the old tales, they tell of a beautiful folk, far to the west, who found many things that were not known before. Who can grow up in Judea without handling this or that, a vase, a cloth, a tool — a way of speech too — and not know it was born out of Greeks? Such Greeks we never knew, only the bastard power-drunk lords of the Syrian Empire in the north, who made their own definition of what was Hellene and taught it to us through suffering. Thus they "Hellenized" us, not with beauty and wisdom, but with fear and terror and hate.

Apelles was the final result, the height and pride of Hellenization. He was part Syrian, part Phoenician, part Egyptian, and a few other things too. He came into Modin the day after my brother John's wedding, riding in a litter borne by twenty slaves. Forty mercenaries marched in front of the litter, and forty mercenaries marched behind it — you could see right there that he was taking no chances in sharing the fate of Pericles.

In the very center of the village, where our market booths are, the litter was set on the ground, and in so doing, one of the slaves twisted his foot and fell. Apelles hopped out of the litter and looked around him. He carried a little whip of woven silver wire and when he saw the slave crouched on the ground, nursing his twisted foot, he leaped at him and opened his back in two places; a small man, but active, Apelles was, fat the way a pig is fat, rolls of pink flesh from head to foot, not pretty, but exhibiting his nakedness for the world, wearing a dainty little skirt and a dainty little tunic, and pleading with the world to examine the little he had under the skirt.

By the time the litter was put down, almost all of Modin, men and women and children, had crowded out to see the new warden. There had been a blessed two weeks without Pericles, an absence unexplained but well regarded; yet the people knew it had to end sometime, as all good things do. We stood there and watched silently as he opened the slave's back.

In our tongue, the word for "slave" and "servant" is the same. No slave can be held for longer than seven years among us, and because that has been written into our law from time immemorial, the sabbatical of freedom to remind us everlastingly that we, ourselves, were slaves in Egypt, we have become almost a people without slaves — in a world where there are many slaves for every free man; where all society, where every city, rests on the backs of slaves, we alone have no slave markets — and it is forbidden to have a block for the sale of men or women. In our law, if a master strikes a slave, the slave can claim his freedom; among civilized people, it is different — and therefore we watched with interest this first manifestation of the character of the new warden.

His mercenaries pushed us back with their spears, and in the circle of space they made, Apelles strutted a bit and then struck an attitude. He drew in his chin, pushed out his stomach, and placed his feet wide, his hands clasped behind him. He licked his lips and then spoke — in lisping Aramaic with the high-pitched tones of a capon.

"What village is this?" he asked. "This is a foul place — what village is it?"

No one answered him, and he took out a lace handkerchief and passed it delicately under his nostrils. "Jews," he lisped. "I detest the smell of Jews, the look of them, the air of them — and the pride of them, filthy, bearded beasts. To make it plain, I repeat, I do not like Jews. And you — " pointing a fat forefinger at David, the twelve-year-old son of Moses ben Simon. "What is this place called?"

"Modin," the boy answered.

"Who is the Adon?" he snapped.

My father stepped forward and stood silently, wrapped in his striped cloak and his enormous dignity, his arms folded, his hawklike face utterly expressionless.

"Are you the Adon?" Apelles demanded querulously. "Hundreds of stinking villages and hundreds of head men — Adons, the lord of this and the lord of that!" His sarcasm almost whined. "What is your name? You do have a name, don't you?"

"My name is Mattathias ben John ben Simon," the Adon replied in his deep, ringing voice, deepening it even further to contrast the squeak of the capon.

"Three generations," Apelles nodded. "Was there ever a Jew, whether he be the dirtiest, meanest beggar or slave, who couldn't reel off three or six or twenty generations of his ancestry?"

"Unlike some folk," my father said softly, "we know who our fathers are." And Apelles stepped forward and slapped him full in the face.

The Adon didn't move, but a cry, almost of anguish, came out of our people, and Judas, standing beside me, lurched forward. I caught him and stopped him, and the leveled spears stopped the others. It was only the beginning of my acquaintance with Apelles, but already I was recognizing that sick and perverted lust for blood that made so many wardens turn so many Jewish villages into shambles.

"I don't like insolence and I don't like disobedience," Apelles said. "I am warden and my duty is to spread through and among your benighted people some understanding and some appreciation of that noble and free culture that has made the name of Greece synonymous with civilization. It is hardly likely that the West will ever understand the East, or the East the West, but for the sake of mankind in general, certain attempts must be made. Naturally, this costs money, and the money will be forthcoming. I don't want to be a hard master. I am a just man, and justice will be the rule. However, the representatives of the King must walk in safety; we cannot have it otherwise. Pericles did not walk into a cloud and vanish. Pericles was murdered, and that murder cannot go unavenged. Each village will have to share a degree of the responsibility. Thus will law and order be established throughout the land, and thus will peace and security prevail."

He paused, passed the handkerchief under his nose, and suddenly called out:

"Jason!"

The captain of the mercenaries, dirty and sweating under his brass armor, strutted up.

"Any one of them," Apelles lisped.

The captain of the mercenaries walked along the line of villagers. He stopped opposite Deborah, daughter of Lebel the schoolmaster. She was eight years old, a bright, lovely slip of a thing, alert and white-faced now, her dark hair plaited in two long braids down her back. In one quick, calculated motion, the captain of mercenaries drew his sword and thrust it into the child's throat, and with never a sound she fell in the spurting pool of her blood.

No one moved; only the anguished wail of the mother, the cry of the father — but no one moved. What Apelles wanted was only too apparent. Then a noise came from the people. Then Apelles climbed back into his litter, and the mercenaries, swords and spears ready, gathered around it. Then the slaves picked up the litter, and Apelles left Modin.

The screaming of Deborah's mother followed him, pitching itself higher and higher and higher.

It was strange to see Lebel in his house of mourning, rocking and lamenting where the body of his daughter was laid out, this little pinch-faced man who for so long had taught me the *aleph,* the *bes,* and the *gimel,* driving in his lessons with a rod — a rod that fell so often on Eleazar that he grinned with embarrassment if a morning went by without it — this little man bereft of all his dignity and power, twisted and mutilated with grief. In another room, his wife wept and the women wept with her, but Lebel sat among his sons, his clothes rent and torn, ashes streaking his face and beard, rocking and whimpering . . .

"The Adon will be here for *min'cha,*" I said.

"The Lord has abandoned me and abandoned Israel."

"We will hold services then."

"Will it bring back my daughter? Will he breathe life into her?"

"With the sundown, Lebel." What else could I say?

"My God has abandoned me . . ."

I went to the house of Mattathias, and he sat there at the big table of cedarwood which had been the center of our family's life for as long as I remembered, where the morning bread was eaten and the hot milk sipped at night, where the Passover was celebrated and the fast of Atonement broken; there he sat, his head in his hands, still mantled in his long striped cloak. Eleazar and Jonathan crouched by the hearth, but Judas paced back and forth, tearing bitter music out of himself.

"Here is Simon," the Adon said.

"And Simon knows!" Judas cried, whirling and facing me, stretching out his hands toward me. "Is there blood on my hands, or are they clean?"

I sat down, poured milk from the pitcher, and broke bread.

"But you held me!" Judas cried, standing over me. "When that dog struck my father, you held me! And when the girl — "

"Would it be any better if you were dead?"

"It's better to die fighting!"

"Yes," I agreed, eating out of ravenous hunger. "There were eighty of them, armed and in armor, and there are less than eighty men in Modin, and no spears and no swords — and no armor except what we took from the mercenaries. So it would have been short and sweet and the blood would have been enough to cover the village. We have knives and our bows and arrows — " I chewed and gulped milk, and the bitterness poured out. "And the bows and arrows are buried, because we, who were known not so long ago as the People of the Bow, pay with our lives if a bow is found among us."

"So we live on, this way," Judas said.

"I don't know. I'm Simon ben Mattathias, a peasant, a farmer; not a seer, not a prophet, not a Rabbi — I don't know."

His arms spread, his hands flat on the table, Judas stared at me. "Are you afraid?"

"I've been afraid — I was afraid today. I'll be afraid again."

"And someday," Judas said, slowly — and I began to realize that this nineteen-year-old brother of mine was something different from other men — very slowly, "I'll ask those who aren't afraid to follow me. And where will you be then?"

"Enough," the Adon said. "Must you always be at each other's throat? There is sorrow enough in our land. All of our hands are washed in blood. Go tonight to the house of Lebel, and beg his forgiveness and God's forgiveness, even as I will do."

I went on eating, and Judas paced back and forth. Then, suddenly, he stopped, faced the Adon, and said:

"I ask no man's forgiveness from here on!"

Time passes, and ours is a healing land under a healing sun. I found Judas, one day not long after, sprawled on the hillside with the goats, and he looked up at me and smiled. The smile I remember well, for the smile of Judas, my brother, was not something easily forgotten or easily resisted.

"Come sit with me, Simon, and be my brother," he said.

I sat down beside him. "I am your brother."

"I know — I know, and I hurt you and I don't know how. All my life, I hurt you, Simon. That's true, isn't it?"

"It's not true," I said, won already, his the way anyone he desired to be his became his.

"And yet when I myself was hurt and it had to be made better, when I wept and my tears had to be dried, when I was hungry and I wanted bread, it was not to the Adon I went, not to my mother who was dead, not to John — but to you, Simon, my brother."

I couldn't look at him; I didn't want to look at him, at those strong clean features that might have been cut from stone, at those wide, pure blue eyes.

"And when I was afraid, I came to you to hold me in your arms and quiet my fear."

"When will you and Ruth be married?" I asked.

"Sometime — how did you know, Simon? But you know everything, don't you? Sometime — when things are better."

"They won't be better."

"But they will, Simon, believe me."

Then we lay silently on the grass for a while, I staring at nothing, but Judas with his eyes fixed across the valley to the tangled passes that led down to the coastal plain.

"How do men fight?" he said suddenly.

"What?"

"How do men fight?"

"That's a strange question — "

"That's all I've asked myself," Judas mused. "Day in and day out, I've asked myself nothing else. How do men fight? Why don't you answer me, Simon? How do men fight?"

You had to answer him. Whether you were Judas's brother or his servant or his follower, you could not have the relationship with him that other men had with you. He took you into himself; he absorbed you; you found yourself hanging onto his words as if the words themselves were entities.

"How do men fight?" I repeated. "With weapons — with armies."

"With armies," Judas said. "And armies are mercenaries, always mercenaries. Men for hire — in all the world, mankind is divided into three groups." He stretched out on his back, arms spread, staring at the sky, at the blue Judean sky, where the thin, lacy clouds shred themselves back and forth, like new flax on a loom. "Three groups," he said softly: "the slaves, those who own the slaves, and the mercenaries, those who kill for hire, who murder for hire — for Greece, for Egypt, for Syria — or for that new master in the West, for Rome. You've heard that, Simon, for Rome; and Rome makes them citizens and pays them less. But it has always been that way, mercenaries — " He lay silent for a moment. "You remember, when we were children we watched the Syrian mercenaries marching south to attack Egypt? War among the *nokri*, always the same. A king hires ten or twenty or forty thousand mercenaries, and he marches against a city. If the king of that city can hire enough mercenaries, they meet on a plain somewhere and hack at each other until it is decided. Otherwise, they close the gates and a siege begins. There's profit in war, and nothing else. Only — Simon, has it ever occurred to you why we free our slaves after seven years?"

"It's the law," I said, "and it's always been that way. For we were ourselves slaves in Egypt — and how can you forget?"

"The Adon would answer me like that," Judas smiled. "Egypt was a long time ago. But consider — instead of three, there are four kinds of people on this earth, the slaves, those who own them, the mercenaries — and the Jews."

"We hold slaves," I said.

"And we free them — marry them, make them a part of us. Why is it that we don't have mercenaries?"

"I don't know," I said. "I never thought of it."

"Yet we don't. And when war comes, when the Syrian or the Greek or the Egyptian comes down on our land, we take our knives and our bows and go out to meet them, a rabble against their trained, armored murderers, against their faceless men who were born for war, bred for war — and live only for war. And they cut us to pieces, the way they would have cut us to pieces in Modin the other day."

"We can't have mercenaries," I said after a while. "If you hire mercenaries, you must make war; otherwise, where will the money come from to pay them? We fight only to defend our land. If we fight as the *nokri* fight, as the strangers fight, for gold and for slaves, then we will be like them."

"I could break Apelles in two," Judas mused. "I could squeeze him like a ripe melon. Never has he done a day's work, used a muscle. When he bathes, a slave lifts his parts — providing he has any — to dry beneath them. Yet he comes with eighty mercenaries, and the power of eighty thousand stand behind him."

"That's right."

"And he calls me a dirty Jew — and he slaps my father's face — and he cuts the throat of a little girl; and this he does in three hundred villages, and I remain silent."

"That's right."

"Until it's more than we can bear, and we go out like a rabble against them — and they slaughter us."

What could I say, but to stare at this brother of mine who saw it as I had never seen it?

"We don't keep slaves," Judas went on evenly, "because when you hold slaves, you must have mercenaries to hold them down, and you must have gold to pay your mercenaries — and you must always war, always, because there is never enough gold — until someone else is stronger, and then you must have the walls of a city to wrap around you. And we have none of those things, neither cities nor slaves nor gold nor mercenaries."

"We have none of those things," I agreed.

"Only our land. But there must be a way, a way to fight without being slaughtered, a way to turn our land into walls. There must be a way . . ."

Early one morning, I woke in the gray part of life, in that absolute pause between day and night which is, as the Rabbis tell us, a perpetual reminder of the time when there was only the void — unbroken, unseparated, neither day nor night nor month nor year. We slept, as always, in the big single room of our house, on the floor on our pallets, my brothers and I and the Adon, only five of us now that John had married. I rolled over on my side and saw the Adon standing before the window, a dark silhouette — and in his hand he held the sword of Pericles, which he must have taken from its hiding place under the roof beams during the night. As I watched, almost without a sound, he drew the sword from its scabbard and held it — not as a man holds a strange thing. Minutes went by, and he stood there, holding the bare sword, yet I felt neither fear nor apprehension, only a deep curiosity as to what lay in his mind, so old, so closely wedded already to the minds of all the old men, all the venerable of old Israel.

He hefted the sword, as if he was taking the weight of it, the feel and balance of it, so that he would remember when the time came. Then, still moving silently, he went to an alcove where we kept the big earthenware jugs of olive oil. He took off the cover of one of these jugs and placed the sword inside, in the oil, and then put the cover back. There it was safe and close to hand.

I rolled over and slept.

It was about two weeks after that, a little less perhaps, or a little more, that three women, half-naked, disheveled, their feet bleeding, staggered into Modin. One of them carried a dead baby at her bosom; one was young and one was very old — and they were the beginning of a stream of refugees that poured into Modin and into every other village in the neighborhood over a period of four or five days.

They all told the same short, tragic story. They were from Jerusalem; they were city people. Many of them had given up thinking of themselves as Jews. They were prepared to become Greek and more Greek. They were civilized people. They were cultured people. They had passed beyond the wearing of beards, of linen pants, of striped cloaks. They wore tunics, they went bare-legged. Many of them underwent painful operations to remove the signs of circumcision. Many of them spoke Greek and pretended to be ill at ease with the Hebrew or the Aramaic. Therefore, what happened was all the more terrible to them.

Antiochus Epiphanes, the King of Kings, who ruled all the land from Antioch, appointed a new general for Jerusalem. His name was Apollonius, and on a larger scale he was to Jerusalem what Apelles was to Modin. He came in with ten thousand mercenaries instead of eighty, and he was largely unappreciative of the culture of the New Jew. In any case, on the Sabbath day, he told his mercenaries to go into the streets for their pay and to take it with their swords — on God's day, the day when no Jew will raise an arm for his defense. All day long, the mercenaries killed; they killed until they could no longer lift their arms. They cut off fingers for rings, arms for bracelets. They turned the city into a butcher shop, and the half-crazed, half-hysterical survivors told us how the streets ran ankle-deep in blood. Then they broke into the Temple and sacrificed swine on the altar.

And of one man who told the tale my father asked: "And where was Menelaus, the high priest?"

"Apollonius bought him."

My father hated and always had hated the high priest, who wore a Greek name and Greek garb, but this he would not believe.

"You're lying!"

"As God is my witness! For three talents, he bought him — and Menelaus prayed over the swine's blood."

"It's true," others said.

My father went to his house. He went to the hearth, took a handful of ashes and rubbed them into his face and hair. Then, with the tears flowing, he said the prayer for the dead.

Judas told me. "Bathe and dress yourself," he said. "The Adon is going to the Temple, and we go with him."

"Is he mad?"

"You ask *him* that. I've never seen him the way he is."

I went to my father with the words on my tongue, *Are you mad? Will you risk your lives and ours? Is there profit in putting your head into the lion's den?* — all this and more

I had on my tongue; and when I saw his face, I said nothing.

"Bathe, Simon," he said to me gently, "and anoint your-self with oil and spices, for we go to God's Temple."

So again and for the last time, Mattathias and his five sons went to the Temple in Jerusalem. As so many times in the past, we walked in a line, the old man, the Adon, first, and then my brother John, and then I, Simon, and then my brother Judas, and then my brother Eleazar, and lastly, Jonathan.

And we were men, and the old times were done. Even Jonathan was no boy; a few weeks had taken the fragile grace of him and begun to make it into something hard and wiry and resilient. He would cry no more. I recalled then, looking at him, how once he had lied and Judas had beaten him for it; they were both of them new. The retiring arro-gance, the humble arrogance, of Judas — the shy arrogance that knows so well its own beauty and charm, the worst kind of arrogance — that was beginning to turn into some-thing else, into a singleness of purpose and intent that I only glimpsed at the time. If I had hated Judas, if I had always hated him, the hatred was at last beginning to wash away. Already, age meant nothing with Judas; he was age-less; he would be ageless until the day he died. John and Eleazar were simple and direct and understandable, but Judas was beyond my understanding already and Jonathan was mercurial, changing, and he would go on changing.

We strode along through somber land. There was little joy in the villages we walked through, and less when they knew where we were bound. Those who recognized Mat-tathias and asked, "Where to, Adon?" and were told, "To the Holy Temple," shook their heads worriedly.

As we neared the city, there were more and more mer-cenaries in evidence. We saw them sitting and drinking at

the wayside taverns. We saw them with their women —
there are always women for mercenaries — and we saw them
marching in cohorts.

And then we were there. The Adon had rent his garments
and said the prayer for the dead, so now he betrayed no
reaction nor slackened his pace as we went into the crazy
and incredible ruin that Jerusalem had become.

The walls were not merely torn down, but savagely and
madly and raggedly torn — and crowned with a seemingly
endless row of pikes, each of which supported a Jew's head.
And the stink of decaying flesh filled the whole city. No one
had cleaned the dried blood from the streets; furniture had
been thrown from windows and balconies, and broken
pieces of chairs, tables, beds and crockery were everywhere.
The shells of burned houses made a pattern, and now and
again you saw a severed arm or a leg that the burial details
had missed, all rotten and covered with flies. Dogs ran in
the city, and occasionally a group of mercenaries clanked
through, eying us suspiciously, but making no move to
harm us; otherwise it was deserted.

As in that long ago, as in that first time when as children
we came into the glorious city of David, we climbed up
and up, toward the Temple. The Temple still stood; that we
could see; and beyond it we could see the Acra, the enormous stone tower the Macedonians had built to house their
garrison. The Acra was untouched; in fact, it was being
strengthened with additional walls and buttresses, and
there was a good deal of movement around it, but the
Temple had been dealt with as insanely as the city walls.
The mighty wooden gates had been burned. The precious
hangings were torn down, and all over the polished walls
obscene phallic symbols had been drawn, hideous cartoons
of men and women having intercourse with beasts — the

better for us to know and understand and appreciate the culture of civilization.

Levites still stood at the gates; or at least they wore the garb of Levites. They moved to stop us as we entered, but when they saw Mattathias, when they saw his face, they shrank aside, and we walked past.

We went into the Holy of Holies, the inner house of God, where the shewbread and the candelabra are. It stank like a butcher's stall. The altar was filthy with dry blood and a pig's head sat there, staring open-eyed at us. A great urn of pork stood to one side, and assorted filth lay on the floor.

At the door, Mattathias halted for a moment — then went on, and then, for the first time in my life, I had the full measure of the old man, the Adon, who was my father. The Temple was he, and he was the Temple. Jews in Rome or in Alexandria, or in Athens or in Babylon, turn to the Temple when they pray; yet at best the Temple is a word or an image for them; they pass their lives and most of them never see it; but when had the Adon not seen it, walked in it, prayed in it? He was a Kohan; scratch the Temple and you cut his flesh. How can I say what it meant to him to see a pig's head on the altar?

Yet he did not falter, but walked to the altar and stood there in the filth. We followed him, and Judas raised his hand to sweep aside the head.

"Leave it alone," the Adon said coldly.

John began, softly, the prayer for the dead, but the Adon cut him short. "Not here! Do you pray for the dead here?"

Minutes went by, and still he stood there, his back to us. Then, at last, he turned around very slowly. The impassiveness of his face amazed me. His cloak was thrown back, and the pure sunlight, entering through the roof, played brilliantly on his pale silk jacket. His beard was quite white now, his long hair white too. Calmly, he looked at us, his glance passing from face to face, as if he were mildly inquiring for some quality he was certain he would find; and at last he fixed his gaze on Judas.

"My son," he said softly.

"Yes, Father," Judas answered.

"When you cleanse this place, cleanse it well."

"Yes, Father," Judas whispered.

"Three times with lye, as the law says. Three times with ashes. And three times with cold, clean sand from the River Jordan."

"Yes, Father," Judas said, his voice hardly audible, his eyes welling with tears.

"And three times more, with cold water and loving care."

"Yes, Father."

Then the Adon went to John and kissed him upon the lips; then to me; then to Judas, to Eleazar, and to Jonathan. Then he said: "We have no more to do here. Let us go home."

We left the Temple, but at the gate the Adon paused, grasped one of the Levites by the arm, and said, "Where do you dwell?"

Shrinking, the man answered, "In the Acra."

"Are there other Jews there?"

"Yes."

"How many?"

"About two thousand."

"Men of wealth?" the Adon went on. "Men of property? Men of culture?"

"Yes — men of culture," the Levite said.

"An island of Western culture," the Adon said softly. "One bit of Athens in the land of the Jews. Is that it?"

The Levite nodded, uncertain as to what to make of the Adon's gentle manner.

"Friends of the King of Kings?"

"Yes," the Levite said, "friends of the King of Kings."

"Good. And they are safe and secure with walls wrapped around them and with ten thousand mercenaries to protect them from the ill-nurtured anger of their people. And is Menelaus, the high priest, with them?"

"Yes, yes."

"Tell Menelaus that Mattathias ben John ben Simon was here from Modin to taste the glory of civilization, and tell him that I brought with me my five sons. Tell him that some-day we will return."

And then we walked back to Modin.

PART TWO

The Young Man, the Maccabee

AND IF YOU ARE NOT JEWISH, BUT from the outside, a stranger, as we say, of the *nokri*, how then shall I tell you what is meant among my people when we say "the Maccabee"?

It is an old, old word among a people who have a curious veneration for words. We are the people of the Book, the Word, and the Law; and in the Law itself it is written, "Thou shalt not hold a slave and have him ignorant." In a world where very few can read and write, the merest water carrier among us reads and writes, and with us a word is not a thing to be spoken foolishly or in an offhand way. And *Maccabee* is an old, old word, a strange word; yet were you to read the five books of Moses and all the other writings of old, you would look in vain for the word *Maccabee*. It is nowhere written.

It is the nature of the word: it is not a title that a man may take, but a gift that only the people may give. In my father's time, there was no Maccabee, nor in his father's time, nor in his grandfather's time; but if you speak to the old men, the Rabbis, of Gideon, they will not term him Gideon ben Joash, which was his name, but speak of him softly and gently as "the Maccabee"; yet how many were there like Gideon? Not of David will they speak thus, nor even of Moses who stood face to face with God, but of

Hezekiah ben Ahaz, and perhaps of one or two others — of them, they will say "They were Maccabees."

It is not a word like "Melek" or "Adon," or even like "Rabbi," which means "my master," only in a strange and venerable way that is hard to explain. The Maccabee is no man's master, and no man is his servant or his slave. Once in a long, long while there comes out of the people a man who is of them and from them and with them; him they call the Maccabee, because they love him. Some say that, in the beginning, the word was *makabeth,* which means "the hammer," and such a man was a Hammer for the people to wield; and others say that the word once meant "to destroy," because he who bore it destroyed the enemies of his people; but I know only that it is a word like no other word in our tongue, a title, worn by a few men — and I knew few men who deserved to wear it.

Rabbi Ragesh said that there was only one — and to him he gave it.

We came back from Jerusalem to Modin, where the walls of our valley pushed the world away. In the hills, each valley is an oasis which can even close out the sounds of men and women in pain, and time drove by in that rhythmical sweep, measured by sunrise and sunset, by the five crops a year we take from our soil, by the ripening, the reaping, the planting, the sowing. Yet it was different, and every day was the last day.

One day I came from the fields, hoe in hand, sweating and dirty, barefoot and barelegged, my pants rolled to the knee, and I saw the Adon taking the sword out of the jar of olive oil. Judas stood by the window, dressed for traveling, for hard traveling in the hills, leggings over heavy sandals, his striped cloak folded back over his shoulders and belted to him. On the table, there was a package of bread and dried figs and raisins. I looked from one to another, but neither spoke. I went to the basin and washed my hands and face, and as I dried myself, Eleazar entered from the courtyard behind the house, carrying Judas's horn bow, which had been buried there, and a handful of arrows.

"Here," he said, handing them to Judas. "And I'll ask you once more — can I go?"

"No," Judas said shortly.

The Adon was wiping the sword. "It will weigh you down," he said. "You're not used to a sword, my son."

"There are many things for me to learn. The sword, I think, is least difficult. Will you fetch me the scabbard?" he asked Eleazar.

"Where are you going?" I demanded.

"I don't know."

"Where is he going?" I asked my father.

The old man shook his head. Judas ran a bowstring through his fingers, rolled it and placed it in his pouch. The short bow and the arrows he thrust into his belt under his coat.

"Answer me!" I said angrily. "I asked you where you were going!"

"And I told you — I don't know."

"Who does know?"

"I'm going into the hills," Judas said, after a long moment of hesitation. "I'm going to walk through villages. I'm going to look at the people and talk to them."

"Why?"

"To see what they will do."

"What do you expect them to do?"

"I don't know. That's why I am going."

I sat down on the bench by the table. Eleazar returned with the scabbard, and Judas sheathed the sword and slung it over his back, under the cloak. There was an incredible lack of self-consciousness about all his actions, a fact that still irritated me, yet I couldn't help but reflect how magnificent he looked, his great cloak sweeping back over his shoulders, the spread and strength of him, the superb poise of his head, his close-cropped reddish-brown beard, and his hair falling to his shoulders under his tight, round cap. I watched him, considered him, and brooded about what he intended, while Jonathan came in with Ruth. Judas and Ruth went out to the court behind the house together, and in a little while they came back.

"I'm going with you," I said to Judas finally.

"I want to go alone," he replied. You didn't argue with him; he had that quality that turned argument away. John came in, and we were all there. He kissed them, and then he motioned for me to go out with him.

Outside, he looked at me for a while, and then he put his arms around me. As always with him, my hot, bitter anger ran out.

"Don't let anything happen," he said.

"What do you expect to happen?"

"I don't know, Simon, I don't know. I'm trying to see in the dark. Take care of them."

The days went by, and each day it became a little worse — not a great deal worse, but a little worse. In the little village of Goumad, which is only an hour's walk from Modin, Apelles's mercenaries put a whole family to death, because three arrows were discovered behind a rafter in their house. The man of the house, Benjamin ben Caleb, was crucified. That was a new thing in the land, a Western importation of Antiochus, the King of Kings. Living, Ben Caleb was nailed over the door of his home, and for a whole day, the mercenaries stood around, listening to his cries and smiling appreciatively. Then, a day or two later, four girls were raped in Zorah, a village to the south of us. One of the village people who tried to defend them was slain. In Galilee, in Samaria, and in Phoenicia, where Jews lived in cities among the Gentiles, it was worse, and terrible tales of pain and suffering drifted back to us in Judea. Yet strangely enough, life in Modin went on much as it always had. We took in the crop; we threshed the wheat and dried the fruit; children were born and old folk died; we filled our presses with new olive oil, and at night we sat at the table after supper, talking of when it had been better and how it would be worse, singing our old, old songs, and listening to the old men tell stories.

It was four days after Judas had left, in the evening time, and a dozen of the village folk sat at the board of Mattathias, drinking wine, munching nuts and raisins, and discussing that most ready of subjects, life's bitterness under the heel of a foreign invader. We are a people who have had perhaps a little more than our share of misery, in one place or another, and we have learned to turn it into laughter; it had to be that way, otherwise we would have long ago perished. I remember well that Simon ben Lazar was re-telling that already overworked tale of Antiochus and the three wise fools, one of those painful, bitter stories that thread through so much of the literature of an oppressed people, and I remember that I was letting the words slip by, so that I could watch Ruth with all my heart and both my eyes. She sat with her mother, holding her head as always high and alert, as if she were listening — God help me, I thought she was listening for Judas — and the lamplight slanted off her face, making a sheen on her skin like polished bronze. How well I remember her that night, the tilt of her head, the shadows under her cheekbones, the coiled braids of her red hair, such a woman as I have not known before or since — and for who else but Judas? Who else could stand beside her and look paired, face, stature and heart out of the ancient blood of the Kohanim?

It was then that a goat cried out, and I heard it and slipped away unobtrusively, so as not to break up the warm flow and spirit of the folk, but fearing that one of the jackals from the hills might be in the corral. I went through the back door, the court, and up the hillside to the stone enclosure where the beasts were kept. It was not a goat, after all, but two rams locked in the horns and one of them crying with pain. I separated them — and then the evening was so cool and pleasant, the moon so round and bright, that I was loath to return, but sat myself under an olive tree where I could watch the moon and smell the clean sea breeze.

It must have been a half hour that I was sitting there before I heard someone call my name, "Simon, Simon?"

"Who calls for Simon?" I asked, although I knew well enough, my heart pounding and my hands suddenly wet.

"*A moonstruck lad,*" Ruth said, coming around the edge of the corral, half-singing the words of the song, "*who sits and dreams of a lovely lass* — were you bored, Simon?"

"I thought there was a jackal in the corral. You shouldn't be here with me."

"Why?" She stood in front of me, her bare toes playing with my sandals, smiling impishly. "Why shouldn't I be out here with you, Simon, who came to protect the goats from a jackal? And if it were not a jackal but a lion, such as David found?"

"There hasn't been a lion in Judea these three hundred years," I answered sullenly.

"You never smile, do you, and nothing is ever funny, is it, Simon ben Mattathias? You are the unhappiest man in Modin — in Judea, I think — in the whole world, I suppose. I think I would give years of my life if a lion were to step out from behind me and swallow you."

"It's hardly likely," I said.

"If you will spread your cloak, I would like to sit down." she laughed.

Shaking my head, I spread the cloak, and she sat down beside me. Apparently, she waited for me to speak, and I didn't know what to say — so we sat there silent, as the moon climbed into the sky and the moonlight flowed like molton silver over the Judean hills. And at last she said:

"You once liked me, Simon — or I thought so."

I stared at her.

"Or I thought so, and for so long," she mused, "every time I came into the house of Mattathias, I asked myself — Will Simon be there, will he look at me? Will he smile at me? Will he speak to me? Will he touch my hand?"

Sick with rage and frustration, I could only say, "And Judas is gone four days!"

"What?" She turned to me, incredulous.

"You heard me."

"Simon, what have I to do with Judas? Simon, what's wrong with you — what did I do to you? You've been like stone, like ice — not only to me, to your father, to Judas!"

"With no reason?"

"I don't know what your reasons are, Simon."

"And when you went out with Judas before he left — "

"I don't love Judas," she said tiredly.

"Does he know that?"

"He knows it."

I shook my head helplessly. "He loves you," I said. "I know it. I know Judas, every gesture, every look, every thought. He's never had anything but what he's wanted to have. I know that damned, cursed humility of his — "

"Is that why you hate him?"

"I don't hate him."

She took both my hands in hers, rocking them on her lap, telling me, "Simon, Simon — Simon ben Mattathias, Simon of Modin — oh how many names I have for you! — my Simon, my strange, beautiful, wonderful, wise and foolish Simon, it's always been you, no second one, no third one, only Simon and a dream that he would love me someday — no, not to love me, but to be near me, to look at me sometimes, to speak to me sometimes; and even that I can't have, can I, Simon?"

"And Judas loves you."

"Simon, will your whole life be Judas? Is there anything besides Jonathan and Eleazar — and John too? What kind of guilt do you bear for them? Judas took me in his arms — and I pitied him. I don't belong to him. I don't belong to anyone, Simon ben Mattathias — I could only belong to one man."

"You pitied him?" I whispered. "You pitied Judas?"

"Simon, I pitied him, can't you understand?"

"No," I said, "no — " She sat there in the moonlight, and how can I tell you what she was and what she looked like? I took her in my arms, and then I wrapped the folds of my cloak over her, and we lay there under the olive tree . . .

Afterwards, we walked in the night, hand in hand, climbing from terrace to terrace, until at last we were on the wild hilltops where the wind sighed in the evergreens and where all the air was fresh and fragrant and scented, I, Simon, and this woman who took away all fear of death, of the future, of misery and sorrow — and made me know only that I lived the way I had never lived before, young and proud and strong, the son of Mattathias, with tears and laughter mingled inside of me.

"And I had to make love to you," she said. "And I had to plead with you, and beg you to take me in your arms."

"No, no."

"Yes, I had to."

"Oh, my darling, no, because I can remember. I can remember how I cut my knee once, and you washed it and bandaged it, and I told myself I would win the whole world for you and bring it to you — "

"To Modin?"

"Yes, to Modin. And when you brought wine to the Adon — "

"I spilled it once."

"My heart broke for you. And when you cried, I cried inside of, all over inside of me."

"And when you were beaten because Judas broke the great goblet, I cried that way for my Simon, for my beautiful, good, gentle Simon."

"Don't say that!"

"Why? Why not? Simon, I love you. I love a man. First, I loved a little boy, and now I love a man — "

Yet when I left her, I could only think, How will I tell Judas?

There were four weeks of poignant happiness. It was no secret; in a place like Modin, where half the town is related to you in one way or another, there are no secrets, and anyone who saw Ruth when she looked at me — or me when I looked at her — knew all there was to know.

It is hard to put anything down of those four weeks, yet I have to, if you would understand what came afterwards to me, Simon, and to my brothers — especially he who came to be called the Maccabee. I sometimes think that a Jew is a stranger on earth, someone who abides for a while and must perforce count each day as if it might be the last. We bind each other with bonds that are stronger than iron, and we make many things sacred that are not sacred among other people. But most of all is life itself sacred, our most terrible crime being an act which is matter of course with all other peoples, suicide — and because of this strange sacredness of life, love becomes almost an act of worship. We open our hearts wide, when we open them.

It was that way with Ruth; it was that way with me. We became a part of each other. I don't know what the Adon thought then; I was alive, and my heart was making its own song, and whether or not he condemned me, thinking, as I so often thought, that I had struck at Judas, I don't know. I had Ruth and I had the whole world. We climbed the hills and lay in the fragrant turf under the cedars. We waded bare-legged in Tubel, the sweet brook, or stretched on the grass to watch the goats. It was the easy time; the harvest was in and we were not yet ready for the planting, so that work which might have fallen heavily on me with Judas gone could be neglected. John and Jonathan spent much time in the synagogue, a long and ancient stone building that served as a school by day and a village center at night and a house of prayer when the sun was rising or setting, studying and poring over the scrolls, but I was not so minded when the sun shone and the birds sang and my heart sang back. I was in love, and an hour without Ruth was dark and endless.

We learned each other then. She made me probe myself,

reach into myself and see what that subtle and bitter thing between Judas and me was, what it meant. How well she knew me, this tall and beautiful woman! How little I knew her! I remember once when I spoke to her — and I did not speak of it again — about Judas, and she turned on me almost in a fury:

"You said you knew Judas — you don't know him! And you don't know me. I'm not a person to you, alive, a human being!"

I looked at her, long-legged and high-bosomed and regal — and more of a person than anyone I had ever known.

"Is it the old times?" she said. "A man had ten wives and ten concubines, and if a child was a girl, her name was not even recorded! If I have a daughter — "

"You?"

"If I have a daughter," she said, "will it be precious to you, and good?"

"If you have a daughter," I said.

"Simon, Simon — what are you afraid of? Judas is a great and beautiful man, and so are you. I've always known that. When I came into your house, I came into the house of Mattathias and his sons, and it was like no other house, no other house. Shall I get down on my knees to you, Simon?"

"Oh, my darling, my darling."

"Simon, when you know me, you will not be afraid any more. I promise you. I'll be strong for you, Simon. There are bad times coming; I know that, and I know where the sons of the Adon will be; but I'll be strong for you, Simon. We have such a long life ahead, so much of it, so much — and someday it will be as it was, with the whole land quiet and gentle in the sunshine . . ."

She loved the land the way I loved it, the way a Jew can love the land and the fruit of it. She was fertile and I would have sons and daughters to follow me — and the old seed would be planted again and ever again. I told the Adon that in a month we would be married.

"You're a man," he said, "and past the marriage age. Why do you tell me?"

"Because you're my father and I want your blessing."

"Yet you didn't ask me."

"I love her and she loves me."

"Where is your brother?" the Adon said.

"Did I send him away? Did he tell me where he went? Is that my whole life — Where is my brother? — always, Where is my brother?"

"Is it your life?" the Adon asked somberly. "Your life is God's, not mine, not yours. There is grief all over Israel, yet nothing matters but your happiness."

"Is that wrong?"

"Do you talk to me of right and wrong, Simon ben Mattathias, or of what is just and what is unjust? Have I whelped you so poorly that you are not a Jew, that the Law is not a covenant with you? Have you forgotten already that we were slaves in Egypt?"

"A thousand years ago!" I cried.

"And was it a thousand years ago," the Adon said coldly, "that you went to the Temple and saw what I saw?"

I told Ruth.

"He is an old man, Simon," she said. "What do you expect? When he went to the Temple, his heart broke." Her eyes searched mine. "Simon, Simon — "

"God help me!"

"Simon, do you love me?"

"As I never loved anything on earth."

"It will be all right, Simon, I promise you."

I avoided Mattathias's rooftree when I could. I sat in the house of Moses ben Aaron, who had loved me since I was a child, and listened to his rambling tales. This was her home and she was with me, her hand ready to touch mine, her eyes ever looking for mine. Moses ben Aaron had traveled and seen things, a rare matter with us who are close rooted to our own soil and not a people of commerce like the Greeks or Phoenicians. He had been to the great wine bazaars in Gebel and Tyre, and even to Alexandria where they will pay almost any price for a Judean vintage. He had seen the purple slaves of the Mediterranean coast, and the yellow-haired German mercenaries of the Romans. He had seen black men and brown men, and he liked to talk about it. Yet always he said:

"Simon ben Mattathias, there is so much a man can travel and no more, for when his belly is full of slavery and cruelty, he has to go away from the *nokri* and come to his own; otherwise the world spins, as if the God of Abraham and Isaac and Jacob turned his face away, and there is nothing but the greed for money and more money, power and more power . . ."

With Ruth, I talked of the child that would be ours. Deborah if she were a girl and David if he were a man. If she had been beautiful before, there was a new glow to her beauty now. Even in our village of Modin, where they had seen her in swaddling clothes, where they had seen her grow and mature, even here she was new and people turned their heads to look after her, and said, "That is a queen of old Israel, a red Kohan of the ancient times." And when the old men met me on the street, along with "Shalom" (Peace) they said to me, "Breed a race of kings, God willing."

When we were alone on the hillside, she would sing in her

deep, rich voice that love song that comes from a time out
of memory:

> For love is strong as death . . .
> Many waters cannot quench love,
> Neither can the floods drown it:
> If a man would give all the substance of his house for love,
> It would utterly be contemned.

So it was and so it finished; that was a long time ago,
and tears dry like everything else. I spoke before of how
it became worse, not all at once but bit by bit, so that in
the two or three weeks that elapsed between the visits of
Apelles the warden, or one of his men, we could forget,
we could resume our lives. Modin was spared longer than
other villages. Our taxes became heavier; we were insulted
more frequently and the insults became a little worse, and
once the Rabbi Enoch was whipped almost to death. But
it was nothing that we couldn't bear. And then, when Judas
had been gone five weeks, Apelles himself returned with
one hundred men and called all the village folk into the
town square.

A curious man, Apelles; he thrived on cruelty the way
normal people thrive on love and gentleness. It was not
merely that he was perverted; the perversion reversed things
in him. He had become fatter since he was warden; he had
become jollier; he was the image of a full and satisfied man.
The killing of Jews, the whipping of Jews, the torturing of
Jews, was meat and drink to him — and you could see that
as he hopped out of his litter, tossed back his yellow mantle
and flicked his little pink skirt. He was a happy man, and
he smiled at us before he explained his current visit.

"A nice village, Modin," he lisped, "but too fruitful, too
fruitful. We must see to that. My friend, the Adon!" he
called.

My father came forward and stood in front of the people. The past months had wrought a great change in him. His beard was white. His gray eyes were paler than ever, and all over his face there was a network of deep wrinkles. Nor was his giant frame as upright as once; he had lost height; there was a quality of defeat and default about him that had increased slowly but steadily in all the time Judas was gone. Now, wrapped in his striped cloak, he stood silently and impassively before Apelles.

"You will be pleased to know," Apelles said, his voice high and eager, "that the King of Kings has devoted considerable thought to the Jews. At the last meeting of his council — and I am proud to note that I participated — a decision was reached to hasten and complete Hellenization of the province. Certain measures must be taken, and decisions will be enforced — lawfully and justly, of course, but enforced — and, naturally, defaulters will be punished."

Apelles took a deep breath, wrinkled his nose, and arranged and patted the folds of his yellow mantle. One fat little hand sought in his sleeve and found his handkerchief and touched it delicately to each nostril.

"But there will be no defaulters," he smiled. "You will recognize that the vile superstitions of your religion and what you call your Law place an insurmountable barrier before civilization. Dietary rules in particular are considered an affront to all Greeks; you will cease to practice them. Reading and writing serve merely to extend and deepen all other vile practices of Jews; your schools will be permanently closed. And since the repository of superstition and ignorance among you are your five books of Moses, these books will be neither read nor intoned. To enforce the last provision, my men will enter your synagogue, obtain your scrolls, and publicly burn them. By order of the King," he finished — with one delicate flick of his handkerchief.

Ruth stood beside me, and I recall the pressure of her fingers on my arm as Apelles finished speaking. But I watched the Adon; I never took my eyes off him, and I knew that somewhere in that crowd Eleazar and Jonathan and John were watching him — as everyone else was — for him to say whether this was the end or not. And as had happened the last time, the Adon never moved. Not by the flicker of a muscle or an eyelid did he betray what he felt. A mercenary stood by him; mercenaries ringed the people; and twenty mounted mercenaries sat on their horses watchfully, bows strung, arrows loosely held in their fingers.

We stood there while four of Apelles's men went into the synagogue, tore down the draperies behind the pulpit, and brought out the seventeen scrolls of the Law that belonged to Modin. How well I knew those scrolls! How well every man and woman and child in the village knew them! I had read from them from the time I was able to read; I had pressed my lips to them; I had fingered the ancient parchment and traced out the black Hebrew words. Eight of the scrolls had been brought from Babylon hundreds of years ago, when the Jews returned from the long exile. Three of them were said to date back to the kingdom of David, and one was said to have been David ben Jesse's own, annotated by his own hand. With what loving care they had been preserved, each of them receiving every seven years a new envelope of the finest silk, stitched with stitches too small to be seen by the naked eye, and embroidered all over! How well they had been hidden through catastrophe, fire and flame! And they were now to be burned by the perverted servant of a pervert — in the name of civilization!

A moan of agony went up from the people as the scrolls

were thrown carelessly on a pile of hay. A mercenary went into one of the houses, returned with a jug of olive oil, knocked off the head, and poured it over the scrolls; another mercenary found a coal in a fireplace, fanned it, and then set the oil-soaked pile on fire.

Borne by his slaves, Apelles was already on his way — and still the people watched the Adon. I think it would have been the end of the village, of every living soul in it, if my father had been anything else than the man he was. I can't tell what went on inside of him; I can only guess. I watched him and saw his body tense, become rigid, and vibrate a little — but not enough for the people to notice, since they said afterwards that Mattathias stood like stone. It was not stone, but a man whose heart bled as Apelles and his mercenaries marched away. The horsemen waited; watching the pile of burning scrolls, watching the people, they sat with notched arrows, dirty men on ill-kept beasts, men who never bathed, never hoped, never dreamed, never loved — brutal, ignorant men whose trade was murder, whose pleasure was a night with a prostitute or a twist of hasheesh, whose relaxation was drunkenness, debased, dehumanized men with special hatred for Jews, since come what might, Jews would never hire them; these men sat on their horses and waited, and there was one scroll apart from the fire, an inch from the flames, not burning yet but yellowing and browning at the edge; and as they waited, a nine-year-old boy — he was Reuben ben Joseph, the son of a simple farmer — ran forward, nimble as a squirrel, seized the scroll, and turned to flee.

One arrow caught him in the thigh, and he rolled over like a flung stone, and Ruth, my tall, brave, wonderful Ruth, had reached him in three strides and raised him in her arms. The mercenaries let go with the rest of their arrows, wheeled their horses, and galloped away — and I only remember that I ran after them, shrieking like a madman, knife in hand, until Eleazar caught me, wrestled with me, and held me until the knife fell from my fingers.

Ruth was dead, but the boy lived; she had held him protected with her arms and body, using herself as a shield from the arrows. She couldn't have suffered very much, for two of the arrows pierced her heart. I know. I drew them forth. I picked her up from where she lay and carried her to her father's house, and all night long I sat there by her body; and in the morning, Judas came.

There are some things I cannot write of, nor are they particularly important to this tale of my glorious brothers. I cannot tell of my feelings through that night, which was a night without end that somehow ended; and then the people went away and Moses ben Aaron and his wife slept from sheer exhaustion, and I was alone. I don't think I slept, but there was a lapse of sorts. My head was in my arms on the table, and then I heard a step and looked up, and the dawn was in the room and Judas stood there.

It was not the Judas who went away five weeks before. There was a difference which I did not see all at once, but sensed rather — sensed that a boy had marched away and a man come back. The humility was gone from him, yet he had become humble. There was a gray streak in his auburn hair and there were lines on his face. And on one cheek, there was the raw welt of a half-healed scar. His beard was untrimmed, his hair shaggy, and the dirt and grime of travel were still on him. But all that was the surface, and underneath something else had happened — yet what was on the surface made him seem vastly older, larger, a somber giant of a man, not beautiful as he had once been beautiful, but almost splendid in a new way.

For what seemed a long, long time, we looked at each other, and then he asked me, "Where is she, Simon?"

I took him to the body and uncovered her face. She appeared to be sleeping. I covered her again.

"There was no pain for her?" he asked simply.

"I don't think so. I drew two arrows from her heart."

"Apelles?"

"Yes, Apelles," I said.

"You must have loved her a great deal, Simon," he said.

"She had my child in her womb, and when she died, everything in me that ever wanted anything died too."

"You'll live again," he said evenly. "This is a house of death, Simon ben Mattathias. Come out in the sun."

I followed him outside, and we stood there in the village street. The village was waking, giving its daily evidence of the tenacity of life. Somewhere, a child laughed. Three chickens fled through the dust, their wings beating. Jonathan and Eleazar came out of the house of Mattathias, and they joined us.

"Where is the Adon?" Judas asked them.

"He went to the synagogue with John and Rabbi Ragesh."

"Bring me water," Judas said to Jonathan, "so I can wash before I pray." Jonathan brought him a basin of water and a towel, and he washed there, before Moses ben Aaron's house. The men of the village greeted Judas quietly, as they went by on their way to the synagogue, and the women stood at the doors of their houses, some of them crying, some of them looking at us pityingly.

"Go ahead," Judas told my brothers, and he walked behind with me, his arm around my shoulders.

"Who told you about Ruth?" I wanted to know.

"The Adon."

"Everything?"

"The rest I can guess, Simon. Simon, I ask only one thing — that when the time comes, Apelles will be mine, not yours."

I didn't care. Ruth was dead and nothing would bring her back.

"Promise me, Simon."

"As you wish — it doesn't matter."

"It matters. This is the end of something — it's the beginning too."

We came to the synagogue and entered. The ark stood bare and desecrated; no one had replaced the torn hangings. The men of the village stood in a circle around the Adon and someone else, and when Judas came forward, the circle opened, and I saw next to the Adon a small, wonderfully ugly man, sharp-eyed, alert, a little past fifty, perhaps.

"The Rabbi Ragesh," Judas said, "and this is my other brother, Simon ben Mattathias."

Ragesh spun to face me. He was incredibly alert and quick, with tiny blue eyes that seemed to sparkle always. Grasping both my hands in his, he answered,

"*Shalom.* I greet with pleasure a son of Mattathias. May you be a refuge for Israel."

"And unto you peace," I answered dully.

"This is a black day in a black year," Ragesh went on. "But let your heart swell with hatred, Simon ben Mattathias, not with despair."

Hatred, I thought, and I was being schooled. There was a time when I knew love and hope and peace, and now it was only hatred, and there was nothing else left, only that.

The Rabbi Ragesh was a guest, and he led the prayers.

In the cool morning, the men stood motionless, wrapped from head to foot in their striped cloaks, their faces cowled as Ragesh intoned:

Sha ma Yisroel, Adonai Elohano, Adonai ehchad . . .
(Hear, oh Israel, the Lord is our God, the Lord is one.)

My eyes sought for Moses ben Aaron and found him, and then the sun rose and flooded the old synagogue with light. We prayed for the dead. I was also dead; I lived, but I was dead. We finished, and by now almost all of the village was in the synagogue, the women as well as the men, and children too.

"What does the Lord ask?" Rabbi Ragesh said, intoning it like a prayer. "He asks obedience."

"Amen — so be it," the people said.

"Resistance to tyranny — is that not obedience to God?" the little stranger demanded gently.

"So be it," the people said.

"And if a serpent strike at my heel, shall I not crush it underfoot?"

"So be it," the people said, the women weeping softly.

"And if Israel is stricken, shall it not raise itself?"

"So be it," they said.

"And if there is no man to judge Israel, shall it believe that God has forsaken it?"

"So be it," the people said.

"Or shall a Maccabee rise up out of the people?"

"Amen," the people said, and Ragesh answered them, "Amen — so be it."

He walked forward through the congregation to where Judas stood, placed a hand on either shoulder, drew him forward and kissed him upon the lips.

"Talk to them," he said to Judas.

I told you how Judas was humble, yet the humility was gone. He went to the front of the synagogue and stood there bathed in a great beam of sunlight, his travel-stained cloak hanging from his broad shoulders, his head bent, his auburn beard glowing as if there were a fire in it. I looked from him to my father, the Adon, and the old man wept unashamed.

"I walked through the land," Judas said, very quietly, so that the people had to crowd up to hear him, "and I saw how the people suffered. As in Modin, it was everywhere, and there is no happiness in Judea. And wherever I went, I said to the people, What will you do? What will you do?"

Judas paused, and in the deep stillness of the synagogue there was only one sound, the weeping of the mother of Ruth. His voice louder, deeper, more resonant, Judas said:

"Why do you weep, my mother? Is there nothing but tears for us? I don't come here for tears; I have wept enough and Israel has wept enough. I saw the strength of the people in all their thousands, but there was only one man who knew what to do, the Rabbi Ragesh, whom the people of all the South call their father. In the village of Dan, he asked the people, Is it better to die on your feet — or to live on your knees, you who are Jews and have made an ancient covenant not to bend your knee to anyone — even to God? So when the mercenaries came, he led the people into the hills and I went with him. For ten days we lived in caves. For weapons, we had only knives and a few bows, yet we could have fought. But Philippus came with his mercenaries on the Sabbath day and the people would not fight because it was God's day, and the mercenaries cut them down. Yet I fought and Ragesh fought — and we live to fight again. Then I ask my father here, Mattathias, the

Adon — I ask him what God demands! Shall we be slain, or shall we fight?"

The people turned to the Adon, who looked at Judas — and that way, minutes went by, and at long last, the Adon said:

"The Sabbath day is holy, but life is holier."

"Hear my father!" Judas cried, his voice ringing.

The women still wept, but the men's faces were turned up to Judas as if they had never seen him before.

How can I say what I felt, what I was, and what I became then, when this woman, who was all women, died? How can I say that — I, Simon, the son of Mattathias? It is recorded by the scribes who set down those things that I took a wife — but that was after, long after. Now there was only a cold hatred inside of me, and there was something else inside of Judas. Eleazar, the good-natured, the huge man, stronger and easier-going than anyone else in Modin — he too was not as he was before, nor was my brother Jonathan, still hardly more than a boy. Even John was strangely different, the gentle, passive John — the almost saintly John, who had already fallen into the old routine of so many Jews, a day's work in the field, a bath, supper with his family — and then study with the scrolls in the synagogue, the holy scrolls that made us the people of the Book, the Word, and the words, where it is written:

How goodly are thy tents, O Jacob, thy dwelling places, O Israel . . .

The warm aura of that, the enfolding quality of it — "Thy tents, O Jacob, thy dwelling places, O Israel!" We are a people of peace; consider it now, we have a greeting as ancient as the ages, in this fashion, *"Shalom,"* to which one answers, *"Alaichem shalom."* And thus it is: "Peace" . . . "And unto thee, peace." Whatever the other nations say, when we raise a glass of wine, we have but one toast, *Lachiam* (Life), for is it not written that three things are holier than others — Peace, Life, and Justice?

We are a peaceful folk and a patient folk with a long memory — so long that it reaches eternally to that time when we were slaves, when we were bondsmen in the land of Egypt. There is no glory in war for us, and we alone have no mercenaries. Yet our patience is not endless.

I must tell you how Apelles returned, and why his name too is written down by our scribes, so that Jews may always remember. But before he returned, the sons of Mattathias gathered under the old man's rooftree, the five of us and the Adon — and there too was Rabbi Ragesh and Ruben ben Tubel, the smith. A strange man, Ruben the smith, short and wide and so powerful that he could bend an iron bar in his hands, and dark, dark of skin and hair with black eyes, and covered all over, from head to foot, with wiry black hair. His family was an old one, out of the tribe of Benjamin, and back to a hundred years before the exile his people had been workers in iron, always people of the forge and hammer. During the exile, his family was one that had not left Judea, but lived for three generations in caves, like beasts. He could work all metals, and like so many Jewish metal workers, he knew the secret of the Dead Sea silicate, how to blend it and melt it and blow it into glass. He was not a learned man, and even as a child I remarked and snickered over the difficulty with which he read from the Torah — but when I had laughed at him once openly, the Adon fetched me a sharp blow across the ear, telling me, "Save your laughter for fools, not for a man who knows secrets you will never dream of."

On this evening, the Adon asked him to come. It was not often that he was under our roof. His wife had scrubbed his linen until it shone on him, white as snow, yet he entered gingerly, and when the Adon motioned for him to join us at the table, he shook his head. "If it please the Adon, I will stand."

My father, who was so strangely wise with all men, did not press him, and all through our talk, he stood. His stillness, his deep and implacable calm, contrasted oddly with the nervous vitality of Rabbi Ragesh, who could not sit still, who was up and down and all over the room, pacing back and forth, darting at us suddenly, emphasizing his words by constantly clapping a clenched fist into an open palm, as when he said:

"Resist! Resist! Resist! That must be like a watchword, like a beacon up and down the land — wherever there are Jews — resist! Smite the conquerer — "

"And he smites back," the Adon said softly.

"Oh, I am sick of that kind of talk!" Ragesh cried.

"My blood boils as hot as yours," my father answered coldly. "I stood in front of all my people, and Apelles struck me, and I stood there so that the people could live to see another morning. And when I came to the Temple and a pig's head sat upon the altar, I swallowed my grief and my anger. It's easy to die, Rabbi! Show me a way to fight and live!"

"There will be no turning back," John agreed, his long face sad and troubled. "It will not be as it was in the South, Rabbi Ragesh, where a few folk went into the hills and died. The whole land will rise up when they hear that the Adon Mattathias ben John has raised himself against the

Greek. Then, when they come down on the land with twenty, or thirty, or a hundred thousand mercenaries — who will remain in Israel to weep?"

"And we fight back!" Ragesh cried. "What do you say — you, Simon?"

I shook my head. "You ask the wrong man when you ask someone who cares less for life than for death. But it would be slaughter — as it was when our fathers fought and our grandfathers. They take a mercenary at the age of six; they raise him in a barracks; day and night, he practices the art of killing. That is all he knows and all he lives for, to wear forty pounds of armor, to fight in a phalanx under heavy shields, to wield a battle ax or a sword. And against that we have our knives and our bows. And as for heavy weapons or armor — Ruben, how many men could you arm with the metal here in Modin, with spear, sword, shield and breastplate — just with that and no greaves and no helmet and no arm-pieces?"

"In iron?" the smith asked.

"In iron."

Ruben considered, calculated on his fingers, and then said, "If you hammered out plow blades, sickles and hoes — twenty men under light armor. But it would be a long task," he sighed. "And where would our crop come from when we hammered out our plows?"

"And even if it were possible," I said, "and God gave us iron as he gave us manna, when we were a landless folk in the desert, where would the men come from? Could we raise out of Israel a hundred thousand men? Then who would feed them? Who would till the land? Who would be left? And if we raised a hundred thousand men, how many years would it take to train them to fight?"

"We know how to fight," Judas said.

"In a phalanx?"

"Is that the only way to fight? What happened two years ago when the Greeks put their phalanx against the Romans? The Romans used the pilum and smashed the phalanx to pieces. And someday, someone will train mercenaries with a new weapon — no, it's not new weapons we need, but a new kind of war. What kind of fools are we that when this king or that king marches his mercenaries into our land, we go up against them on a level plain and die! We send a rabble to be cut to pieces by a machine! That's not war — it's slaughter!"

The Adon leaned forward, his eyes alight. "What are you thinking, my son?"

"Of how men fight — and for a year I've thought of nothing else. They fight for booty, for loot, for gold, and for slaves. We fight for our land. They have mercenaries and arms. We have the land and a free people. Those are our weapons — the land and the people, our arms and our armor. We have our bows and our knives — we need nothing else. Spears, perhaps, and Ruben could hammer out a hundred spearheads in a week. Could you, Ruben?"

"Spearheads, yes," the smith nodded. "A spear is not a breastplate or a sword."

"And we fight our way — and they fight our way," Judas cried, looking from face to face. "When Rabbi Ragesh led his people into the caves — and I did not know then, Rabbi — and they followed, the people waited to die. That's not the way. We've died for too long. It's their turn now."

"How, Judas, how?" John said.

"Let them look for us! Let them send in their armies! An army cannot climb like a goat, but we can! Let there be an arrow behind every rock — in every tree! Let there be rocks on every cliff! We'll never face them, never oppose them, never try to stop them — but cut at them and cut at them and cut at them, so that they can never sleep without expecting our arrows at night, so that they never dare enter a narrow pass, so that all Judea becomes a trap for them! Let them march their armies through the land — we'll be in the hills! Let them come into the hills — every rock will live! Let them look for us, and we'll spread out and fade like the mist! Let them put their army through a pass, and we'll cut it up as you cut a snake."

"And when they come to the villages?" I asked.

"The villages will be empty. Can they garrison the thousand towns of Judea?"

"And if they burn the villages?"

"We will live in the hills — in caves if we have to. And the war will become our strength, just as the land is our strength."

"And for how long?" John said.

And Ragesh returned, "Forever — if need be until the judgment day."

"It will not be forever," Judas said.

And Eleazar, resting his great arms on the table, leaned forward toward Judas, his head lifted and smiling; and Jonathan was smiling too, not with mirth but with something he saw, his young face aglow in the lamplight, his eyes shining.

I could not sleep and I went out into the night — and there was a man on the hillside, and when I went close to him, I saw that it was the Adon Mattathias, my father, wrapped in his woolen cloak and looking at the valley as it slumbered in the moonlight. "Welcome, Simon," he said to me, "and come and stand by me, for an old man is better with his son by his side." I went to him, and he put an arm around my shoulders. "What do you look for, Father?" I asked him, and he answered, shrugging, "It could be the angel of death who walks so often in Judea — or it could be these silver hills, and to look at them once more, Simon, for they cleave to me and this is the old land of my fathers. And you come out here because grief and hatred is a knife in you that cuts at your heart. Would you believe me, Simon, that I loved a woman as much once, and she died in child-birth, and my heart hardened like a rock and I cried out to the God of Israel, May you be damned, for you gave me five sons and took away the only thing on earth that I love! A just God weighs a man's grief against his tongue, for con-sider how singularly have I been blessed in these, my withered years. My five sons have not turned against me, for all of my coldness and hardness, nor has one of them raised a hand against another, and of even the sons of Jacob, blessed of memory, that could not be said. How then, Simon, will your own heart turn to stone?"

"Do you want me to laugh with joy?" I asked.

The old man nodded, his long white beard sweeping his chest. "I do, Simon," he said. "We are each of us here for a day. How long ago was it that Mattathias kissed a woman under that olive tree? I close my eyes, and it was no more than yesterday, and we are here for an instant on the body of old Israel. God wants no tears, but laughter, and the dead sleep well. For the living there should be a joyful time, otherwise fight no more, Simon — and how can you fight, or hope, or believe, if you cleave to the dead?"

"With hatred," I said.

"Hatred? Believe me, my son, it's poor fuel for a Jew. How is it written in the holy scrolls they burned? *And pro-claim liberty throughout all the land unto all the inhabitants thereof: it shall be a jubilee unto you; and ye shall return*

*every man unto his possession, and ye shall return every man
unto his family.* Did Isaiah command the people to hatred,
or did he tell them to let justice well up as water, and righteousness as a mighty stream? Save your hatred for your
enemy, my son — for your own people, there must be love
and hope, otherwise put down your bow before ever you lay
a shaft on the string. Look now, Simon, did God give
Ragesh, that tempestuous little man, the only right to say
who is the Maccabee? Only the people can make out of
themselves a Maccabee and raise him up. Yes, they will follow Judas because he is like a flame — and I, who am his
father, say it to you, who are his brother, that never before
in Israel was there such a man as Judas — no, not even
Gideon, may God forgive me; but the flame burns out,
and who will take the ashes and make new life grow out
of them? Simon, Simon — "

"Come inside," I said, for the old man leaned heavily
upon me, shivering a little. "The night air is cold."

"Yes," he said, "and I've talked on like an old fool, long
and not too wisely."

And we went down the hillside, the Adon leaning on my
shoulders.

To the house of Moses ben Aaron I went, the next day,
and the vintner had become like one of his own grapes,
squeezed dry, and of no good to anyone; and his wife sat
like a shadow, a black shawl over her head. "Come in,
Simon," he said to me, "come in, my son, and take off your
shoes and sit with us. We will think, for just a while, that
my daughter is here with us."

"We will not think that," his wife said dully.

"A cup of wine for the son of Mattathias," he said, pouring it for me. "Thus I would send her into the house of the

Adon with a new vintage. Let Mattathias ben John taste and judge — Simon, Simon, this is a lonely household."

"Must you talk of her?" his wife demanded. "Can't you let the dead sleep?"

"Now peace, woman. Do I disturb her sleep? This is the man who loved her — this is Simon ben Mattathias. Of what else should I speak to him? When she was a child, he played with her, and when she grew to be a woman, he held her in his arms. What else should I speak of?"

"Of Apelles," she said.

"May he rot in hell! His name soils my tongue!"

"Of Apelles," she repeated.

"Talk to her, Simon," he pleaded to me. "Talk to her, because she takes no food, not wine, not bread, but only sits like a shadow. Talk to her."

"I've heard enough talk," the mother of Ruth said. "Do I need talk from the sons of the Adon? I was like a mother to them, but of my own I had only one child. Simon, what will you do when Apelles returns to Modin?"

Both of them stared at me, and I nodded. I poured another cup of wine and held it out to her. "Drink, my mother. The time of mourning is over."

She rose, took the cup of wine, and drained it.

In a little shed, built out from a fragment of stone wall as old as the hills, was the anvil and forge of Ruben the smith. Now, as in my own childhood, it was a favorite place for the children. Your mother sent you with a leaking pot or your father with a broken hoe blade. The work was done, but you stayed as the day faded away, caught, trapped, taken by the broad little man, soot-blackened, his mighty arms the personification of the metal he worked, his great hammer a fearful engine of destruction, his bellows the living mouth of a dragon. He lived in a world of sparks and heat, and under his hands the dead metal came alive. He liked children, and he told them his strange stories, like no other stories. Well do I remember coming there once with Ruth, and how she clung fearfully to me while Ruben told us of Cain, the black-browed, red-handed Cain, who was plunged down to the nether world where first he saw the imps work metal — and how he rambled on and on until finally Ruth burst into tears. "Weep not, little girl," he said, melting all at once, and picking her up in his bare, hairy arms, "Oh, weep not, my golden one, my queen in Israel, my beautiful one." But she fought him until he let her go, and then she ran and hid in our corn crib, where I found her and comforted her.

It might have been yesterday when I came to his workshop, for the children were there still, as close as they dared come, while he worked with his hammer, and Judas, stripped to the waist, clamped his metal for him. "And here is Simon," Ruben said, down with the hammer, *clang, clang, clang,* "also to teach me my trade? I was burning metal before you were weaned, either of you. And I've seen a thing or two, for twice I went north to the mountains with Moses ben Aaron, to buy the iron where they dig it from the earth, where the slaves crawl into the ground like moles, all naked — and blind, too, and at night they sleep fenced in, like animals, whining and whimpering. That I saw with my own eyes on the slopes of Ararat, where the ark settled to earth, where the Greeks bring slaves from the whole world over to mine the metal for them. Yet when I make a spear, it is no good, too short in the haft, too heavy in the head — "

"A weapon must serve a man, not man a weapon," Judas said.

"You hear him, Simon ben Mattathias," Ruben smiled, the hammer showering sparks as he beat at the iron — "me, he tells of spears and weapons. When you toddled, Judas, when you were in swathing, I was in Tyre and a Roman cohort came — the first, mind you — and I felt their pilum, six pounds of metal and six pounds of wood behind it. There is a weapon, by all the devils! I have seen the spear of the wild men who live beyond Ararat, three feet of metal and shaped like a leaf, and I have seen the nasty, snake-like spear of the Parthian. Or your Syrian spear, a shovel to scoop out the flesh, or your Greek weapon, fourteen feet long for three men to hold, or your miserable Egyptian spear with its bronze head, or your Bedouin lance. The Roman captain said to me then, Who are you? I answered, A Jew out of Judea, a smith, a worker in metal whose name is Ruben ben Tubel. I hadn't his language or he mine, but we found them to translate. I never met a Jew, he said. Said I, I never met a Roman. He said to me then, Are all Jews as strong and ugly as you? And are all Romans, I answered him, as foul of mouth to strangers? That is a dirty weapon in your hand and a dirty tongue in your head. For I was young then, Judas ben Mattathias, and never afraid of anything that lived. Well, he took a pilum from one of his men and there was a donkey on the street with a bit of a sweet-faced lad pulling it. Look, Jew, he said, and drove the pilum through the donkey with one motion, so that the wood pressed the donkey's side and the iron pole stood two feet beyond. There's our weapon, Jew, he said, while the lad screamed with fear and grief, and there's good pay and better glory in the Legion. I told you I feared nothing then. I threw a silver coin to the lad, and I spat in the Roman's face and walked away. Yes, he might have killed me, but they were strangers there — "

True or not, the children loved his tale, their eyes fixed upon him, their faces rapt. Judas held up the spearhead, long, slender as a reed, still glowing red from the heat.

"Temper it!" the smith said, and Judas plunged it into a bucket of cold water. Through the steam, I heard the smith ring it with his hammer.

"Too frail," he said. "Too frail. Armor will stand it."

"But flesh will not," Judas answered evenly, "and it will find its way. Make them, Ruben, make them."

And in the month of Tishri, when the sweet breath of the new year was all over the land, Apelles returned. So things have a beginning and an end — even Modin.

Judas laid his plans well. He was tireless; day and night, he worked, planned, schemed, and day by day, the store of long, slender spears mounted. A village condemned was Modin. We dug our bows out of the ground. We made new arrows. We turned our plows into spears. We put a razor edge upon our knives. And already, even now, it was to Judas that people brought their woes. "And six children, Judas ben Mattathias — " "We will make provision for the children." "And what will a man do with his goats?" "Our stock goes with us." It was Lebel, the teacher, who pleaded his case. "I am a man of peace, of peace." He came to the Adon, his bloodshot blue eyes wet with tears. "Where is the place of a man of peace in Israel today?" And the Adon called for Judas, who listened and nodded.

"Will our children grow up like savages in the wilderness?"

"No," Lebel said.

"Or Jews who cannot read or write?"

Lebel shook his head.

"Then make peace in your heart, Lebel!"

Then Judas told the Adon that the few slaves in Modin must be freed. "Why?" "Because only free men can fight like free men," Judas said. The Adon said, "Then ask the people —" And thus was our first assembly in the open valley. From the near-by villages of Goumad and Dema, people came to listen, and the synagogue would not hold them all, so Judas stood on the fragment of ancient stone wall to speak, and he said to people:

"I want no man who is faint of heart to follow me! I want no man who cares more for his wife and child than he cares for freedom! I want no man who counts the measure when he pours it out! I know a road that leads in only one direction, and who travels it must travel light. I want no slaves or bondsmen — turn them away or put weapons in their hands!"

"Who are you to talk like that?" some of them cried.

"A Jew out of Modin," Judas said. There could be an incredible simplicity about him — yet a cunning measure of the people he spoke to. "And if a Jew should not speak, then I'll be silent" — and he began to climb down. But they shouted at him:

"Speak! Speak!"

"I don't come with gifts," he said simply. "I come with blood on my hands — and there will be blood on yours when you listen to me."

"Speak!" they told him. And afterwards, when twenty men from Goumad came armed, to seek him out, they asked in the village:

"Where will we find the Maccabee?"

And the people of Modin directed them to the house of Mattathias. Thus it was in the days before Apelles came back . . .

I told you how the road ran through our village and through the valley. There was much that Judas did, but this I took on myself, and each morning I posted one of the village boys on a high crag, where he could see the road for miles. Eastward, over hill and dale, through a necklace of villages, the road traveled to Jerusalem, but westward by stages it went down to the forest and through the forest to the Mediterranean. One day it was Jonathan, one day another of the boys, and as long as it was light they perched on the rocks, straining their young eyes for the glitter of a breastplate or the flash of a spear. I knew it must come and come soon; no secret can be a secret in a land like ours, where every bit of news travels like the wind through the valleys and the villages.

I had none of Judas's sublime faith. There were the weak and the strong, the poor and the wealthy, and it was well enough to talk about the warden and his men, but what would happen when the test came? Already Eleazar and Jonathan worshiped Judas; his every word, his every wish was their law. How can I deny that I envied the way they listened to him, the way they watched him! When I saw that, the old hatred, the old bitterness, the old resentment welled up in me — so that I asked myself over and over again, Why isn't he like other men? I soaked myself in guilt, because I knew deep in my heart that if Judas had been here, Ruth would be alive — and somehow I held it against him that there was never a word of reproach, never a word of blame for me, never a word of anger. Yet when John came to me looking for sympathy, I turned on him.

"Are you for this too?" he wanted to know. His wife was heavy with child.

"For what?"

"For war, for death? Walk in righteousness, it says, walk in peace. But when Judas speaks, we stop thinking."

"What would you think of, John?" I demanded.

"At least, this way we live."

"And is life so dear?" I cried. "Is it so good, so sweet, so just?" I caught myself. Was I like the Adon already? Was this my brother or a stranger? Yet in spite of myself, I said the cruelest thing I knew, "Are you a son of Mattathias, or a bastard? Are you a Jew?"

It was like the lash of a whip, and John cringed visibly; it was worse than the lash of a whip, for this was a saintly man who had never lifted up his voice against any living thing, but accepted God's will with that gentle Jewish Amen, so be it; and he stared at me for a while before he dropped his head and walked away. . . .

And then Apelles returned.

In the morning, Nathan ben Borach, thirteen years old and fast as a deer, came leaping down from the hillside, calling, "Simon! Simon!" But all the people heard, and when I reached him, I had to push through the press of the people. "From where?" I asked him. "From the west." "And how far?" "Two or three miles — I don't know how far. I saw the gleam you told me to watch for, and then I saw the men and I came."

"We have time," Judas decided, quieting them. "Go to your houses and bolt the doors and close the shutters — and wait." He had a little silver whistle that Ruben had made for him. "When I call you, come — those who have spears with spears and the rest with bows. Watch your shafts when you drop them and shoot well."

"And the men from Goumad?"

"It's too late," Judas said, "and this will be for Modin."

"We could go to the hills now," someone said.

"And we could bend our knees to Apelles. Go to your houses, and those of you who have no heart, stay there, stay there."

They did as he said, and doors closed and the village became silent. The Adon and Rabbi Ragesh and Judas and Eleazar and I stood in the square and waited. I had my knife in my belt, and under his cloak Judas wore the long two-edged sword of Pericles. Then Jonathan ran from the house and joined us. I would have sent him back, but Judas looked at me and nodded — and I held my peace. A moment later, John joined us, and with him was Ruben ben Tubel, cloaked and clenching his hammer under his cloak. Close together, the eight of us waited, until presently we heard the beat of a drum and the metallic clash of armor — and then the mercenaries came, first a rank of twenty, then Apelles in his litter, then sixty more in three ranks of twenty, no horsemen now, for which I breathed a sigh of relief, but walking among the mercenaries a Jew, a white robed Levite whom I recognized as one of the Temple attendants from Jerusalem.

The slaves set down the litter, and Apelles hopped out, grotesquely magnificent in a golden mantle and a little red skirt. How well I remember him as he stood there in the cool Judean morning, the apostle of civilization, his hair carefully set and curled, his cupid bow lips delicately rouged, his pink cheeks carefully shaven, his jowls underlined with a golden necklace, his capon bosom swelling the golden mantle, his fat thighs setting off his flounced skirt, his little feet encased in high silver sandals that wound up his dimpled calves.

"The Adon Mattathias," he greeted us, "the noble lord of a noble people." My father nodded, but said nothing. "And is this a welcome?" he lisped. "Are eight men a fitting delegation for your warden?"

"The people are in their houses."

"Their pigpens," Apelles smiled.

"We will call them if you wish," the Adon said, gently and respectfully.

"Presently, presently," Apelles agreed. "You suit my mood. There is a civilized way of doing everything. Jason!" he cried, waving at the Levite.

Hesitantly, the Jew joined him. The man was afraid. His face was as white as his cap, and his tiny beard and his two tiny mustaches trembled visibly.

"Now welcome, Joseph ben Samuel," my father said gently, "to the poor hospitality of Modin."

"*Shalom,*" the Levite whispered.

"An ancient greeting, a warm greeting," the Adon said. "And peace unto you, Joseph ben Samuel. Our house is enriched with an elder of the tribe of Levi."

"He comes to the sacrifice," Apelles lisped smilingly. "The great King to his poor wardens saith thus, 'My heart is heavy with this dark folk and their dark worship. An unseen God makes a secretive and vile people.' So saith the King to me, his poor warden, and what else should I do but obey his orders? Yet I brought the good Jason here, a Levite, so that you might sacrifice in your own way." He clapped his pudgy hands, and two mercenaries fetched a bronze altar they had been carrying and set it down before us. It was a slim thing, about four feet high, and crowned with the figure of Athene.

"Pallas Athene," Apelles said, mincing around the altar. "She was my own choice — Wisdom. Knowledge comes first and then civilization. Is that not so? Later Zeus and the swift Hermes. A complete man is a full man, is that not so?

Make a flame, Jason, and burn the incense — and then we will have the people forth to see the Adon do honor to this noble lady."

"Yes, make a flame, Joseph ben Samuel," my father said. "Pallas Athene — later Zeus and the swift Hermes. Make a flame, Joseph ben Samuel."

Looking at the Adon, never taking his eyes off the Adon, the Levite approached the altar. Then, with one quick step, my father reached out a long arm, seized the Jew, and in a motion so quick I could scarcely follow, drew his knife and plunged it into his heart.

"There is your sacrifice, Apelles!" he cried, hurling the dead Levite against the altar. "For the Goddess of Wisdom!"

The shrill sound of Judas's whistle broke the morning air. The two mercenaries who had brought the altar leveled their spears and came at us, but Eleazar raised the altar and flung it at them, bowling both over. Apelles turned to run, but Judas was on him, his first grasp short and stripping off the golden mantle. Half naked, Apelles tripped and fell, rolled over, and then squealed wildly as he saw Judas above him. With his bare hands, Judas killed him, lifting him by the neck and snapping it suddenly, as you do with a chicken, so that the wild squeals stopped and the head lolled.

Then, for the first time, I saw Judas fight. The mercenaries were driving down on us, their brazen shields lapping, their shovel-like spears leveled. Judas drew his sword; I picked up the spear of one of the groaning mercenaries Eleazar had struck, and Eleazar had gotten from somewhere a wine mallet, an eight-foot pole with twenty pounds of wood at the end of it, used for mashing grapes in a deep cistern. The blacksmith joined us with his hammer, but it was Eleazar who broke the first rank of spears, charging in and using the long heavy pole as a flail. Judas was beside him, sword in one hand, knife in the other, never pausing, never still, quicker than I had ever dreamed a man could be, a stroke here, a cut there, always in motion, always making a circle of steel around him with the sword.

It was not a long battle, and my own part was small. The spear of a battle-maddened mercenary tore my cloak, and I closed with him and broke my spear on his shield. We rolled on the ground, he trying to draw his sword, I cursing the neck plates that impeded my fingers. He half drew his sword, and I stopped trying to throttle him, but beat his face in with my clenched fist and continued to beat at the bloody face even after he was dead. I took his sword, and all of this seemed like hours but could only have been a minute or two at most, yet the people of Modin had already poured out of the houses, some with spears and some with bows, and the world was full of that wild screaming that goes on in a battle — and the mercenaries were no longer in orderly ranks with lapped shields, but in clumps and clusters, and a good many of them on the ground and others running.

But around Judas and Eleazar and Ruben they made a knot, as if these three must be torn down and offered to whatever Gods mercenaries worshiped, or the world would end surely; and there I went, where my brothers fought, and there too the Adon came, knife in hand, cloak torn and bloodstained. I killed another man — I remember yet the blasphemous ease of slaughter — running through the small of the back, severing his spine just beneath his armor; and I saw the Adon drag down another, an old wolf, truly, and terrible in the strength of his wiry arms — and then it was done, and Judas and Eleazar and Ruben and my father and I stood panting and gasping for breath with twelve dead and dying men at our feet, and what remained of the mercenaries fled.

They fled through the streets and the Jews followed them with arrows and slew them. They fled into the houses where they were hunted down and fought like wolves until they were slain. They fled up the hillside, pricked all over with arrows, and yet they were dragged down. We took no prisoners; these were mercenaries we fought. The last one was dragged out of a cistern where he crouched, soaked in olive oil, and a spear was driven through his heart.

And then the battle of Modin was done. Only eight Jews were dead, although at least fifty, including my father, bore wounds of the fight; but every mercenary had died. Apelles was dead, as was the Levite. Of the *nokri*, only the slaves who bore the litter remained.

So I tell it here, I, Simon, the least of all my glorious brothers, and as I tell it, the fighting in Modin was finished, and Ruth was avenged, hollow as vengeance is, and the blood ran in our village street, and the whole valley was like a charnel house, with ninety dead men sprawled through it. It was the end and the beginning; for after that fight, no man of Modin was ever again the same, and even to this day it is said of the few of us who are left, the pitiful few out of Modin — "He was in the valley when we first slew the mercenaries."

In an hour, we, the people of peace, of the book, had learned to kill, and we learned well. With Judas, I faced the huddled knot of slaves who had borne Apelles's litter. Coldly, Judas told them that they could do one of two things; they could join us, accept circumcision, become Jews and fight by our sides, or they could go out of Judea forever. Uncomprehendingly, they stared, and Judas re-

peated what he had said, and still they stared uncomprehendingly, their mouths wide, their frightened eyes still
mirroring the brief, bloody, savage fight in which no quarter
was asked and no quarter was given.

Where could they go? They were branded breast and
face as slaves; slaves they had been and slaves they would
always be, and there was no hope and no courage left in
them. All over their bodies, they bore the marks of Apelles's
metal whip; but Apelles they knew, and we were strange,
bearded devils whom they did not know; so finally they
trudged out of the valley, westward to the sea, where some
new master would find them and put them into bondage
once again.

There was much to do, and curiously enough there was
little mourning — very little for Jews who are so close knit,
man and wife, parents and child, making a sanctuary out
of the family. We buried our dead. We gathered together
the bodies of the mercenaries, stripped them of arms and
armor, and put them together in one grave. Only one
body was desecrated — that of Apelles. Moses ben Aaron,
wounded and bloody all over from the fight, cut off the
head of Apelles. First some of the people tried to stop him,
but the Adon said sternly:

"Leave him be and let him make his own peace with
God!"

The vintner moved like a man in a dream, walking here
and there in the village street, holding the head by its
curly, oiled locks, dripping blood behind him. His wife
ran after him, screaming; it had been her deep hatred for
Apelles that left him unmoved once, but now she cried at
him:

"What terrible curse will you bring down on us? Are you
a man or a devil?"

"A devil," he answered dully. "Get away from me, woman!"

At last, he stopped in the market square, where the worst fighting had taken place, where the bronze altar lay. His face set, he righted the altar and jammed the head of Apelles onto the slim statue of Athene.

"This way I worship," he said, and spat into the dead face and then turned away, this mild and philosophic little man, who a year ago would have cringed at the sight of blood. What happened to him, I will tell in its place.

We finished our preparations. We gathered our stock, our goats, our sheep, our donkeys. The donkeys we loaded with our household goods, and whatever else we could carry, we took with us. What we could not carry, we destroyed. The cisterns of sweet olive oil, we befouled. The great tanks of wine, we smashed. It was farewell and good-by to everything we had known, to the whole, deep, straightforward current of our lives. It was farewell to Modin, to the little valley that had nurtured us, to our sacred scrolls which were ashes, to the ancient stone synagogue, to the terraced and fertile fields which we had built and our fathers before us and their fathers before them. It was farewell to the graveyard where Jews had lain for a thousand years. It was farewell, yet no one protested now and no one wept. And then, when most of the night was done, the caravan started — and once more we were the wanderers, the homeless ones.

So the village moved out of Modin and northward, and now we were armed. We carried spears and swords and bows, and we were a grim band as we wended our way through the terraces, higher and higher. In Goumad, where we paused to rest and where the people brought us milk and fruit and wine, we told the story of the fight, and when we left Goumad, twelve families of that village were with us. We did not recruit; we did not harangue. When they asked "For how long?" we answered "Until we are free." Until the land is cleansed over, three times, as it is written.

With nightfall, we camped on a lonely mountainside, and as the sun set, we prayed and remembered the dead. Now, after the weariness and strangeness of the day's journey, some of the children began to weep, and their mothers comforted them, singing to them, "Sleep, my lamb, my woolly lamb; slumber, little waif of God. Never fear the darkness; your pure heart fills it with light . . ." that song which was old already when Moses heard it from his mother's lips.

I sat by a fire, and Judas plucked my arm. I followed him, and we climbed up the face of the cliff, higher and higher, until we saw the Mediterranean, all bathed over with the final, rosy hue of sunset. Then Judas pointed down through the valleys to Modin, and I saw a glow that was not of the sunset. The village was burning. For over an hour, we stayed there, watching it, never speaking, but watching it burn, and at last, Judas said:

"They will pay — for every lick of flame, for every drop of blood, for every hurt."

"It will not bring Modin back."

"We will bring Modin back."

We had planned where we would go. Two days north of Modin, twenty miles as a bird flies, but two days weary journey for a strong man on foot and twice that for our village, on the very border of Judea, is the Wilderness of Ephraim. Once, centuries ago, before the Exile, this was a more populous and fertile land than even the terraced hills and lush valleys around Jerusalem. In those days, many thousands of Jews lived there, for the bottom lands were deeper and richer than anywhere else in Palestine; but in the time of the Exile, it was depopulated, and only a sprinkling of hardy folk had returned to its lonely ravines. Judas had been there, and Ragesh too, and years before, my father and certain others of the old men. But I saw it for the first time on the afternoon we went into it, the great, dark, wooded peaks, with grim Mount Ephraim towering over all, flinging its menacing ridges eastward to Mount Gaash; the tangled forests, cedar and pine and birch, the bare cliffs and the deep, dark gorges.

A woeful silence fell over us as we approached. Conversation stopped, and even the persistent, unconquerable laughter of the children died away. We went into a narrow valley, wended our way downward and downward through lush green woods, and the broad sunlight broke into bands and then into flecked splotches. Deer darted past, and once a jackal barked, and there were other noises in the woods that were strange to us. At the bottom of the valley was a swamp, from which cranes and herons darted up as we pushed through. For hours, we trod the muck of that swamp and then we came up to higher land, and then turned up into a cleftlike, sheltered valley, full of dead leaves and pine needles, unholy in its quiet, and almost never visited by the sun.

We who had left home were home, and it was the beginning.

PART THREE

Eleazar, the Splendor of Battle

IT WAS NOT A CHEERFUL PLACE, THAT WIL-
derness of Ephraim, and as the days passed, it became
less cheerful. The ashes of Modin were scarcely cold when
a hundred other villages of Judea became flaming reminders
of the Greek passion for civilization, and singly, in pairs, by
the fives and the tens, refugees trickled into the little valley
where we hid. "Marah," someone called the place, because
it was born out of bitterness and sorrow, and the name took
hold.

To Marah came people because there was no other place,
particularly, for them to go, and because they had heard
that in Marah the sons of Mattathias were. Apollonius,
chief warden of Jerusalem and Judea, lined the valley
road from Modin to Hadid with the heads of Jews, seven
hundred of them mounted on poles, to wipe out the insult
of Apelles's head on the altar. With five thousand mercenaries, he ranged Judea from end to end, killing and burning
and destroying. And we hid in the mountains, paralyzed at
first, until the bitterness of the people demanded of Mattathias, "What will you do?"

"We will fight," Judas said; but it was one thing to say
that now, hidden away in the hills and another when the
enemy came into your own village. The old man, the Adon,

said nothing. How he had aged in the past year! His hair was snow white; his cheeks were sunken, and his high-ridged nose was all that remained to show his fierce and unremitting will. For hours he sat alone, chin on hand, brooding, thinking, dreaming of God-knows-what; and it seemed to me, often enough, that when the people came to him with their complaints, he listened with unhearing ears and looked with unseeing eyes.

When Judas and I came to him, one day, he demanded of us, "Which of you did Ragesh call the Maccabee?"

"What would you have us do?" Judas asked, a note of bewilderment in his voice.

"And what would you have me do? I sit here, an Adon of a wilderness, and I dream of my youth. Am I a young man that you ask me what to do?"

"The people are afraid and lonely and bewildered," I said.

"*You* are afraid, not the people," the old man said to me, contemptuous.

"What should we do?"

"Bring me your brothers and any others who are not afraid, and I'll show you what to do," the Adon answered coldly. Judas faced him, staring at him; then Judas turned and walked away and I followed. It was not a change in Judas, and there was still the same cold hopelessness and emptiness inside of me; but the world had changed, and we were a homeless, tiny group of a tiny and insignificant folk, a handful of folk who farmed the valleys of Judea and called themselves Jews and worshiped an invisible God and made themselves different from all other people — and now had ranged themselves against the might of the Syrian Empire with its one hundred and twenty walled cities, its Greek aristocracy, and its untold thousands of mercenaries. That was what had sunk home, in me, in Judas too, in everyone among us as we fled into Ephraim — the war machine that was backed by a hundred thousand talents of wealth, a hundred thousand mercenaries, and a hundred thousand more if those were slain — and beyond Syria were the other Greek empires, and there was Egypt ravening in the south for the lush wealth of our valleys; and it came to the whole world, which could pause in its affairs to eliminate Jews, because to all nations and all peoples the Jew was the same, an abomination whose ways were not their ways.

We found our brothers, and Ragesh too; Ruben the smith, Moses ben Aaron, and a handful more who could rouse themselves out of their misery to follow the Adon. We armed ourselves with bows, knives — and swords, those of us who wanted to know the feel of this strange weapon, and we came to the Adon. He didn't greet us well. "Where there should have been a hundred, there are twenty," he said, and then he said nothing else for hours, leading us a swift pace southward — a lean, tireless, angry old man.

We came into Shiloh on the road to Jerusalem, a pleasant little village on a mountain stream, a village that tore at our hearts, it was so like Modin. It was a way-stop, with an inn, for Shiloh, then as now, was famous for its amber-colored raisin wine and the honey cheese it prepared. As we came striding into the town, walking close, grim-faced and dusty, the people looked at us with surprise and fear. Arms and all, we were covered with our cloaks, but who was there in Judea who did not know, by description if not by sight, the towering, white-bearded figure of the Adon Mattathias? And who did not know that he and his sons were outlaw, cursed by the Macedonians and by the high priest Menelaus as well?

Surprise there should have been, but not such fear, even

though this was a place where Apelles had worked well, even though a tall altar to Zeus stood in the square, garlanded with fruits and dirty with new blood; even so, there should have not been such fear in their faces, though cowardice is not a rare thing in such times and surrender is easier than a burned home and a cave in the mountains of Ephraim or the lonely Wilderness of Bethaven.

And then we saw the mercenaries at the inn, sitting on the grass outside, comfortable with loaves of bread and goblets of wine and fresh boiled chicken that they crammed into their mouths, the fat running down their unwashed jowls. A dozen of them, there were, tribute to the gentle charm of a bent knee, and they had two slaves with them to carry spears and shields. The better for comfort, they had laid aside their heavy breast armor, unlaced their leather jerkins and turned back their skirts, so that their manliness might be as well displayed as their filthiness. Then as now, the mercenary is an everlasting mystery to the Jew — this landless, nationless, cityless creature, who is born and raised and hired out only to kill. Since these labored for Greeks, they abided by the regulation on shaving, but there was always the dark growth of a few days on their cheeks. For them, water was neither to be taken by mouth nor by skin; an abomination to them, they liked better the smell that surrounded them, the dirt that encrusted them — which were good comrades for their incredible ignorance.

There was a poor, half-witted girl of Shiloh, whose name we later learned was Miriam, an orphan waif from Jerusalem who had found shelter in the town, but not too much more than that as it seemed, and they were playing a game with her as we came along the street, passing her from man to man, playing at childish and perverted and miserable exhibitionism, laughing and shouting at each other in the crude and vulgarized Aramaic patois that is the common speech of the Macedonian hirelings — this they were doing until we came up and halted there, twenty Jews, tall and unsmiling, dust-covered from the road and cloaked, head and foot, led by one lean, hawk-faced, white-bearded old man, calm, but with something awful that pervaded his quiet, something the mercenaries could not but sense, even as they must have sensed an extension of that quiet to the village, suddenly still and almost deserted of people.

"Get on, you old crow," one of them said, and the others laughed; but their laughter was unnatural now, and the girl Miriam curled up on the ground and wept. The inn-keeper came bustling out, a fat man, clean-shaven, but a Jew from his speech.

"What is it now?" he said. "I want no trouble here and no beggars from the road!"

"And we look like beggars?" the Adon asked softly. "Who are you, innkeeper, that you call us beggars? If we are out of the dry lands and thirsty, is there no draught of wine for us?"

As my father spoke, the officer of the mercenaries came to the door of the inn and stood there, sipping at a glass of wine and prepared to be amused by the bout between the innkeeper and us.

"You see my house is occupied," the innkeeper said, but less certainly, looking at us narrowly and uncomfortably.

"And thus the blessed Abraham spoke when the three strangers came to his tent?" the Adon went on, even more softly and gently. "Or did he come forward with sweet water to wash their feet? Or did his wife, Sarah, cook food with her own hands that they might eat? Your doors are closed to your own people — if you still have people — but open to this filth, to these creatures who kill for hire."

The mercenaries and their officer could follow only a little of what was said, for my father spoke in the old Hebrew instead of the Aramaic, but the innkeeper went white.

Shaking visibly, he managed to ask, "Who are you, old man?"

"The Adon Mattathias!" the girl screamed.

My father threw off his cloak, as did we, drawing our swords, except for Jonathan whose bow was strung, who crouched as the captain of the mercenaries leaped forward shouting, who loosed an arrow that sank into his throat and ended his screaming in a terrible, blood-choked cry. The innkeeper fled into the house. The mercenaries lay where they were, half drunk, paralyzed at this sudden and awful appearance of twenty armed men led by a fierce and angry old patriarch, and we slew them where they were, without mercy and without pity. It was a bitter thing to do, a terrible thing to do; but these were not men whom we could take captive, talk to, entreat, move, change — these were mercenaries.

When it was finished, when only the two slaves remained, huddled together and crying with terror, the girl Miriam crawled to my father and embraced his legs. We watched him, and he stood for a moment, motionless, bloody sword in hand; then he let go his sword, drew the girl to her feet, kissed her lips and said:

"What is your name, my child?"

"Miriam."

"Who was your father? Who was your mother?"

"I don't know," she sobbed.

"And how many like you are there?" the old man sighed. "Do you know where the Wilderness of Ephraim is?"

She nodded.

"Then wash and go there, and when you meet a Jew, ask him to take you to the place of Mattathias and if he asks you who your father is, tell him Mattathias is your father."

"I'm afraid — I'm afraid."

"Go now!" he told her sternly. "Go and don't look behind you." And then he said to us, "Fetch me the innkeeper!"

People had come up now. First the children — and then more and more, until a half-circle of Jews contained the inn yard, frightened and silent and staring at the shambles of the dead men. Eleazar and Ruben went into the house; we heard them stamping through it, and then they emerged dragging the innkeeper, who was limp with fear, who wept and moaned. They threw him at the feet of the Adon, and he crawled forward on his belly, inch by inch, until he could kiss the straps of my father's sandals.

"Stop it!" my father roared. "What are you — Jew or Greek or animal that you crawl on your belly to me! Stand up on your feet!"

His only response was to lie there, moaning and rolling his fat bulk from side to side. My father spurned him with his toe, walked away and turned to the people.

"And look you, now — I would have slain him and with my own hand, but let him live and remember that he crawled on his belly like this, and tell it up and down the land, so that his life will become a hell and he can look no man in the face. Our people have been slain and tortured until the whole land sounds with their cries, but his own rotten life is so much that he will press his face to the dirt for it. He is a brave man when the conquerer stands behind him — as are you all, you wretched and miserable people! God's curse on you!"

The women began to sob. Here and there, someone said, "No — No." And men covered their faces with their cloaks.

"Will you not look at me?" the Adon cried. "Am I worse than the mercenaries?"

An old man pushed through them and up to my father. "Take back your curse, Mattathias ben John ben Simon! What have we done to deserve your curse?"

"You have bent your knee," my father said coldly.

"Have you forgotten me, Mattathias?" the old man demanded. "Jacob ben Gerson — have you forgotten me?"

"I remember you," my father said.

"And I have not bent my knee, Mattathias. Nineteen they slew here in Shiloh, and four of them were circumcised infants, so that we would heed the Greek ways and circumcise no more — and then we made our peace with them. Take your curse away."

"What holds you here, old man? Is life so sweet? I've had my threescore years and more — and so have you. What holds you here?"

"Where shall I go, Mattathias? Where shall my people go?"

"Go to Ephraim!" my father charged him, his voice bitter and unyielding. "Go to the wilderness, where we have camped under tents like our fathers and where we make a strength out of ourselves! But bow yourself to no man, not even to the Lord God, for He doesn't ask it." And then, pushing past him, the Adon went to the altar, threw it over, stalked past it, past the people and through Shiloh. We followed him and said no word, except when Judas whispered to me:

"There's a fire in him — and if he were young, Simon, if he were young — "

"He's young," I said curtly. "He's young and they don't have to call him the Maccabee."

"What do you mean?"

"And you don't know what I mean, Judas?" I murmured.

He grasped my cloak and demanded, almost pitifully, "And you, too, Simon — in the name of God, what have I done to you that you should hate me so?"

"Nothing."

"And you hate me for nothing?"

"Nothing," I said. "Nothing — and come. He won't wait, the old man."

We turned off the road, crossed the valley, and mounted the hillside. High up, where we could see for miles in every direction, we made our camp, ate our bread and washed it down with wine, and then lay down in our cloaks around a smoldering brushwood fire. Night fell, yet I could not sleep, so filled was my mind with the day's events, with the brief and savage slaughter at the inn, with the dread picture of the old man, my father — and with memories before that too, our pleasant sweet childhood in Modin, Ruth and her love for me, and my love for her — what it was, memories of what are now less than memories, so short and strange and little known is life. As always in that time between night and day, where there's no comfort of slumber, life became like a dream, a moment, something to be grasped at and sought and sought — just as I would always seek, and have sought, indeed, for the kind of love I knew in that moment at Modin, that brief and sun-soaked moment when there was neither yesterday nor tomorrow but only now. And the remembering, the fear and the loneliness, became too much, and I rose and went to the dying and sullen pit of our fire, heatless now in the cold melancholy of early morning. As I stood there, someone touched my arm, and I whirled to see the Adon, looking at me like an old hawk. Had he not slept?

"Find your brother, Simon, and come with me," he said.

I woke Judas and we followed the Adon up the hillside to a rocky escapement. "Look there," my father said, pointing down the valley away from Shiloh and toward Jerusalem, and following his hand, we saw in the blackness a suggestion of light, like a few flung and dying embers. "What would you say?" he asked.

"I would say you should have killed that swine, the innkeeper," Judas replied angrily, "for that's a camp of mercenaries. No time was wasted to bring them."

"And yet you were silent enough at the inn," the old man murmured.

"I was silent."

"And now — Judas, whom Ragesh calls the Maccabee," he said ironically, "what now?"

Silent and stony-faced, Judas stood and stared down the valley.

"What now, Judas Maccabeus?" my father demanded contemptuously. "They sit there in the valley, and when dawn comes they will go into Shiloh and make ashes of it. If I had slain the innkeeper, Judas Maccabeus, I would have done so with my own hand and my own sword — but you who talked so well of war, how many children will die in Shiloh tomorrow?"

Without answering, Judas strode toward our fire, and I turned on my father furiously. "Would you break every living thing around you, old man?"

The hand that grasped my shoulder was like an iron claw, and for days after the marks were there, and the old man, the Adon, said to me, in that soft and awful way of his:

"Honor me, Simon, for you are out of my loins and still less of a man — and by all that is holy, I'll have soft words from my sons! What is strong doesn't break!" And then he walked off after Judas.

When I reached the fire, everyone was up, and a moment later, we moved through the night after Judas. With no words spoken, the Adon fell back, and Judas led. Already, the night was breaking, and eastward there was a gray haze of dawn, and it was just light enough to make out the path we followed. Southward, Judas led us, climbing higher, until we walked on the crusted edge of the hills, and he led us quickly, never pausing for care or breath, but quickly, almost headlong, until in not too long a while we hung on a ledge over the camp of the mercenaries, square beneath us, some six or seven hundred feet down, sprawled in sleep on the road itself where the road and the two hillsides of the valley merged. Here too was evidence of the contempt the Greeks had for this bucolic and peaceful folk, the Jews, the peace-worshiping Jews who knew neither how to war nor to defend; for there in relief of Shiloh were only two twenties of footmen, with no guard over them as they slept, no sentries, but only stacked weapons and piled armor and deep sleep.

Now Judas didn't hesitate; he gave his orders swiftly, almost bitterly, sending a handful of men under Jonathan, the boy Jonathan, the quick, eager, restless boy Jonathan, a few hundred paces north; John went with them, but the boy Jonathan led, and they were to go down until they were a spear-length from the road and wait; and a handful more went south with the Adon. Eleazar and I and Ruben remained with Judas, who led us to a great boulder, a mighty boulder that perched on the ledge and had perched there since God first cast the hills on this sweet and ancient land. "Can you move it, Eleazar?" he asked, and Eleazar, smiling, crouched under it, spread his arms to gain purchase, and then heaved. Dawn was coming, the rosy, wonderful Judean dawn, and in the faint, new light Eleazar's mighty frame unfolded itself like Samson of old. He had shed his cloak, stripped off his coat and cast his sandals. Clad only in his linen trousers, he was all of man's strength, the muscles bunching, tightening, and then driving in one savage effort that unhinged the stone and moved it, as it had not moved since first the earth began. It shook, and we joined our arms to his; it stirred, and Eleazar urged it as though it lived; it rocked, and then it turned over and fell. One moment, it paused at the edge of the ledge, then over and down with a crash that shook the hills like thunder, splitting in two and starting a hundred other rocks that bounded and roared and drove down on the sleeping mercenaries — asleep no longer, but frightfully awake, seeking about them, crawling, running, picking up whatever arms were at hand, screaming in terror as the rocks plunged on them.

Swords drawn, we four followed the rocks. At least ten of them must have been killed and crippled by the landslide, and perhaps half again as many fled wildly along the road in either direction, to be slain by the arrows of our two little groups; yet four times our number rallied and stood and faced our little group with sword and spear. Again I saw my brothers fight, Judas, so swift and terrible and deadly, and Eleazar, the gentle, amiable Eleazar who was one with battle, who loved it and fought like a demon out of hell. There were only four of us, and we were not rocks upon their sleep, but men of flesh and blood, and there were fifteen or sixteen of them. Let it not be said that a mercenary cannot fight; that alone they *can* do, well; and I learned it that morning, fighting for my life, with Judas on one side of me and Ruben on the other — even as we fought again, so many long years later — but with Eleazar now, who slew two men and cut down a third, and without whom then, at the beginning, when we had scarcely learned to fight, we should have surely perished. Battle is forever; time stands still; and the strength goes from the body like water from a hole in a bottle. Back to back, four square, we held them off and seven of them were down, but I was cut and bleeding and so was Ruben from a long spear thrust. They came at us again with spears when Jonathan and his men reached us, and then it was over. Two fled up the hillside, Eleazar after them, barehanded and barefooted, springing from rock to rock, like a great cat. One he reached and slew with a crushing, awful blow of his fist, but the second turned at bay with his long, shovel-like Syrian spear. He thrust at Eleazar, who avoided the blow, caught the spear with a lightninglike movement, and jerked. The mercenary fell forward and Eleazar was upon him. It happened quickly, so quickly that we stood and watched; panting, bleeding, we watched, as if there were an unwritten but known pact that this was for Eleazar ben Mattathias and no other, for Eleazar to struggle with him, roll over once, and then come erect with the mercenary's throat in his two hands, come erect and lift, so that the man hung there, screaming and clawing until he died and Eleazar let go of him.

We dragged all of the bodies to the road and piled them there, after we had taken what weapons we could carry. Almost all of us were wounded, cut and bleeding, even my father, and some badly; but we were all alive and able to walk — and there was no mercenary who lived. We piled the bodies and Judas said:

"This way, and again and again until they come into our land no longer."

And then we washed our wounds and laid down to rest.

So it began and we learned the new war, the people's war that is not fought with armies and wealth, but with the strength that comes out of the people; for we went again to Shiloh and told them how it was. Twelve men of Shiloh joined us, and we gave them arms out of what we had taken from the mercenaries; for the rest, sentries were posted on the hills around the village, so that when the mercenaries came again they would be warned and they would take their possessions and flee.

Then for nine days, we raided among the hills and valleys of northern Judea. In those nine days, we learned our warfare; we learned to fight in a different way than people had ever fought before. We traveled by night, in the starlight and the moonlight, and in the warm days we slept in caves or in sheltered wooded thickets. We moved quickly, and Judas began to use a tactic which later became the basis for all our operations, attack from the rear and sudden appearance in the rear of an enemy who pursued us. It was a rhythm of motion, and once it had begun, Judas allowed no pause, no rest. We learned other things too, for at first we weighed ourselves down with the heavy spears and swords of the mercenaries, many of us putting on their breastplates as well, but whatever we gained with the unfamiliar weapons, we lost in a lack of mobility, and toward the end of our raid, we had abandoned all our armor. The mercenaries were not bowmen, and where they had detachments of archers, the bows were heavy, five-foot-long staffs of curved wood. These too, we took at first, attracted by the deadly look of them, but soon threw them away for our small and practical bows of laminated ram's horn, which we had used all our lives for hares and jackals and wild birds. When we could, we attacked before the dawn — otherwise at some time in the night. Nor was it all victory. The two fights at Shiloh made us overconfident, and lent us contempt for the mercenaries; we paid a price for that, a ter-

rible price, for flushed with our success we attacked a column of sixty mercenaries outside of Bethel, three twenties
of them and in daylight, so that they could mesh their
shields and drive a phalanx at us. By then our number had
grown to thirty-nine, yet we would have all perished had it
not been for the terrible fighting fury of Eleazar and Judas,
who beat back attack after attack, even when only nine of
us still stood on our feet, so that finally what was left of the
mercenaries and what was left of us drew apart, panting and
weak from the fight, each group too hurt to do more; and we
were able to lift our wounded and bear them away.

That was the end of our raid, but in the nine days all
Judea had been set aflame and seething and turbulent,
and there was no family, no matter how far removed, but
knew the name of Mattathias and his sons. And the Greeks
licked their wounds and no longer regarded the Jew as a
meek and gentle scholar who would sooner die on the
Sabbath day than lift a hand in his defense. No longer did
their mercenaries travel the roads of our land alone or in
tens or even in twenties, but they withdrew into their
walled fortresses, and when they moved, they moved as
armies, and when they slept their sentries paced anxiously
back and forth. No, it was not all on our side, for they took
their revenge, killing and burning and looting and lighting
up the whole land at night with the flames of burning villages. But the people fought back; they died in their burning
villages with knives in their hands, and everywhere, by the
thousands, the people retreated into the mountains, the
wild, wooded hills of Judah, of Bethaven and of Gilead. And
from everywhere, from all over the land, a steady trickle of
the strongest, the most bitter, the least afraid, found their
way to Ephraim.

*   *   *   *   *

Among the men we bore back was my father, the Adon Mattathias, with a sword cut deep in thigh and the cruel gouge of a shovel spear in his shoulder. With my own hands, I dressed his wounds, feeling his pain under my fingers but seeing no sign of it in his white, hawklike face. As tenderly as we might, we bore him back to Ephraim, none but his sons carrying the litter; yet at last when we reached the little valley where our people were, with our mixed tale of battle, victory and defeat, his wounds were already infected and giving pus. He lay in a tent we had raised for him, and one of us tended him constantly, yet he grew no better, only worse. The Rabbi Ragesh, who had studied healing with the sages of Alexandria, put glass drains into his wounds, so that they might remain open and allow the discharge to run off, but the Adon chided him gently, saying:

"Ragesh, Ragesh, you make a great thing of a small matter. Life has been a bitter thing too long for me to cling to it. Like an old Jew, I will go to my Lord with my knees stiff and a willful heart and I'm not afraid."

"You're not going to God, Mattathias," Ragesh smiled, "while we need you. A little while — "

"You don't need me. I have five strong sons, so take your devil's instruments, Ragesh, and leave me to my pain."

Day by day, his fever increased, until he lost all knowledge of where he was and what had happened and wandered in his own youth when all the land was sunny and peaceful and he sat with the scrolls in the synagogue and studied under the ancient scholars what the wise men of Babylon had written. His flesh fell away in those days and the skin of his face stretched itself tight and thin. There was only one brief moment when his fever broke and he was lucid and clear, and then he called for us, his sons — and we gathered around him, John holding him up so he could see us, Judas caressing one thin hand, and Eleazar kneeling before him and weeping like a child. There was little light in the tent and outside the rain pattered down, but even through the sound of the rain it seemed to me that I could hear the soft, lost murmur of the people — all of the people in Ephraim, who had gathered about the tent where the old man, the Adon Mattathias, lay dying.

"Where are you, my sons, my strong and stout-hearted sons?" he whispered, speaking in the old Hebrew instead of the Aramaic and casting his words in that splendid formal manner in which our ancient scrolls are written. "Where are you, my sons?"

"Here," I answered him. "Here, my father."

"Then, Simon, kiss thou my lips," he said, "for I would give thee the little strength that remains in me. Heed me now, Simon, for thou art strong and willful and terrible, even as I was."

I kissed him and he lifted a hand and stroked my face, and he felt the tears and shook his head. "Nay, nay, art thou a woman that thou must weep over the death of a man? We are flesh and born to die, Simon, so weep no more."

"No more," I murmured.

"Now heed me, Simon, for I charge you!" His voice rose, and that old, imperious note of the Adon crept into it. "We are a small folk, a tiny folk, yea — a people cast into a wilderness of strangers, and how shall we survive unless we bring forth goodness? For our ways are not the ways of others, and our God is like no other God. Blessed be the Lord God of Israel and the people who keep his covenant, for what saith He?"

I shook my head dumbly.

"What saith He, Simon? Surely, He says, Walk in the paths of righteousness, and love goodness and hate evil. So He chose us, a stubborn people, a stiff-necked people, and it was His covenant that we should bow our knee to no one — no one, Simon! Hold your head up — otherwise let Judea be a wilderness!" The effort exhausted him; he lay back in John's arms, breathing hoarsely, his eyes closed. Then he said:

"For you, Simon, your brothers. Thou art thy brother's keeper, thee and no other, and I charge you with them, I charge you with them. And should there be a man or a woman or a child in Israel that wants sustenance, that needs succor, that cries for help or mercy, then turn not away thy countenance, Simon ben Mattathias, harden not thy heart, harden not thy heart — "

Then he said, "Judas — oh, my son, Judas!"

Judas bent his head, and my father raised his hands and kissed them. "Thou are the Maccabee," the old man said, "and the people will look after thee and thou wilt lead them, Judas. Deny me not."

"I will do as you say," Judas whispered.

"Even as Gideon led, thou wilt lead. And thou, John, my first-born, gentle and good, and thou, Eleazar, who will teach us the splendor of battle when man fights to free himself, and thou, Jonathan, my child — my child Jonathan, come and let me put my arms around you and kiss you — and then I will say, *Hear, O Israel, the Lord is our God* . . ."

Then he lay back, and the harshness went out of that grim, hawklike face, and with the snow-white hair and the white beard to shroud him, he slept. I raised the tent flap and went out into the rain to where the people waited.

"The Adon Mattathias is dead," I told them. "May God have mercy on him, my father." And then I went back to weep with my brothers; and above the sound of the rain I could hear the people weeping.

We bore his body back to Modin, my brothers and I and the Rabbi Ragesh, that whimsical, eager man whom the people of the South loved, almost as much as the people of the North had once honored and respected the Adon — or loved him perhaps; I don't know; I was his son, and it is not easy to be the son of a fierce and righteous man. Or it may be that they knew him better, for whenever we came to a village and it was told that we bore the body of the Adon Mattathias ben John, the people crowded up to the simple cedar coffin in which he lay, that they might touch it or press their lips to it, so that they could tell this to their children and their grandchildren. And everywhere, whether in a village half ruined to which people clung, or in a little valley where the people hid and lived, there were old men who saluted the coffin with both hands pressed to their foreheads — in the old, old way that Jews had saluted their melaks, or kings, in the time when there were kings — and then wrapped themselves in their striped cloaks, head and eyes hidden, swaying back and forth and chanting, not to my father but to the Lord he had worshiped: "Magnified and sanctified be Thy glorious name forever and forever." And in other places, the children took the wild flowers, the bright and wonderful wild flowers that make our whole land like a garden, and strewed them over the coffin.

Two by two, we carried his body — until at last we stood upon a hilltop and looked down the lovely terraces to that sweet and fertile place where Modin had been, but where now only a few walls and chimneys stood among the ashes. We bore him to our crypt, cut into a hillside, and laid him with the dust of his father and his grandfather. "Rest as all men must rest," Ragesh said, but I was forlorn and frightened and alone in this graveyard of Modin, this dead place of dead memories. Who takes up the sword perishes by the sword, even the Adon who once in my mind was the figure of a grim and just God. Tired and forlorn, I sat on a hillside with Ragesh and my brothers and broke bread and drank from a skin of wine. Already, the terraces were a jungle of weeds, and the fruit on the trees, unpruned and untended, would shrivel and be sour. I had thought on our way here that the spirit of Ruth would pervade this place and join me, but no spirit was there, only the bitter pang of memory, and as I looked at my brothers, looked from face to face, I saw that their memories too were sad and lonely. Judas was like a man bereft, and it shook me to realize how young he still was. Already, there were streaks of gray in his close-cropped beard and his long auburn hair, and a strange and brooding sorrow had begun to line itself on his beautiful features. Ragesh too watched him as he sat there, digging at the earth with a stick, eyes cast down; and suddenly he asked Ragesh:

"Why are we what we are?"

Shrugging, the Rabbi smiled and shook his head.

"For all other people, there is peace, but for us who hate war so and want only to live in quiet, there has never been peace, only our blood spilled over this land for a thousand years."

"That is true," Ragesh nodded.

"And there's no life for me," Judas said bitterly, "or for any son of Mattathias, may he rest in peace. But no peace for us, no woman, no home, no children — "

Again Ragesh bowed his head, but Judas turned on him and cried, "And you dared to call me the Maccabee — I'm cursed, I tell you, cursed! Look at my hands — already they're covered with blood, and there's nothing but blood ahead of me. Did I want this? Did I ask for it? David wanted to be king, but I don't want that — and what have I ever wanted that was granted to me?"

"Freedom," Ragesh said softly, and then Judas put his face in his hands and wept.

It will not be remembered so; in other ways will it be remembered — the things that took place in the five years that followed; but for me the memory is of my glorious brothers, of the great charge that Eleazar led against the phalanx, smashing it open as no others but the Romans smashed it, for the fight Judas fought with the Greek Apollonius — Apollonius who boasted that with his own hands he slew eleven hundred and fifty-nine Jews, Apollonius who directed the great blood-letting in Jerusalem when first they defiled the Temple, Apollonius who had brought to him in one night twenty Jewish virgins and despoiled them all, the better to prove his own manhood and the superiority of Western civilization.

Yet I must tell of the misery and hopelessness in the land for the death of the Adon Mattathias. We came back to Ephraim, and the people were frightened and afraid, sinking into beastlike defeat, for indeed they lived like beasts in the caves and the brushwood shelters. In our valley and in the narrow defiles that led up from the brooding, land-locked swamp — called by some the pit of sorrows — more than twelve thousand Jews now lived, and most had come with only their grief and the clothes they wore, without tools, food or weapons, but always with children, the numberless laughing children that are thicker than olives in Judea and once were rounder too. They came into a place dry and wooded, yet pestilential from the rot and odor of the great swamp. All through the spring, the snows would melt from the slopes of Ephraim and the other mountains, and the water would drain down into the swamp from which there was no outlet, lying there for the next ten months in a deep ooze of decay. As I said, once, long ago and before the Exile, this had been one of the most pleasant and fruitful places in all Palestine; then the spring freshets were caught in stone reservoirs and spread carefully over ten thousand terraces during the ensuing months, and the land blossomed like a garden. But now the terraces were gone, as were the reservoirs — and the whole place was one of the least accessible and most forbidding wildernesses west of the Jordan. Here the bark of the jackal mixed itself with the cry of the wild heron, and here was the tiny part of Judea where men were free.

It was not an easy freedom that we came back to. After the first surge of common misfortune, the camps divided into those who had and those who had not. People were close to starvation while other people hoarded food; a thousand petty fights and jealousies had sprung up; an informer had been tracked down and slain, and his family pledged revenge; the stout in heart were murderously bitter toward the defeatists, of whom there was no lack, and the defeatists in turn blamed the advocates of resistance. Within Ephraim, there was a little party of Jerusalemites who held themselves apart from the village folk; whereby, the village folk made the life of the few city people hell indeed. With the sinking of morale had come a physical letdown — dirt, misery, privation of all sorts — this is what my brothers and I came back to, and it was not I who knew what to do or where to turn but Judas who called a council of all the Adons and Rabbis in the refuge, demanding that they meet with him in the tent of Mattathias. Twenty-seven of them came, but nine

held aloof, whereupon Judas told Eleazar and me to go
with men of Modin and Goumad — men who then and later
were rocks upon which we stood often enough — and fetch
them. It was not a pleasant thing; -it is not good to see
Jew against Jew, yet that was seen before; we brought them,
and there was one, Samuel ben Zebulun, Adon of Gibeah,
who demanded of Judas:

"And who are you to drag me here in this fashion, you
with the pap of your mother not yet dry on your cheek?"

He was a proud and resentful man, past sixty; but Judas,
standing at the end of the tent, did not answer but looked at
him until the Adon could not meet his eyes and turned away
angrily.

"Then choose someone to lead you," Judas said coldly,
"and I will follow him if he fights. And if he doesn't fight,
others will. And if all of you should go and make your peace
with the Greek, then I and my brothers will fight, so that
the name Jew will not be a shame and an abomination to
the *nokri*."

"Is this the wisdom of youth?" Nathan ben Joseph, a
Jerusalem Rabbi, demanded caustically.

"I have no wisdom," Judas replied angrily, "but I know
two things the Adon Mattathias taught me: to love freedom
and to bend my knee neither to man nor to God."

"Peace, Judas, peace," Ragesh said.

"And these two things that constitute the wisdom of
Mattathias," said Samuel ben Zebulun, "brought ruin upon
Judea, so that our land is laid waste and the people weep
in their agony. Save me from the wisdom of Mattathias!"

The words were hardly out of his mouth when Judas was
upon him, seizing his cloak in two clenched fists and telling
him, in a hoarse and awful whisper, "Say what you will of
me, old man, but speak no word of the Adon Mattathias, not

good and not evil, for I tell you, you're not worth the fringe of his garment — no, nor fit to serve him or answer his most menial demand!"

"Judas!" the Rabbi Ragesh cried, and the word was enough, so that my brother let go of the old man, bowed his head and left the tent.

We followed him, Eleazar and John and Jonathan and myself, and I walked ahead, putting my arm around Judas and shaking him gently, "All right, so easy, easy — "

"I can't do it, Simon. You saw what happened to me. I can't do it."

"Then who will do it? Name him."

"You."

I shook my head. "No, no, there's only one man in all Israel they'll follow the way they would have followed the Adon himself, may he rest in peace. Who knows it better than I do, Judas, for is it not true that all my life I hated in you what was not in me?"

"What, Simon, what?" he pleaded.

I answered, "The power to make people love you more than they love life itself."

"Yet," he said, moodily and hopelessly, "the one thing I wanted was given to you."

My brothers were with us now; we sat down under a tree, and I told Judas: "There are five of us, the sons of Mattathias, and we are brothers. You were right, Judas, for if the rest should go away and abase themselves, we will do what has to be done. I don't know if it's the blessing or the curse of the old man, the Adon, but it's in us, in all of us, different as we are. But they won't go away, Judas. We came out of them, as the Adon did, and what we are they made us. How else should it be? Was it ever given to Greek or Egyptian to raise up a Maccabee?" Eleazar stopped me, for he saw the Rabbi Ragesh coming. "Enough, Simon," Judas said, and I saw the reflection of his torment on his face.

There was no forgiveness in the eyes of Ragesh as he said to Judas, "Thus do you honor age in Israel! It was you I called the Maccabee!"

"Did I claim it?" Judas asked miserably. "Did I claim it?"

"Claim it when you deserve it! Now go back, for they will still have you!"

We rose, and with Judas, we returned to the tent. "I ask your forgiveness," he said to the old men assembled, and they answered, "Amen — so be it."

They listened to Judas as he spoke. On the floor of the tent, they sat, their legs crossed, hooded in their long striped cloaks, these old men listening to a boy — for Judas was hardly more than that — even as their ancestors had sat in their goatskin tents in the long, long ago. I watched them as Judas spoke, and how well do I remember their faces, those lined, harsh, hawk-nosed intolerant faces; those bearded, weathered faces that spelled Jew in so strange and definite a way, not by eye or feature but a pattern of thought and a pattern of life that had imprinted itself on eyes, nose, mouth, and cheek — these Adons and Rabbis and venerable patriarchs; for thou shalt honor the gray hairs on a man's head — and did they not see that Judas, who was youth in all its beauty and glory, was graying too? They were against him at first, but as he talked he melted them, and watching it I thought once more of the incredible simplicity of my brother — and something else beside that — for under all there was an imperious direction. Whether they knew it then or not, Judas laid down there the iron law for a nation that would spend three decades in terrible struggle to liberate itself. And when those decades were done, how many of these old men would be alive? But they did not think of that then; they looked at this boy who was all of the legends of Israel, David in form and Gideon in purity and directness, Jeremiah in passion and Isaiah in wrath, and the harsh lines in their faces eased, and more and more frequently, they said softly, "Amen — so be it."

Yet for all that, Judas betrayed himself, placing the burden on himself and us, his brothers. I am not to judge, yet I would not have done it so, but Judas did it, for better or for worse. In battle and in the training of men, he would command — that was his price — and under him would be Eleazar and the child Jonathan. Provisioning and supplies would be under John, and I, Simon, would judge the people — with an iron hand I would judge them, even as a man was judged in battle — that was his price.

"A harsh price," one of the Adons said, yet Judas had won them.

"I know a thing," Judas said. "I know battle. I know the enemy, whether he be the fat and wealthy Jew, walled up in the Acra in Jerusalem, or whether he be a mercenary in pay of the Greek. For months now, I and my brothers have lived only for battle, for killing and for slaughter. When the killing is over, we will do as you say. When the land is free, we will go away if you so desire — or we will abase ourselves and kiss the hems of your garments. But until then, I put a price on the blood of Mattathias and you have heard it."

"Would you be a king in Israel?" someone asked.

And then I marveled, for before my eyes, standing there, Judas wept as he said, "No — no, I swear it, in the name of God!" They could not face this humility of his. "God forgive you," Ragesh said, and Samuel ben Zebulun, so bitter before, went up to Judas, took him by the shoulders and kissed his

lips. "Maccabee," he said softly, "weep for the suffering before us — and the old men will follow where a child leads
them. Be strong and passionate and terrible and love freedom and righteousness." But still Judas wept, and finally we
all of us went out of the tent and left him alone.

There were six weeks then, in which Judas made an army,
six weeks while we waited for Apollonius, chief warden of
Judea, to feel the fly that was biting him from Ephraim and
to blot it out. At the beginning of that time, a Jew of
Damascus, Moses ben Daniel by name, found his way to
Ephraim with twenty-two mules bearing fine wheat flour.
By then, already, John and I had enforced the decree of
common pooling of all foods in a central place, so that
while no one had too much to eat, no one starved — and the
iron hand, as they came to call it, of Simon ben Mattathias
was felt; an iron hand that to me was soft and useless, and
is, God help me, to this day. I do not make small of myself;
I know myself.

Thus, forty-four sacks of flour were a welcome and a
gracious gift from this man who lived so far from Judea.
A merchant in wheat, he and his family had lived in
Damascus for ten generations, yet they remained Jews, and
each morning and each night turned toward the Temple to
pray — and when they heard that resistance was alive in
Judea, burning like a slow flame, they bethought them of
what they might do. He brought us the wheat, and his
daughter, Deborah, seventeen years old and white as a lily
in a pond, came with him to our dank and lonely Wilderness
of Ephraim. Nor was he the only one, for even then Jews
all over the world, in Alexandria, in Rome, in Athens —
even in far-off Spain — lifted their heads when they heard
the rumor that Judea might be free again.

The evening he came, Ragesh broke open a precious bottle of yellow *semath* wine, and with his daughter he sat in the tent of Ragesh and spoke to my brothers, myself, and a handful of the old men. All of us watched him — all but Eleazar, who had eyes only for his daughter; and she hid her face from the red-cheeked, red-bearded giant of a man.

A worldly person was Moses ben Daniel, such a Jew as I had never known before. Not alone the fact that he came with twelve black men who were his slaves and who adored him, big, smiling men out of Africa, soft-spoken and gentle, yet, as I learned, terrible in battle and deep in affection; not alone the fact that he wore silks such as I had never seen; not alone the fact that his curved sword was hilted with hundreds of tiny pearls: but the man himself was different from any Jews I had known. Unlike the Hellenists, the apostles of the Greek, he never for a moment could forget that he was a Jew — indeed more so than any of us; yet his culture was wider and deeper than the glib culture of any Hellenist I had met. Well read was he, and learned too, so that when Ragesh said, "And if a stranger sojourn with thee in your land, ye shall not do him wrong," he was able to answer in fine, old Hebrew, "The stranger that sojourneth with you shall be unto you as the home born among you, and thou shalt love him as thyself; for ye were strangers in the land of Egypt. . . .

"As so many of us are strangers," Moses ben Daniel said, "and we forget the old land and the old ways and the old soil — but a word like freedom travels on the high wind. Jews meet at the crossroads of the world."

"And what do they say?"

"A little is whispered," Moses ben Daniel smiled, crossing his legs and patting his fine linen trousers into even folds.

"It is hard to live in exile," he nodded, "but it has certain compensations. A man's heart is heavy and his home is an island — and then it comes from somewhere that a Maccabee is risen in Israel."

"But what does Antiochus think?" Judas demanded.

"He knows the name of Judas ben Mattathias," the merchant nodded. "I came with gifts that I should not come empty-handed, for though a stranger is welcome, he can make himself more welcome — is that not so?"

"Is a Jew a stranger in Judea?" Ragesh laughed, and Moses ben Daniel savored the odor of his wine, said the blessing softly, and sipped.

"It honors me," he sighed. "What shall one who lives among the *nokri* weep for, the Judean sky, the Judean hills — or the wine? Now let me tell you — your warden, Apollonius, came to Antiochus, because, as he puts it, a few miserable Jews had risen in Judea. I had it from the best of sources, you may believe me. Do you know the King of Kings?" He looked from face to face.

"We are not honored," Ragesh said. "We are simple peasants who till the land. The great ones, the wealthy ones, the noble ones among the Jews have shut themselves up in the Acra of Jerusalem, where the high priest Menelaus holds court."

"Then let me tell you a little about this King of Kings who rules half the world — as he puts it. He is fat, loosely fat, and his lower lip hangs down and pouts constantly; but he is convinced of his own beauty. He serves many women and he does things to them I won't speak of — he also loves animals. And he takes hemp. When he takes the hemp, he does terrible things to most of those about him, and even men like Apollonius are afraid of him. Yet Apollonius came to the palace, pleading for troops. 'Against whom?' the

King said, and Apollonius answered, 'The Jews, my Lord, to whom I abase myself.' 'Jews?' asked Antiochus, 'Jews? What are Jews?' 'A people who live in Palestine,' Apollonius answered. 'Their country is called Judea,' he went on, knowing full well that Antiochus had a record of every shekel squeezed out of our land. 'Jews — Judea?' Antiochus said, looking at Apollonius in a way that made the warden sweat sufficiently. 'Have you no men?' 'Seven thousand,' Apollonius answered, and the King roared, 'And with seven thousand men you annoy me with Jews! Mercenaries are dearer than wardens.' Thus he said — and it is felt that even here in Ephraim, he'll seek you out, he'll seek you out."

"Apollonius?"

Moses ben Daniel nodded somberly. "How does one serve a king? Poorly, my young friend," he said to Judas. "Kings are not wise — they are very stupid indeed, and this one is not clever enough to know that Apollonius is as good a warden as he might find. He is only clever enough to do awful things to Apollonius if the Greek — he is all Greek, you know, or mostly, which is all these days — if the Greek does not do awful things to the rebels. He does not know that Apollonius was forced to spread himself thinly to hold down a thousand villages, and he does not particularly care. But Apollonius does care to remain as warden of Judea, and for that reason I think he will seek you out — and soon."

There was a long silence then. I watched Judas, and I knew what no one else present knew — how afraid he was. But his voice had all of its light and endearing charm as he said to the merchant:

"And to me, who has never been more than a dozen miles past the border of Judea, Damascus is a wonderland indeed. Tell me about it. Tell me about the King and how a king lives and rules . . ."

Yet that day, the germ was born, the new army, the new war, the new might that would give the word *Jew* new meaning, a different kind of meaning — that would embody the very word with connotations of love or hatred, admiration or disgust, considering upon whose tongue the word lay.

So it is to this day, when I sit here and write, calling to mind this and that of those days so long past, so that I may make truth and understanding for this time — this time when the Senate of mighty Rome sends a legate to seek out the Maccabee. But the Maccabee is dead, and I am an old Jew, like my father the Adon and those before him, an old Jew who troubles his memories. And how, I wonder, is one to sift memory, for what was, instead of the glow of what should have been? I walked not long ago through the streets that border the market place, and there was a singer, one of the real ones out of the tribe of Dan, and he sang the song of the five sons of Mattathias. I covered my face with my cloak and listened and I heard him say, "Now heed ye Eleazar, the splendor of battle; his name was Eleazar and the Lord was his weapon . . ."

But now, sitting here, groping back to then, I see Eleazar as he walked that night with the girl from Damascus, my brother without anger, without malice, going so softly, going so patiently, more the Jew than any of us. I see Judas facing Ragesh that same night, and Ragesh said, "If we go south to the Negeb — " "The Negeb is broad enough," Judas answered. "I would stay here where Apollonius can find us, and we will greet him." "Without an army?" "We'll make an army," Judas said, and Ragesh looked at me. "The people will be the army, and my brothers and I will train them." It was a dream, but there was no denying him. We saw Eleazar then with the girl, walking through the moonlight, and Ragesh said, with almost humble amazement, "And ye are the sons of Mattathias . . ."

We fought our first great battle — great by the tiny skirmishes of the past, yet little enough to what followed — six weeks after the merchant of Damascus appeared in Ephraim, and a week after Eleazar took his daughter as a bride and the twelve black men as dowry. Faithful enough they were to him, to the end; they became Jews, lived as Jews and died as Jews. In those six weeks, we gathered together twelve hundred men under the banner of the Maccabee.

Never had there been a thing like this in Israel before — or in any land, for these men were not mercenaries nor were they wild barbarians, in whom war and life are so intermixed that the one cannot be entangled from the other. No, these were simple farmers, gentle scholars whose devotion had been to the Law, the covenant, and the scrolls of our past. Some, indeed, knew well enough the use of our small, laminated bows and had shot partridges and rabbits with them, but even those had no experience with spears or swords; and many there were like the pupils of the saintly Rabbi Lazarus ben Simon who had a school at Mizpah, and who taught a creed of love that extended itself to the smallest insect, so that his disciples walked barefoot with their eyes upon the ground, that they might not crush the lowliest of God's creatures. These same men now stood in ranks of the twenties, while Ragesh, who had been among the Parthians — who are the best archers in the world — taught them to case the slim Jewish barbs, flight after flight, until a veritable rain of them sought out every crevice in the enemy's ranks.

Other things too, we learned, I and my brothers as well

as the men of the little army that was making in Marah.
From the Ethiopians, the black men who had come with the
merchant of Damascus, we learned to turn spears into
lances, to cast them, to guide them with bits of thin leather,
so that they rode the wind. From Judas, we learned to use
the long sword of the Syrian, for the sword came to him like
a part of his fist, another arm. Moses ben Daniel left his
daughter with us and traveled on to Alexandria, returning
a month later with one hundred Jewish youths, volunteers
from the Alexandrian community, and a gift of ten talents
of gold from the great synagogue. Among the volunteers
were six engineers, two of whom had lived among the
Romans and taught us to make their catapults. Well do I remember how they marched into Ephraim, these strangers
from far-off Egypt, laden with gifts and dressed in beautiful
garments that made our peasant homespun seem simple
indeed. They brought a gift for the Maccabee: a banner of
blue silk, and upon it the star of David, and sewn beneath
the star: *Judas Maccabeus. Who resists tyrants obeys God.*
And I remember too how they crowded forward to look at
Judas — who had already become a legend, and the wonder
and surprise of the volunteers when they discovered that
Judas was as young as most of them and younger than
some.

Yet it was not all easy and not all smooth. We never
had food enough in Ephraim, and always the population
grew as Apollonius vented his wrath on Judea. Wherever
there were Greeks or Greek rule, Jews suffered, and people
came to Ephraim from as far off as Galilee and Geshur,
footsore, starving often enough, a pitiful trickle of refugees
who all repeated the same tale of terror, rape, and murder.
It was my task and John's to care for them. I sat in judgment, from early in the morning until late at night — and

it was not judgment such as an Ethnarch deals out today — and the bickering and the squabbling never ceased. The elders resented my youth; the young ones challenged it — and from that came what they called the iron hand of Simon ben Mattathias.

How often I envied my brothers, Eleazar and Jonathan and Judas, whose work was the comparative simplicity of war! Yet I had my share of war too, as you will see. Once, I shook it off and went to watch Ruben and Eleazar work at an open forge they had set up against the hillside — iron and hammer and fire and these two, the strongest men in Judea, beating the insensate metal and muttering all the while that ancient blessing, as old as Cain, who first worked metal. In the shower of sparks, they greeted me, and I saw that they were happy, Ruben, the wild survivor of those sons of Esau, and Eleazar who had no doubts, no fears, no hatred even, but only a love of all things and a reverence for Judas and myself that was almost worship. It was not his to doubt, it was his to battle and train others to battle; and he said to me, over the heads of the curious crowd that can always be found at any forge — children and adults too, and women, there as much for these two men as for the fire, and graybeards to criticize and the black Ethiopians to admire and applaud — "Now, Simon, these black men are making us spears to throw" — holding up a red-hot blade — "but not for me!"

"What for you, Eleazar?" someone demanded.

He plunged the blade into a pot of water that boiled and sent off clouds of steam, and then he took from behind him a huge hammer. "This is for me — a hammer."

They felt it, a mighty lump of iron, with a handle of twelve iron rods, beaten together and bound. The women tried to raise it, and laughed as it bent them over. The children touched it, and Eleazar watched and glowed with pride. He picked it up and swung it around his head, letting it go and spinning it on its leather strap — until the crowd broke away, laughing with apprehension mixed with delight. Ruben was twice his age and more, but they were alike in the simple wonder with which they approached weapons' iron, their delight at the submissiveness of metal to them and what came forth from their hands. Thus it was with my brother, my brother Eleazar . . .

There came to me a man and wife out of the town of Carmel in the far South, and the man, Adam ben Lazar, tall and dark and hawklike and unbending, as so many of those who live close to the Bedouins are, said to me, "And thou art the Maccabee?"

"Not the Maccabee, who is my brother Judas. Are you new in Marah that you don't know Simon ben Mattathias?"

"I am new, and I come to be judged by a child." But his wife, who was round and lovely, yet worn and terrible with grief, said nothing.

"And yet I judge," I said. "If you want other judgment, go to the Greeks and find it."

"You are bitter the way the Adon your father was bitter, Simon ben Mattathias."

"What I am I am."

"Like him," his wife cried suddenly, pointing to her husband. "The men in Israel were emptied and hatred was poured in. I want him no more, so separate us and make us strangers to each other."

"Why?" I asked the woman.

"Shall I tell you, when every word is wiped in blood?"

"Tell me or don't tell me," I said, "for I make no marriages and break none. Go to the Rabbis or the Kohanim for that, to the old ones, not to me."

"Will the old ones understand?" the man demanded coldly. "Listen, Simon, and then send me where you will, to hell or to the arms of your brother, the Maccabee."

"We are married twelve years," the woman said, "and we had a daughter and three sons," and she said it in almost those singsong tones of the teller of tales in the market place. "Bright they were, and round and beautiful and a blessing in my heart and my house and in the eyes of God. Then the warden, whose name was Lampos, set up his Greek altar in the market place and told the people to come and bend their knees and burn incense. But he" — whirling on her husband and pointing an accusing finger at him — "he would not bend his knee, and the Greek smiled with pleasure — "

"With pleasure," Adam ben Lazar nodded, wooden-faced. "He was the right man for the South. For if there are hard men in Judea, you will find harder if you travel South."

"So he slew my little girl," she said, "and he hung her body on the rafters over our door, so that the blood dripped on our doorstep, and all day and all night, the mercenaries sat there, drinking and eating and watching, so that we should not cut down her body and give her burial — "

Without tears she told this. I judged in the open, sitting on a rock, and sometimes the people listened. Now they listened, and more and more came, and as she told her tale, the people were packed around, shoulder to shoulder.

"This for seven days, and when the Sabbath came, with his own hands this Lampos cut the throat of my little boy and hung the body up beside the girl, the girl who was already foul with corruption and smell. Yet we must live there. All around the house stood the mercenaries, day and night, with their spears linked, so that a mouse could not

crawl through. Then, on the third Sabbath, Apollonius came
to consult with his warden, and it was great sport — " Her
voice dried up; she did not cry or appear to be moved, but
her voice dried up.

"It was great sport and the Greeks love sport," her husband said, nodding. "With his own hands, Apollonius cut
the throat of the third child, for he pointed out to us that a
people who could not bend a knee, to God or man, were an
abomination on the face of the earth. It was merciful to
kill the young, he said, so that mankind could look forward
to a time when it would be rid of Jews forever, and then
all the world would be sweet with laughter."

"And the next week, they slew our first-born and hung
the body beside the others," the woman added in her terrible
singsong tones. "And all in a row, the four bodies hanged,
and the birds came to feed upon them; but we could not cut
them down, we could not cut them down, and the flesh that
came out of my womb rotted away. So I hate him, my husband, even as I hate the *nokri*, for his pride was too much
and it destroyed everything I loved."

She did not weep, but an anguished sigh came from the
people listening.

"His pride was too much," she said; "his pride was too
much."

There was silence then for what seemed to be a long
while, a silence broken only by the weeping of those among
the people who did not hate too much to weep. Yet I
could not judge and I said so, motioning to Ragesh who
stood there, listening. "Come and judge," I asked him. "You
are a man of years and a Rabbi." But Ragesh shook his
head, and like two lost and eternally tormented souls, the
man and his wife stood in the circle of the people — until
Judas pushed through them and stood before her, such

sorrow and love on his young and beautiful face as I have not seen before or since on the countenance of any human being. All she had said of death and the making of death seemed to wither away in the face of this man who was the very embodiment of life, and he took her two hands in his and pressed his lips to them.

"Weep," he said softly; "weep, my mother, weep."

She shook her head.

"Weep, for I love you."

And still she shook her head hopelessly and damned.

"Weep, because you lost four children and gained a hundred. Am I not your child and your lover — then weep for me, weep for me or the pain of your children will lie on my heart and destroy me. Weep for me and the blood on my hands. I am proud too, and I wear my pride like a rock around my neck."

Slowly, it came, a crinkling of her long dark eyes, a bit of moisture there, and then tears — and then long, screaming moans as she fell to the ground and lay there. Her husband picked her up in his arms, weeping even as she did, and Judas turned from them and passed through the people, who made way for him. He walked through them, his head bowed, his hands hanging by his sides.

And two things happened: my brother, Eleazar, married, and word came from Jerusalem that Apollonius had gathered together three thousand mercenaries and would march on Ephraim. Not a great army, but trained, disciplined and merciless professional soldiers — and a host indeed to match with our hundreds. Don't think that we were not afraid, for a Jew is wrapped in a curiously sensitive skin — and our fears seem to go deeper even than the fears of others, as our shame does too, and as that pride does, for which the *nokri* hate us. A pall fell over Marah, and what laughter there had been in Ephraim disappeared as hours passed after the word was brought.

Still, we had some respite. Ours is a small land, but each valley is a world unto itself, and just as the mountains are numberless, so are the valleys; and what is an easy mile as the crow flies can be ten or even twenty arduous miles as a man walks, climbs and crawls. There is a great road that runs from north to south, from the cities of Syria to the cities of Egypt, and there is a road from Jerusalem to the sea, but the rest are paths, winding mountain tracks, sometimes wide enough for a cart and sometimes only wide enough for a single man on foot. The cart roads and paths creep through the valley bottoms, winding here and there; we, who know the land and were bred to it, go across the hills and ridges, but men in armor stick to the valley bottoms and take the long way. Thus it was not a bird's thirty miles from Jerusalem to Ephraim, but three days' journey, even for men on forced march — and we made the most of those three days.

As soon as the news came that Apollonius was on the march, Judas called for a concourse of all the people, the men and women, the little children and the rheumy-eyed ancients — the first of the many assemblies that took place during the resistance. He sent out runners, and almost immediately people began to flow into the spoon-shaped cedar-grown hollow of Marah. That was in early morning, and until late afternoon people moved into the valley, young men and old men, and women with babes at their breasts. The few isolated villages in Ephraim emptied themselves, and the whole populations of near-by Lebonah,

Kaarim and Yoshay treked over the mountains and down into Marah. From the caves, the people came, from their brushwood huts, their tents and crude shelters; and hour by hour, the valley filled.

Never before had I seen anything like it, a flow of people like slow-running water. Later, we had concourses where a hundred thousand came together, but this day in Marah, fifteen thousand Jews stood with their faces turned up to Judas, who mounted a high rock to address them; and it seemed truly a mighty host of people, women with troubled eyes, silent children and eager-faced young men.

It made a noise, the sound of many, like water, turbulent but far, until Judas spread his arms for silence and the noise fell away, leaving only the breathing of the folk and the wind in the high trees. Late afternoon now, a golden cast of sunlight flowed down into the valley; the sky overhead was white, pink-fringed; two hawks circled, lifted and dropped, and the trees bent to the breeze, as if by so doing they could better cast their fragrance down upon us. The ineffable sweetness of our Judean land laid its spell over the whole throng, eased them, so that mothers, tired with their babes, sat down on the earth and the whole crowd softened, unbent itself, taking sustenance it seemed from the sweet land and the sweet air that had nurtured them. Above them, on the lip of the rock, Judas stood, tall, slim-hipped, auburn-haired, all in white, trousers and jacket, his long hair blowing — child and father, young and old, a strange mixture of the gentle and the fierce, the humble and the arrogant, the tame and the wild. . . .

He said those words that are written, "An army of mercenaries march on Ephraim to destroy us — and we will go against them in our smallness and smite them" — speaking Hebrew, the old tongue in which best things are best said

— "hip and thigh, root and branch, for it is the warden of all Judea who leads them. Now we will make our accounting to the King, and when he sends three thousand alive, we will return him three thousand dead, measure for measure." The people fixed their eyes on him; no one moved, and indeed it seemed that no one breathed. "Our cup is full," Judas said, "and truly it runneth over! Why do they come to our land to despoil us? Are we not human that we should watch our children slain and not weep? Let them go away from us and trouble us no more, otherwise we will become a people of awful anger." But he spoke with no anger now, only a simple and direct kind of regret, and the people whispered, "Amen — so be it."

"If you have a house that still stands, go to it," Judas said. "I want only those who have nothing to lose but the chains that bind them. If you have a pot of gold, treasure it and come not with us. If you love your children more than your freedom, go away and no one will mark you with shame, and if you are betrothed, go to your betrothed — for we are betrothed to freedom. But if there is one among, you, just one, who will lay down his life for our cause — and surely, mind you, for what I plan is death and only death — let that man seek me out in my tent afterward. I need only one, only one." He paused, sweeping them with his eyes. "Now, let the twenties form here in Marah. The others must go into the hills, to the caves and the woods and the thickets, and hide there until we have finished fighting."

I went to our tent, and four men waited there for Judas. Four men who were not afraid of death, which all men should fear, but would welcome it, girding themselves with hatred. There was Lebel, the schoolmaster, who had taught me my first letters, who day after day had marked the seventy-seven pages of the Law with quick, birdlike motions of his thin stick, that omnipotent stick that so surely and quickly sought out and rapped the knuckles of any boy foolish enough to doze or whisper; Lebel, the father of Deborah, who had been thrust through the throat by the sword of Jason, the mercenary; Lebel, who had opened each day's lesson with a variation of the first adage — "What does the Lord require of a man, but that he should walk humbly and love righteousness?" — Lebel who was meek and gentle as a lamb.

There was Moses ben Aaron, the father of the one woman both Judas and I had loved. There was Adam ben Lazar, the hard and terrible man from the South, whose pride was too much. And there was Ragesh, the whimsical, questing, curious and philosophical Ragesh, to whom death was no less intriguing a problem than life itself.

I greeted them, "Peace." "And unto thee, peace," they said. But my mind and my heart were tearing at me, and I could not speak, nor they either, until Judas came.

They were none of them young men, but Judas gave them more virginal youth than he himself had as he kissed each of them, saying to them, with something of awe, "You will go to die because I say it is needful!"

"You are the Maccabee," Adam ben Lazar shrugged.

"And Ragesh," Judas said, "you who have neither hatred nor pride, why would you die?"

"All men die," Ragesh smiled.

"Yet I need only one, and it cannot be you, Ragesh, for Apollonius knows you, and will he believe that the Rabbi Ragesh would betray his people and his God and his country too? I want someone to lead them into hell, and for that they will take the life of the man who betrays them, even if he should succeed. I want someone to go to them

and bargain with them for a price. Then he will lead them
where they must be led, into the great swamp, over the hill
of Gerson, where there is only one way in and there will be
no way out. And it cannot be you, Adam ben Lazar, for
how will you walk softly and treacherously, with your eyes
downcast? Lebel, Lebel, should I destroy you? What I
know, you taught me, and shall I repay it thus?"

"I come for favors, not for sacrifice, Judas Maccabeus,"
the schoolmaster said simply.

"And how will you play the part, when Apollonius sees in
your eyes all the gentle goodness of your soul? No — a
renegade should be complex rather than simple, worldly
and without honor. I must have a Greek to send to the
Greeks." He went to Moses ben Aaron, taking both his
hands, "God help me and God forgive me." "So the years
go, and if not now then later," the vintner said. "What I
loved is gone, and you are the Maccabee, Judas. So tell me
what you want me to do."

That night, Jonathan and I and four hundred men
traveled south, across the hilltops, over the narrow mountain trails, driving on until the first rosy gleam of dawn lit
the sky — and then we crawled in among the trees and
thickets, and for five hours, we slept the deep and motionless sleep of utter exhaustion. We traveled lightly, armed
only with our small horn bows and knives, and each of us
carried a loaf of bread and a bag of meal. The instructions
Judas gave me were clear and direct; we were to meet the
advance guard of Apollonius and make life miserable for
them, pick off stragglers, cover them with rocks when they
went into the passes, and give them no peace, day or night.
Only when Moses ben Aaron appeared were we to allow
them to evade us — and then we were to return to Ephraim

as quickly as we could travel. Meanwhile, Judas, Eleazar, and John would set the trap in the swamp.

It was late afternoon before we heard the voices of the mercenaries, the hard sound of their armor and the muffled beat of their marching drums. We had already divided our forces, a hundred under me and a hundred under the boy Jonathan — and ten twenties as mobile units. We spread ourselves along the edge of a defile and waited, and soon they came in sight, three abreast, the column stretching like a long snake fully half a mile down the road, the brazen helmets gleaming in the sun, the long polished spears rippling like water, the standards flying, the breastplates shining. Possibly because they knew they would have to bite into the mountains, there were no cavalry in the column except a splendid white horse which Apollonius himself rode. I saw him then for the first time, a huge, dark-browed man, his armor silvered, his mantle snow white, his black hair falling loose to his shoulders. He was no Apelles, but a leader of men, a dark, domineering, savage and bloodthirsty man, terrible in battle and sick with a hunger for blood.

They had learned something of our ways, for they moved slowly and deliberately, magnificent in their harsh, metallic inevitability, archers thrown out before them, and officers of the twenties constantly scanning the hills that towered above them. They saw us as I set my whistle to my lips and blew, and the harping of our bowstrings mixed with shouted orders and bitter curses. They made a turtle's back of their shields, and in a moment the whole long column had become a plated, crawling snake, a roof of shields covering every man from our sight — except Apollonius who, oblivious to danger, rode his horse back and forth along the line, roaring orders at his men and curses at us up on the ridge. Yet,

quick as they were, they were not quick enough, and the
rain of our arrows left an occasional mercenary either dead
or twisting in pain on the ground. It is not wholly good —
even in terms of murder — to be a mercenary, for those who
were badly wounded were put to death there on the spot by
their own comrades, their throats competently and quickly
cut, and those wounded who lingered behind were slain by
us. Yet the column did not halt or allow itself to be diverted
into suicidal attempts to climb the precipitous slope, but
kept on at a steady, disciplined pace to the vantage and
security of an open place. Before they reached it, we killed
Apollonius's horse. He became the target for a hundred
bowmen, yet he emerged untouched; even though his horse
was feathered with arrows, he leaped from the saddle un-
hurt and kept pace with the column under cover of his
shield.

We followed and harassed them as long as the ridge
paralleled the road, but when they formed in an open place
and detached their light bowmen to attack us, we melted
away, and at a loose run, which their armor could never
match, we circled up into the hills ahead of them.

When they camped that night, I threw my men around
them and we crawled in again and again during the night
to rain arrows over their camp. Twice, they formed the
phalanx and attacked us, but we melted away, and their
formations clattered about, chasing ghosts. Then we camped
a mile or so from them, sleeping by turn, but having always
five or six twenties to see that the mercenaries got no sleep.
In that whole night operation, we lost only four men. Seven
others were wounded, but none of them too badly to walk;
yet when we searched the mercenaries' camp after they had
left, we found the bodies of eighteen of them.

That same morning, Jonathan crawled close to the Greek

camp and saw Moses ben Aaron arrive. He saw him seized
and watched him plead for his life. Then he saw him talk
long and vehemently with Apollonius, until at last the grim
hatred on the face of the Greek relaxed and a hint of a
smile twisted his lips. This, Jonathan told us — and almost
without stopping, we took our way back to Ephraim.

It is hard to tell of a battle, until its end; for at the beginning, it moves slowly, spread out over a deal of ground, and
you see only what is directly before you. Yet I have been in
at the end of many, as you will see, and that is different.
Here I must tell things as they happened — as well as I may
— for who else of my glorious brothers will narrate things as
they were? Or the men of Modin — where are they?

I must tell how Moses ben Aaron died, even as I told of
the death of his daughter Ruth, who was my heart and my
flesh too. This I did not see. We came back to Ephraim,
having marched in two days and two nights over seventy
miles of mountainous country, having fought and retired
bearing our wounded with us, but Judas had neither sympathy nor praise, and ordered me to take my men and hide
them along the defile that led to the deep and lonely morass
of Ephraim. "But we have not slept!" "Sleep when you've
taken your position," Judas said, "and God help the man
who reveals himself until the Greek has passed! He'll die
by my own hand!" I opened my mouth to speak, and then
swallowed the words. Judas was transformed; I saw that; I
saw the awful wildness in him that permitted no crossing,
not even by his own flesh and blood. He stood in the valley
where the people had dwelt, and now it was empty. He was
alone and lord and tyrant of the devastation. "Where have
the people gone?" "They hide until we have won or died."
He took me by the arms, his talonlike grip reminding me

more of the Adon than any gesture or look could. "Simon, Simon, there is only one way into Ephraim and one way out — and you will be there! You will not fail me? You hated me, Simon — now promise!"

"I don't hate you, Judas. How shall I hate my brother?"

"How shall you love him?" Judas said. "Jonathan is with you, and treasure him, treasure him."

We went to the defile then, Jonathan and I and our four hundred, and we hid in the thickets, behind the rocks or in holes we dug in the ground. There was no food and no fire, and we mixed our meal with water and ate it. We slept where we lay, and at last, the mercenaries appeared, Moses ben Aaron leading them, and they marched through the defile beneath us and into the morass of Ephraim.

Then, when they had passed, we slipped down into the defiles, worked like mad dragging rocks and tree trunks across it, and then manned the barricade. An hour went past before they attacked us.

As it was told to me, they went on through the cleft into the dim, sun-splotched loneliness of Ephraim. Almost a mile they marched into that sad, unhappy desolation before the mud caught them, before they realized that from this reed-strewn wilderness there was no way out but the way they had come. It was there, buried in the mud, that we later discovered the body of Moses ben Aaron, cruelly mutilated. It was after they killed him, that they made two more attempts to cross the swamp before turning back. But when they came back to the hard ground, they found that the defile was blocked — blocked by us, while from all sides Judas and his men rained their arrows upon them.

That was as close to panic as the Greek Apollonius came. Twice he led his army into that narrow defile, and twice we fought there behind our barricade. We shot away our arrows and then fought with our spears. We broke our spears, and fought with rocks and sticks and knives and with our bare hands too. From us, from the four hundred under Jonathan and me and Ruben, he took the worst toll, for he drove at us with a close phalanx again and again, until fully half our men were slain or bleeding all over with wounds; yet we managed to hold him, while all the time Judas's men on the rocks above rained their arrows upon him — the short, needle-sharp, devastating arrows that fill the air like snow, seeking out every nook and crevice in a mercenary's armor.

It seemed forever that we manned that barricade, but it could not have been too long; yet there, in that defile, Apollonius lost at least half of his men. Half of our four hundred to half of his three thousand. He fell back to the hard, open ground — and we in the pass leaned on our weapons, bleeding and panting, weary unto death and yet drunk with our triumph, almost hysterical with rage and triumph and terror, our dead all around us and the dead of the mercenaries strewn like a carpet along the length of the defile. For the first time, Jew had met Greek, knife to sword, and stopped him and smashed him and beat him back — and for all of our exhaustion we pressed down the defile to the meadow where they stood.

Apollonius had formed his phalanx four square. We were outnumbered, they could have driven through us then; but they had no heart for it, and hardly was the square made when Eleazar and Judas led their men against it, shouting as they poured from the hills. They were fresh, and Apollonius had marched his men all day and dragged them through a mire and led them into two costly attacks. We wore no armor and the mercenaries were burdened down, each of them, with nearly a hundred pounds of plate and weapons. We knew this place as we knew our own faces, and they were lost in a strange and frightening wilderness, a place where already the long shadows of evening were beginning to close in, where mountains towered on every side and where all the spirits and demons they feared were evoked.

Eleazar led the charge. With his great hammer, he flung himself onto the phalanx, beating the wall of spears aside, churning into the phalanx as the thresher churns into wheat, and behind him came Judas and gentle John, the black Africans and the mass of yelling, battle-mad Jews, people who had suffered and were waiting for this. The phalanx cracked, and all that were left of our exhausted band joined the charge. What remained of order in the battle disappeared, and the mercenaries broke and fled. The charge became a melee and the melee became a slaughter. Some of the mercenaries fought back, but most of them broke and ran, plunging into the mud, floundering knee-deep in the morass, hunted down and killed. Others ran for the hills; a few escaped — a very few, for we fought with a fierce and terrible abandon, and always, wherever the mercenaries held their ground, there was the giant Eleazar and his awful hammer and his black spearmen. For my own part, I was lost with the rage of battle, even as the others were. Never before had I let Jonathan out of my sight and reach, but now I knew only that those who had killed all I loved were before me, and I fought as the others fought, once beside my brother Judas, and again alone, dragging down a fleeing mercenary, and driving my knife again and again into his side, between the plates of his armor.

I rose, and it was twilight and it was done, except for the screaming of the wounded and the fleeing; and a few yards from me, two men stood face to face, the Greek Apollonius and my brother Judas. The sun had already dropped behind the mountains, leaving behind it a great fan of purple and red, and only a bloody glow lit the depths of the morass, glinting from the ponds and coloring the tall reeds. Both Judas and the Greek gleamed red in this somber twilight, the blood from their wounds mingling with the bloody light from the sky. My own weariness was such that the very thought of fighting again made my whole body throb with pain, but in these two men, there was no sign of fatigue, only such hatred as I had never before seen in mankind. Hatred was in their faces, their stance — in their whole being, in their every move and look and gesture. Each held a long Greek sword; Apollonius had shed his shield in the battle, but he still wore breastplate and greaves and helmet. One long cut on his cheek had stained him all over with blood, but otherwise, he was unwounded, while Judas was cut and gashed in a dozen places. They stood the same height, but the Greek was as heavy as Judas was lean, as ugly as Judas was beautiful. Naked to the waist was Judas, and blood molded his linen to his legs. Sometime, in the battle, he had lost his sandals, and he walked barefoot. The Greek was a bull, heavy and ominous and dangerous, and Judas was like the lean, quick leopard that prowls in the hills of Galilee.

I dragged myself toward them, conscious now of my own wounds, the pain of them running from limb to limb, but Judas saw me and waved me aside imperiously. Others approached, and still Judas and Apollonius stood as they were until a circle of men surrounded them, and finally Judas said:

"Will you fight, Greek, or will you run and die the way your men died?"

The Greek's answer was a quick thrust, which Judas parried, and then they fought as I have never seen two men fight, with the abandon of beasts and the rage of demons. Back and forth they fought, their swords making a wild music in the darkening night, their breath coming in short, violent gasps, their feet sucking at the soft ground. They were closed about with Jews now, but the space was wide enough, and when more was needed, the crowd gave back. This was the Maccabee, and no one interfered; I understood that. Even if Judas died there, neither I nor John nor Eleazar nor Jonathan could help him. I saw them all now; but they did not see me. They saw only the two men who fought.

And then, the Greek brought his sword down on Judas with a cut that would have cloven him to his waist, had he not caught it on his own blade, caught it and snapped his sword, so he stood with a stump in his hand for just a fraction of a second, and then hurled himself in, past the Greek's recovery, driving the jagged end of his blade into Apollonius's face. The Greek went down, Judas upon him, cutting again and again at the shapeless face, until Eleazar and I sprang forward and pulled him off.

Sobbing, Judas stood there. He let go his broken hilt, which fell on the Greek's body, and then he bent over and took the sword of Apollonius. It was night now, but we were too weary to move. We laid down and slept there, the living and the dead, side by side.

So it was that we became an army, not like any army that was before, but an army out of the people and the strength of the people, the one army in all the world where men fought neither for pay nor for power, but for the ways of their fathers and the land of their fathers. That night, we slept in the soggy turf of the swamp of Ephraim, and the next day we stripped the bodies of our enemies and buried them — all but Apollonius, we buried, and his body was taken by a group of men to the gates of Jerusalem, where it was flung in the dirt, that the rich Jews who defended the city and dwelt in it might see the madman in whom they had put their trust.

But for us, there was no rest. Our strength increased. Ragesh went off to the South with Jonathan, to raise another army out of the dark, fierce Jews who for hundreds of years had defended their land from the endless stream of Bedouin raiders the desert spewed forth. Village after village rose, slew their garrison, put to death their own traitors, and trekked to join us in the Wilderness of Ephraim. As the weeks passed, our number increased to twenty and then to thirty thousand folk — and finally more than a hundred thousand; and as the people increased, the strength of our army increased. For me, the task of providing for this host of people, organizing them and feeding them, became a staggering burden. Day after day, I worked from dawn to sunset. Patrols covered Judea, emptying cisterns and warehouses and bringing food and wine and oil to Ephraim where we built new storage places for them. Whatever the villages could spare, they gave us, the Jews of Alexandria raised their own defense force and with it convoyed caravans of food to us. In Ephraim itself, in the most inaccessible mountain valleys, we began to clear the brush and forest and repair the ancient terraces that had not been farmed for three centuries.

In this John helped me, his patience without end, his gentle forbearance achieving results where my own hot anger raised walls all around me, the while Judas and Eleazar and Jonathan trained our people to fight. The war that we had learned so well by now, the war that made a trap and threat out of the whole land, every village, every hillside, every valley — went on without pause. From the desert in the south to the mountains of Galilee in the north we raided constantly, one or another of my brothers scouring the country to let Greek or rich Jew know that only behind fortress walls was there safety; but three months went by before we fought our second great battle.

Yet how am I to sort it out? The years began in which battle followed battle; and always there were more mercenaries, and more and still more, a bottomless well of countless thousands of these paid murderers with whom the world abounded; for the world made them and sold them to a mad king in the North whose life presently consisted of only one obsession — that the Jews must be destroyed.

It took time to find a new warden for Judea. His name was Horon, and he led four thousand mercenaries, four hundred cavalry among them, down the great main road to Egypt, swinging eastward and north at Ekron and into our mountains, even as Apollonius did before. It was between Modin and Gibeon that we met him and smashed him, hemming him in between the hills and driving him back. Eight hundred dead he left there at that battlefield, and for two days we followed the broken retreating phalanxes, letting arrows rain on them from every hillside and every cliff, until at last they reached the fortified cities of the coast.

Thus, in the space of three months, we smashed two great armies, and now, except for the citadel of Jerusalem, where rich Jews shared the cramped space with a Greek garrison, there was no road, no path, no village in all Judea where mercenaries could move in a force of less than thousands; and even when they moved in their thousands, they feared the close valleys and the high mountains as they might fear hell itself. From Ephraim, our liberated area now extended south to the very walls of the city, and I remember well the first time Judas and I led five hundred Jewish spearmen to within sight of the Temple. For hours we stood there, silent at the ruin and filth of our holy city — and then retreated when the mercenaries moved out against us.

A new life was growing up in the land. In Ephraim, the terraces were beginning to blossom, as we filled baskets with the fertile muck from the morass and piled it behind stone walls on the hillsides. Even as far as Modin, families were returning to the ruins of their homes, putting in crops and taking out harvests. But it was reprieve rather than freedom, as we learned when Moses ben Daniel came again from Damascus; a different Moses ben Daniel, older, with the light of terrible things in his eyes.

"I come to stay," he said. "There are no Jews left in Damascus. Antiochus is mad — stark, raving mad. He issued an order that every Jew in Syria must die, and Jewish blood ran like water in the streets of the city. Outside the city for ten miles, there is a row of spears, and on every spear, there is a Jewish head. I escaped because I was able to buy freedom, but you can count on your hands how many others escaped. They killed my wife and my other daughter."

All this he said in a cold and matter-of-fact way — in the same way that Jews would speak of terrible things, such things and other things. "Every Jew must die," he said tonelessly. "Every Jew in Damascus, every Jew in Hammon, in Sidon, in Apollonia and in Joppa — and in Judea. He will build a mountain of Jewish skulls and he will fill the valleys

of Judea with Jewish bones. Thus he says, screaming it in
his madness, and thus says the proclamation in every city
in Syria. To kill a Jew is no longer a crime, but a virtue —
thus it says."

"And how does he plan to kill every Jew in Judea?" Judas
said softly, while Eleazar clenched and unclenched his big
fists, the tears running down his face as he listened.

"He will come down with more men than ever marched
into Palestine in all time — a hundred thousand, he says,
although I do not think he will find money enough for such
an army. But, however, it will be a mighty host — I tell you
that, you young man whom they call the Maccabee. Even
before I left, Damascus was filled with slave dealers —
dealers from Athens and Sicily, and Rome too, and the
King's treasurer was hounding them for advances against
concessions. In the great jewelry mart, four hundred rubies
from the King's own treasure were on sale, and everywhere
around the city mercenaries were camped, and still more
arrived — "

"And they make us an angry and awful people," Judas
whispered.

So it was that the third army came against us. How many
men it comprised, I don't know, for it stretched out over
seven miles of road, and it was a host such as had never
been seen in Judea before. There was no counting it. This
one said fifty thousand, and another said eighty thousand
— but this I know: With Ruben and Eleazar and three of
the black men, I went to the ridge of Mount Gilboa and
saw them coming into the land. It was not a sight to make
a man brave, men swarming on like locusts, mercenaries
without end, miles of wagons, slave dealers, prostitutes and
other camp followers — like the migration of a whole nation.
Here was every mercenary who could be scraped into

service from Syria, and many from Egypt and Greece and Persia. And against them, we had six thousand.

Their very size saved us. In its entirety, this mass of men and women and animals could only crawl down the coastal road, a few miles a day. From the hills, we watched them, and whenever they detached details to raid the countryside for food or booty, they were met in the passes by swarms of Jewish arrows. In their path, we poisoned the wells and cisterns and burned every bit of food we could not carry away, and always at night, around their sprawling camp, our signal fires blazed. When they slept, Eleazar and his black Africans would lead little parties into their very camp itself, cut throats and sow confusion and escape into the very vastness of their multitude.

As far south as Hazor they came. Their number had swelled itself, for the slave dealers had managed to gather up two or three thousand Jewish captives, as well as five or six thousand of the *nokri* who lived on the coastal plain. They were not particularly discriminating about who they put in chains, for they labored under their cash advances to Antiochus, and our spies told us of the discord and bitterness between the motley of slave dealers, the lords of prostitution and the Greek officers of Antiochus. In addition to all this, the trash and refuse of the coastal cities, the miserable, dying cities of that land which was once the proud and mighty Philistia, sold themselves to Gorgias, the Greek commander, as mercenaries. Gorgias was a wavering, uncertain specimen of the same mongrel type as Apelles, and he had only one fear — of returning to the north without having reduced Judea and destroyed the Jews. Thus, he welcomed every addition to his ranks, swelling his original army, as we heard, to over a hundred thousand men. At the same time, he waged war like a madman against every defenseless Jew who still dwelt on the coastal plain.

At Hazor, this host paused, their camp sprawling over miles of the plain, while we gathered our six thousand at Mizpah in the foothills, less than ten miles away. They were good men, our six thousand. As they stood on their arms, Judas and I walked through their ranks, he praised this one and remembered some deed of that one. He had that uncanny facility of memory which never allowed him to forget the name of a man he knew, or a name he had heard or a deed he had seen, and now he took hand after hand, stopping occasionally to embrace someone who had been with us in the old days, when we raided with our tens or our twenties. He glowed with pride at the ranks of tall, lean, hard men, men who could walk thirty miles over the mountains on a piece of bread or a handful of meal, and fight at the end of that time, living and fighting like lean and angry wolves. They crowded around him as he spoke, their eyes glowing.

"We have a venture and a deed before us," Judas said, "that was never given to Israel before — for when did such a host come into our old and holy land? Not David and not Solomon faced such might, yet the Lord is our right hand — and we will smite them and destroy them and drive them back whence they came. Their case is not so good. They are hungry and angry and already they fight among themselves. And we have stung them a little," he added smiling. "We'll sting them again."

A roar went up, which Judas quieted with arms spread.

"Would you have them hear you?" he smiled. "They sit down there in the valley, even now, looking up at our hills — and sooner or later they must gather their courage and come through the passes. Thus will we fight: I lead, and under each of my brothers a thousand men will march. If we should fail, then let us die, so that we will not have to bear the memory; but if we live and are separated, we will rendezvous at Modin, where the Adon Mattathias, my father, dwelt, and we will make an assembly there and give thanks to God."

The "Amen" swelled up and shook the trees. . . .

How shall I tell it, when there were so many battles? It is simple to say that Gorgias took five thousand foot and a thousand horse and moved north to Emmaus, probing at our hills. When he left his camp to advance, we went behind him and burned his camp. That was the first but not the last time we cut a force off from its main group, burning its base behind it. So many battles — that it is hard now to separate the one from the other. Yet Gorgias was less than Apollonius. He was in the hills already, with six thousand men, when he heard on every side of him the twittering of our whistles and the sonorous rumble of our *shofars*. When he saw the lights of his burning camp, in the early evening, he already knew the terror of those who march through Judean defiles when the skies rain Jewish arrows. He must have decided to turn then and there and make a night march to rejoin the eighty or ninety thousand he had left behind him. He was a fool and afraid, and that night he learned the full meaning of fear, doing what no other Greek commander would have ever dared, marching by night in the Judean passes, his army strung out, his horses wild with pain from our arrows and riding down his own men. The arrows never ceased, all that night. In the narrow passes, landslides of stone increased his agony, and once, where the valley bottom narrowed to a space hardly more than a yard wide, Eleazar and Ruben the smith held the pass, the Africans and the men of Modin behind them, and the

Africans had a new score to settle, loving the wife and daughter of Moses ben Daniel who were slain in Damascus. For three hours, Gorgias hurled his mercenaries against the pass, and for three hours the great iron hammer of my brother Eleazar beat them back. In the night, in that pass, the bodies of the dead lay shoulder high, and those who held the way waded ankle-deep in hot blood — until the screaming, terror-stricken mercenaries clawed their way up the cliffs to die by our knives and our arrows. Ever since, that valley pass has exuded a fearful stench, for we filled it with the bodies of more than two thousand mercenaries, making a fit memorial for Antiochus, the mad King of Kings.

Some escaped, but not many. Gorgias and a handful found their way back to the coastal plain, but the rest we hunted down in the night and through to the dawn, dragging them down almost within sight of the mighty encampment. . . .

For eight months that followed, the huge, sprawling army of the Greeks camped there on the Plain of Philistia, and in that time they made nine separate efforts to penetrate the Judean hills, and nine times we clawed them to pieces and sent them reeling back to the shelter of the plain. Hunger, demoralization and disease preyed upon them, and during that eight months they raped the cities of Gaza and Ascalon, supposedly under their shelter and protection, handing over the whole population of both places to the slave dealers to settle the long overdue debt of the King of Kings. Yet inland, only ten or fifteen miles away, at Mizpah and Gath and other villages of the sort, Jews rebuilt their terraces and cultivated their land in peace.

We learned a good deal in those eight months of almost unceasing battle. We learned finally, and for all, that a mountain folk cannot be rooted up from the soil that bred them. We learned that a Jew will fight a little better than a mercenary, since our fight is for God and land and the other for money and loot. And we learned to use, when we had to, the weapons of the Greek, sword and spear.

There was no longer, in Judea, a question of who led the people. Judas was the Maccabee — it became his name then, the name he gave to all of us his brothers; and the people, ready to follow in the beginning because there was no one else to follow, came to love him in the end as no man in all of Israel, before or since, has been loved — indeed as no man in all the world was loved by those he led. I remained what I was and am — Simon ben Mattathias, a Jew like other Jews; but my brothers grew into a glory never before known: John, whom the people looked on like a father; Jonathan, young and cunning and wily, raiding like a devil and a wolf combined; Eleazar, the splendor of battle, the terror of battle; and Judas, the Maccabee — Judas, my brother Judas, Judas whom I hated and loved, Judas who was the embodiment of the people and the soul of the people, who had no life apart from them, the gentle in judgment and the terrible in battle, Judas whom I never knew or could know — and whom, I think, no one else ever knew or could know. I loved one woman and lost her, and I became something cold and bitter and apart, like the Adon, my father — yet, I do not know, looking back, that Judas did not love her more. How can I set up my small and dry capacity to love against the ever-flowering warmth of him, my brother, who loved so many and was loved by thousands? Never, in all this time I write of, did I see him do a small thing, a miserable thing, a mean thing; never did I hear his voice raised in anger — except against the enemy, and even there the anger was softened by pity and remorse. In that time and in the years that followed, many of us became hardened by war; better than anything we had ever known, we learned to kill; but Judas was never hardened. The soft and gentle edge of his character was never dulled. When four men were caught as traitors and almost slain on the spot, it was Judas who saved them and let them go. When a dreadful sickness broke out among us, terrifying even the strongest of heart, Judas nursed the sick with his own hands. When food was scarce, Judas ate little or nothing.

The women worshiped him, yet there was no woman for him but the woman who had carried my child and died. I think, sometimes, that over and beyond all of it, he was the loneliest and saddest man I have ever known.

At the end of the eight months, Lysias, regent of Antiochus, came in person to lead the attack, bringing with him from the North four thousand cavalry. Our own numbers had grown to over ten thousand tested and hardened men, but Lysias took twenty thousand foot and almost seven thousand horse, marched them through the dry lands of Idumea, and led them up through the South toward Hebron. It is true that the valleys were wider there, but still he had to come into our Judean hills, and like Gorgias he made the tragic mistake of relying upon cavalry in country where it was often difficult for men to walk two abreast. His horsemen were his own worst enemies, yet he clung to them, even though again and again they went mad with pain from our Judean arrows. From the moment he entered the Mountains of Judah, we harried him, and finally, at Beth Zur, we blocked his way. For three days, he tried to carry the pass, and for three days we slew his men and filled the valley with his dead. He began to retreat, and then his retreat became a route, and all the way back to the Shephela, we drove him, cutting off group after group, giving him no peace and no rest and no sleep and no pause. Only when he reached the plain itself and could assemble what was left of his phalanx, did we leave off killing — and yet we followed him, bold now, a fringe of trotting bowmen at the edge of his massed shields, day and night. From Judea came thousands of bundles of the slim, straight cedar arrows, and they rained like water on his camp. When he charged with his phalanx, we melted away, and when he sent out what remained of his cavalry, we slew the horses with our arrows. . . .

A year had passed since the great host of the King of Kings had made its way into Palestine to destroy Judea and the Jews. Now it began its march back to Syria in the North, leaving behind, in the course of that year, no less than thirty thousand dead. And as the monstrous, unwieldy mass of mercenaries, slave dealers, slaves, pimps, and whores moved north, we followed them; and all the way, from Philistia to the Plain of Sharon to Galilee, our Jewish arrows rained upon them — that they might remember their scorn for us, and the perversions they had visited upon us.

So it was that, in the month of Marheshvan, in the soft and lovely Judean autumn, when the cool wind blows day and night from the Mediterranean, when the valleys are carpeted with poppies, the land was liberated. When the first scent of winter stings the evergreen of the mountain-tops, when the last fall planting is put into the earth, and when the *shekar*, the strong and heady wine, is ready for the drinking, the land was freed — not forever; there was no one among us foolish enough or hopeful enough to think we had seen the last of the Greek, or that the madman

Antiochus would so readily give up the rich and perennial and beautiful treasure chest of Judea. There were a million mercenaries available for hire, and there were cities enough from which he could squeeze blood and gold to hire them; but for all of that, it would be months and perhaps years before he could recover from the blows we had dealt him — and in that time, we had respite.

It was a golden autumn, as if the whole land, every rock and every grain of sand, every flower and every blade of wheat, gave thanks to God for that, the most precious of all things, freedom. From the Wilderness of Judah in the South and from the Wilderness of Ephraim in the North, thousands of families began their trek homeward, to the ruined farms and villages they had left. In the sweet eventide, you could hear their singing in the deep valleys and along the mountain tracks, as they gave thanks for the liberation. And other thousands converged upon the holy city of Jerusalem, for word had gone about that the Maccabee would enter it and cleanse the Temple.

For two whole days, Judas, and we his brothers, and his captains as well as the leading Adons and Rabbis of the land, held council as to what should be done with the last remaining enemy within Judea, the Greeks and wealthy Jews who, with their mercenaries, held the citadel within Jerusalem. Some, like Ragesh, proposed conciliation, an attempt to bargain with them on the basis that they leave the land, but this I opposed, and my brothers backed me.

"We do not bargain with traitors and swine," I said, and Judas agreed, adding, "There was a swine's head on the altar, and they worshiped it. So there will be time enough when they crawl on their bellies to us, as I once saw a traitor in Shiloh crawl, to decide whether they should live or die."

Others wanted to mass all our power and storm the
citadel, particularly the Alexandrian Jews, who felt that
their engineers would come from Egypt with machines
enough to overcome any obstacle, but Judas opposed this.
"There has been bloodletting enough," he said. "All our
fighting has been in the valleys — and how are we to go
up against stone walls twenty feet thick? Let them rot there
in the citadel — and let them see with their own eyes how
the people cleanse the Temple . . ."

So we returned to the Temple, even as the Adon said we
would return. We marched first to Modin, which was rising
again from its ashes, and there we cleansed the synagogue,
and the Rabbi Ragesh led the prayers. Then with two
thousand picked men, led by the veterans of Modin and
Goumad, all of them in full armor for this occasion, bearing
sword, spear, and shield, we began the procession to the
Temple. First came the Kohanim, four red-bearded old men
who had been driven from the Temple five years before, all
stalwart patriots who had fought with us. Strangely like
the Adon they were, in their blue and white vestments.
Then came twenty Levites, all in white and over their
shoulders snow-white cloaks, and they walked barefoot with
their heads bowed in shame, for too many traitors and too
many of those who had shut themselves up in the citadel
were Levites. After the Levites, Judas walked, he too barefoot, a red cap upon his head, and from beneath it his beautiful auburn hair lay upon his striped cloak. Like the Levites,
he was unarmed and without adornment, and like them
he walked with his eyes upon the ground, even though again
and again as we passed through a village, people pressed
forward to kiss his hands and to hail the Maccabee. Behind
Judas we, his four brothers, marched; and like the fighting
men who followed us, we were clad in the heavy panoply

of war. We carried neither spear nor shield, but we wore
polished brass breastplates and long Greek swords, and on
our heads were four brazen helms with blue plumes, and
behind us marched our two thousand men.

Yet that was not the end of the procession, for a concourse
of people followed us, increasing as we neared the city, and
under the broken walls of Jerusalem thousands more waited
our arrival.

How could I help but thrill with pride as I looked at my
glorious brothers — Judas so tall and handsome; Eleazar like
a great, tawny lion; Jonathan so lithe and quick and eager,
like a lean deer in the first flush of his young manhood, the
new beard curling on his brown face; and John in his gentle
and loving sadness?

We marched on, over hill and dale, as I had walked the
first time with my father so long ago, but the city was not
the same. It was a crazy ruin of filth and desolation. Grass
grew amidst the rubble; doorways gaped, and the empty
streets gave it a sad and tomblike aspect. Wild dogs slunk
back into the houses as we passed, and everywhere there
was evidence of crazy, senseless vandalism — the better to
remind us in time to come of the higher civilization that had
paused so briefly, leaving its mark upon this place. Wherever you looked, you saw dry, sun-bleached human bones,
with here and there a skull. As we climbed higher and
higher, nearing the Temple, the signs of vandalism increased
— and as we approached the mount, we could see movement
on the walls of the Acra, tiny figures who watched us from
the walled security of their citadel.

The people saw them too, and noticing the looks of hatred
I felt it boded ill for the Jews who had shut themselves up
in that place. At first, we were all noise and shouting, filled
with the triumph of our victory and our return, but as we

entered the city, our tones became more subdued, hushed as we climbed higher — and silent as we entered the Temple area, for here what was done was not human but monstrous.

Even to the last, the place had been traduced with swine's flesh, for it lay about, rotting and filling the place with an awful smell. The wonderful carved wooden gates of the Temple were burned; the priceless marble in the corridors was gouged and smashed; and the ancient scrolls of the Law were torn to bits and scattered about. As a last gesture, the mercenaries, or the Greeks, had taken three children, cut their throats, and dragged their bodies through the inner chambers as they bled, flinging them dead onto a pile of the blue silk hangings that had once separated room from room. Thus it went, senseless destruction, perversion and madness — the frenetic madness that seems to come only from blind hatred of Jews.

And on the altar itself, there stood a marble statue of Antiochus, the King of Kings, the apostle of civilization and all the gentle virtues of Western culture. Even the sculptor, with whatever fears and rewards pursued him, could not remove the sense of bestiality that pervaded the image of the King of Kings. . . .

It was not a time for mourning. I dispatched Eleazar with a thousand men to guard the Acra, and I led the others to see what could be done about repairing the aqueduct and filling some of the great siege cisterns with water. When I returned, a thousand Jews were scrubbing the Temple with lye and ashes, Judas among them.

It took us three weeks, and there was no scarcity of labor. From all over Judea came Jews to lend their arms to rebuilding the Temple. Stonecutters took marble from the lower city and recut it to replace the slabs that were damaged. The aqueduct was repaired and a stream of water flushed out the place. Rings, bracelets, trinkets of every sort poured into the common coffers, to be melted down and shaped into new *m'norah* by Ruben the smith. The best woodworkers in Judea fashioned new gates, and from every village came offerings of silk for the hangings. All day, and all night by the light of torches, workmen swarmed over the Temple, and finally, on the day of the twenty-fourth of Kislev, it was finished, rebuilt, cleansed and beautiful again.

And on the morning of the twenty-fifth of Kislev, the new Temple was consecrated, and there sounded in its halls once again that ancient, ancient declaration:

"Hear, O Israel, the Lord is our God, the Lord is one!"

In the *m'norah*, the lights were lit, and for eight days the ceremony of dedication continued. During those eight days, almost every inhabitant of Judea came to Jerusalem — and for those eight days, a thousand armed men with bows strung stood around the citadel, day and night.

PART FOUR

Judas, without Peer, without Reproach

ND NOW I MUST TELL WHAT IS HARD-
est to tell, how the end came to my glorious brothers. The
Greeks, who have many gods and many versions of the
truth, and many notions of liberty, too, have a goddess
whom they call the Muse of History, and they are very
proud that they set down the truth when they write of their
history; but the making of history among us, who are
Jews, is like the searching of a people's soul. We are not
obsessed by the truth, since our past and our future too is
a pact between ourselves and our covenant and our God
— and all those things in which we believe; and what else
should we state but the truth? Would we hide the fact
that Cain slew Abel, in cold and terrible anger, or that
David ben Jesse sinned as few men have sinned? We are
not like the *nokri*, for we were slaves in Egypt; and for all
time to come, through our children's time and their children's, we will not forget that; and we will bend our knee
to no man and not even to God. Can you separate freedom
from truth? And with what other people is it said, as we say,
that resistance to tyrants is the highest and truest obedience
to God?

And so I write, seeking in the past, that is given to no
man to visit again, but only for God and for His immortal

records; and the memories come like clouds driven by the winds, so that I want to put aside the parchment and lay my head on the table and cry out:

"Oh, my brothers, my glorious brothers, where are you — and when will Israel or the world see your like again?"

Already in the synagogues there is a new scroll, the scroll of the Maccabees, as they call it — as if there could be more than one, more than Judas, my brother Judas, who of all men was without peer and without reproach — and in this scroll it is written thus:

Then his son Judas, called Maccabeus, rose up in his stead.

And all his brethren helped him, and so did all they that held with his father, and they fought with cheerfulness the battle of Israel.

So he got his people great honor, and put on a breastplate as a giant, and girt his warlike harness about him, and he made battles, protecting the host with his sword.

In his acts, he was like a lion, and like a lion's whelp roaring for his prey.

For he pursued the wicked, and sought them out, and burnt up those that vexed his people. Wherefore the wicked shrunk for fear of him, and all the workers of iniquity were troubled, because salvation prospered in his hand.

He grieved also many kings, and made Jacob glad with his acts, and his memorial is blessed forever.

Moreover, he went through the cities of Judah, destroying the ungodly out of them, and turning away wrath from Israel; so that he was renowned unto the utmost part of the earth, and he received unto him such as were ready to perish.

So it says: *And he received unto him such as were ready to perish.* Judas, Judas, how few of us there were, in the end, who were ready to perish! We became weary — and weary you never were. We lost hope, when you knew that the strength of a people is something that cannot die. Yes, and I remember when you returned again to Modin, to the broken rooftree of Mattathias, and put away your weapons and worked side by side with me and with Jonathan to rebuild the house and the terraces, and Nicanor came there in all his splendor and found you in the field with your hands on the plow, you, the Maccabee, the Kohan, the priest of the Temple, and I remember how, as you spoke with him, the first captain of the King of Kings, you bent again and again to pick up a lump of that good Judean earth we tilled, breaking it, and letting it slide through your fingers. . . .

Yet I must tell before this of how Eleazar died. I am an old man, wandering in the past and trying to understand the things that make a Jew a Jew, and I must be forgiven for my wandering.

There was short respite when we cleansed the Temple. In his hunger for money to hire more mercenaries and thereby to gain more money, the mad Antiochus led an expedition eastward against the Parthians, and there he died. But his son and his regents lacked none of his insatiable hunger. Westward they could not go, for already the grim strength of Rome barred their path — and said, Go this far and no farther. Eastward were the deserts, and beyond the deserts the terrible arrows of the Parthians. But to the south always was the treasure chest of Judea. The rich and beautiful hill country of the Jews that could, with its boundless fertility, bring back all the glory of Macedonia — provided that the Maccabee was crushed.

Four times more armies were sent into our Judean hills, and four times we crushed them, smashed them, and filled the defiles with the arrow-tufted bodies of our foes — yet how much war can a people endure? We no longer lay in the Wilderness of Ephraim, but had gone back to the farms and the villages. With each invasion, Judas sent out his call for volunteers. At first, they came by the thousands to the standard of the Maccabee, the standard which had never known defeat, but when the awful monotony and suffering of invasion repeated itself again and again, the amount of volunteers dwindled. For each campaign there were a few less; with each campaign; the knife of years of warfare sank a little deeper. We could not, like Antiochus, call upon a numberless swarm of mercenaries. There were just so many Jews in Judea — and no more. . . .

And then, Lysias, the new warden, came with the elephants. I will tell you of the elephants, those great and terrible beasts that no one of us had ever seen before, but first I must explain why we had to go against them with only three thousand men. The best of our men, two thousand, among whom were the battle-scarred veterans of Modin and Goumad — these we had to leave at the Temple, to stand endless guard over the Acra, where month after month the Jewish traitors and the Greeks maintained themselves, defying us to batter down their huge walls. Jonathan and John remained there in command. Another thousand men garrisoned the fortress of Beth Zur, for the Bedouins were growing bold, now that the mercenaries had been swept from the land, and again and again, they came from the desert, camel-mounted, to raid our villages. For Judas to find additional men to patrol the borders of Judea — against the numberless bands of mercenaries who between masters would seek for booty among the Jews; against the Philistines in the West, a bastard, corrupted people; and against the minor Greek satraps, who had broken away after the death of Antiochus, and who could keep neither their hands nor their eyes off the treasure chest of Judea — was a constant and heartbreaking task, for once the Greeks were smashed, it was not easy to persuade men from their farms and their families. It was against this that he had to — and did — raise an army to stop four separate invasions; but when they came with the elephants, that was an additional terror.

We heard only rumors of the struggle for power that went on in the court of the dead Antiochus. The dead madman left an idiot son, to whom they fed perversions, drugs and women, and animals too, for these practices were common in Antioch, and in Damascus. And meanwhile Philippus, the King's regent, fought for power against Lysias, a Greek sailor, who through shrewdness, deceit, and wholesale murder had climbed high in Syrian power. Knowing that the conquest of Judea might well tip the balance, Lysias hit upon the idea of the elephant troops, and he dispatched his messengers, loaded down with gold and jewels, all the way to the valley of the Indus, where they hired two hundred of the great beasts, along with drivers and archers to man the castles upon their backs. It was the Greek's idea that if our hills were a fortress, he would invade them with a new kind of fortress, and once and for all crush the power of the Maccabee and his followers. Thus he came down the coastal road with the elephants and ten thousand mercenaries to back them up, and they swung inland through the Vale of Eshcol to come upon us through the broad Southern passes.

All during their journey South, we had reports of these new, monstrous, ungainly beasts that lumbered along like living castles, carrying wooden walls upon their backs with slits for arrows; and as the rumors spread through Judea, the elephants grew in size and fearsomeness. It was the quality of the unknown, looming over us like devils, and people who through years of warfare against awful odds had feared nothing mortal now trembled at the thought of these moving mountains.

Not knowing at first which route the elephants would take, Judas concentrated what forces he could muster at Bethlehem, from where he sent out scouts. The first rumor was to the effect of the main attack being upon Beth Zur, and Judas and Eleazar set off with two thousand men in that direction. The other thousand, under my command, moved toward the deep pass near Beth Zechariah. We had marched for only an hour or two when we heard the ominous rumble of the elephant troops, a sound like no other sound I had known. The men tensed and paled, and already I could see uncertainty and fear running like cold water through the ranks. Ruben, the smith, was with me, Ruben of Modin, who in a hundred encounters had never shown fear or hesitation; but now, at this new and unknown sound, the blood left his face and the spring went from his step. "They are beasts," I told him. "God made them and man can slay them." "And if they are not beasts?" "Then you are a fool — and a coward!"

Seizing my arm in an iron grip, he cried, "No man ever called me a coward, Simon ben Mattathias!" "I call you that, damn you!" "And why do you curse me, Simon?" "Because we have fought too long to be afraid now. I want you to take half the men and bar the pass — and hold it the way we held it so many times! Hold it against hell itself, until Judas can come to us! But if you leave it before the Maccabee arrives, God help you!" "I'll hold it, Simon . . ." And then I sent our fleetest runner after Judas and Eleazar.

At a quick trot, I led our thousand to the neck of the valley, the northern end where it narrowed to perhaps

twenty yards, and while Ruben and his men worked madly
to erect some sort of a barricade out of stones and fallen
trees, I led my five hundred up the slope, where they could
take vantage points for their arrows. We had hardly time;
we were still clambering up the slope when the first of the
great beasts became visible, moving up the valley at an
ominous and inevitable pace, slowly, yet the more terribly
for that. Three abreast, the elephants moved, and truly
there seemed no end of them. On the head of each, the
driver sat, and behind him there was a box of heavy wood,
slit all over for the archers. All naked were the drivers,
thin, brown men, who sat with crossed legs, dangling a long
stick, pointed and with a hook just below the point, and
occasionally they hooked or prodded the beasts they drove.
Adam ben Lazar was my lieutenant there, and I told him
to kill the drivers first, but I wondered whether it would
stop or divert the beasts. Now, more than a hundred of
them were in sight, and we could see the gleaming spears
and helmets of the mercenaries who marched behind them.
The frightening rumble of their feet filled the whole valley
and mixed itself with the shrill shouting of their drivers,
while from beyond them the hoarse cries of the mercenaries
sounded heady with triumph.

Let me try to tell what happened as it happened; tell it
I must, and other things too, for all the pain in the telling.
I do not blame Ruben; how shall I blame you, Ruben, my
comrade who rests now with my glorious brothers in that
past that belongs to all men? Nothing he knew Ruben
feared, and time was to prove that, but our little cedar
arrows that fell like rain only enraged the great beasts. We
killed the drivers, but the elephants came on. We feathered
the wooden boxes on their backs, yet they came on — onto
the barricade, smashing it under their feet, and Ruben and

his men broke and ran, and it was the first time in years that a Greek saw the backs of Jews in combat.

I ran to help them, and for all their fear, my men followed. We sped along the ridge, leaping down the hillside, yet it was not I who stopped those who fled, but my brothers and their two thousand, pouring into the valley, with Eleazar at their head, Eleazar and his mighty hammer, Eleazar, the splendor of battle, the one man I knew who never feared, never doubted, never mocked, the simple, brave, wonderful Eleazar — and behind him came the eight black Africans who remained of the original twelve, the eight soft-voiced men who loved my brother and had fought beside him through these years.

I was close enough then to hear Eleazar cry, "And are you afraid? Of what? Are beasts born that cannot be slain?"

In that mad rush of the elephants, the men behind Judas halted in fear and wonder; but Eleazar leaped ahead and alone he met one elephant that had outpaced the others. Such a sight was never seen before then or since, for Eleazar's great body arched, the hammer swung back over his head, and then it met the elephant with a crushing thud that sounded above the screaming and shouting. And the elephant, skull crushed, went down on its knees, rolled over and died. But already Eleazar and his black men were surrounded by the beasts. They fought with their spears and Eleazar fought with his hammer until a blow from an elephant's tusk tore it from his grasp. It was not as long as it takes here in the telling. He was dead before Judas and I could reach his side. They were shooting arrows from the boxes, and there were already two arrows in his body, when he seized the spear of a fallen African, ran under one of the great beasts and thrust the whole length of the spear into his bowels. The stampede of elephants came on; nothing could have stopped it then; and in the valley bottom, crushed under hundreds of pounding feet, lay my brother Eleazar and his black comrades.

We scattered. We clawed up the slopes, and always I tried to keep near Judas — and perhaps I wept as Judas was weeping. I don't know; I don't remember. I know only that Eleazar was dead. . . .

By nightfall, we had gathered together eighteen hundred of our men — and we retreated northward. For the first time, the Maccabee had been smashed in battle.

I walked in the night, sometimes alone, sometimes in the press of my men, and I didn't care, so much was the heart out of us. In the beginning, it was only important that I keep near Judas; but as the night wore on, a cloudy, sullen night, I wrapped myself in loneliness, in bitterness, in bereavement — and I separated myself from Judas. I let him go past me and lose himself. Not so much anger as a burning, corroding frustration and fear gripped me. All men were human, but Judas was something else. His tears were a lie; his grief was no grief; his soul was lost and he was like a sword that has only one purpose and one destiny.

Hatred came, slowly; the old awful black hatred of my brother — that was compounded out of such a welter of things, such a complex of things, such a mystery of things, being old and bitter and insatiable, and sunk into that ancient, ancient tale of how Cain slew Abel. And who had slain Eleazar? And who would slay the rest of us, one by one, without peace and without end and without surcease? Eleazar was dead, but already for Judas there were only the men, the army, the struggle, the resistance that had squeezed the last ounce of mercy out of him.

Now, moving slowly through that despairing and unholy night, dragging my feet, careless of hope or tomorrow or anything but the pit of death and destruction into which I felt myself sinking, I recalled how it had been when Judas came back to Modin and stood over the body of the lovely and splendid woman I had loved, how he stood there at first without saying a word, without sign or evidence of grief — and then spoke only of vengeance.

Who had slain her, he would say . . .

"Thy brother's keeper," the Adon, the old man had said to me. "And thou, Simon, thou art thy brother's keeper, thou and no other."

But Judas, whose hands were already so red with blood, so wet and red with blood, could think only of reddening them more — and vengeance was his, not the Lord God's, not the people's, but his and only his. . . .

I was standing still, moving no more. What was the use of moving? Where were we going? The old man was dead, Eleazar was dead — and how long now for the others? Why go? Why flee? I sank to the ground, and here and there, near by, other men were giving up the flight, the purpose — the drive that had driven us so long; and then I heard the voice of my brother in the night.

Let him seek me then. I damned him. I stretched out there on the ground, my face in my hands, and his voice came: "Simon! Simon!"

As the devil seeks a man.

"Simon!"

Without end, for he was the Maccabee — without end.

"Simon!"

God's curse on you, go and leave me!

"Simon!"

I lifted my face, and he was above me, peering at me through the dark. "Simon?" he asked.

"What do you want?"

"Get up," he said. "Get up, Simon ben Mattathias."

I rose and stood before him.

"Are you wounded that you lie in the night?" he asked quietly. "Or is it fear — the damned fear that was always in your heart?"

My knife was out — and one arm at his throat, and still he didn't move but looked at me coolly. Then I hurled the knife into the darkness and covered my face with my hands.

"Why didn't you kill me?" Judas demanded. "For the rotten black hatred in you."

"Leave me alone."

"I will not leave you alone. Where are your men?"

"Where is Eleazar?"

"He is dead," Judas said evenly. "Strong he was, but you are stronger, Simon ben Mattathias. Only your heart is not like his. For victory — you're good for victory, but God help Israel if it should depend on you in defeat!"

"Shut up!"

"Why? Because you can't bear the truth? Where was the sword of Simon when Eleazar died? Where was it?"

The long moments dragged by while we stood there, and finally, finally and at long last, I asked my brother, "What shall I do?"

"Gather your men," he said without emotion. "Eleazar is dead, and we are full of grief. But the enemy is not grieved. Gather your men, Simon."

In the early morning, we sat around a fire, Judas on one side of me, Ruben on the other, and all around us lay our men, some asleep, some awake and trying to comprehend what had been; and Ruben wept the way a child weeps, telling us, "He was your brother, but he was my child, my child, and I betrayed him — and I ran when he stood, and I turned my back to them when he turned his face to them, and why am I alive when he lies dead there in the valley?"

"Peace," I said to him. "For the love of God, stop!" For I felt that if I had to listen to any more of Ruben's grief, I would surely go mad. But Judas said, softly and gently:

"Let him get it out of him, Simon, Simon — let him get it out of him, otherwise it will swell up like a cancer inside of him and destroy him."

"I taught him the forge," Ruben wept. "I taught him the secrets of metal, the ancient secrets, and he burned as pure as the iron when it turns blue with the flame. God gave me no son, but he gave me Eleazar, and I betrayed him, I slew him. May my hands rot and fall off! May my heart turn into lead! May I be accursed forever and forever!" He wrapped his face in his cloak, and he rocked back and forth, moaning and sobbing. . . .

In a way it was the end. There was reprieve, yet in a way it was the end of all my glorious brothers, the sons of Mattathias, who had become like heroes of old to Israel. For the first time, we could not turn and fight. In the old days, with five hundred men Judas would have turned and faced the enemy and laughed at their numbers, and cut at them and harried them and made every valley a hell and every pass a slaughterhouse; but the men left to us would not face the elephants, and there was no other way for it but to go back to Jerusalem and join our brothers behind the walls Judas had erected to defend the Temple Mount.

With Eleazar's death, something had happened to Judas, something had broken inside of him, and when I said to him, "What have we to do with fighting behind walls?" he answered me, "My brothers are there." "And we will be there — and will Lysias have to seek us?" "And shall I make war again?" Judas asked hopelessly. "The people are in their

villages. Shall I tell them to burn their homes and go to
Ephraim? Will they listen to me again?" "You are the
Maccabee," I told him. "Judas, my brother Judas, heed me
— you are the Maccabee, and the people will listen."

For a long while, he was silent, and then he shook his
head. "No, Simon — no. I am not like you, and you are like
my father, the Adon; but I am not like him and not like
you — and I will go to my brothers at Jerusalem. If you
would make war from the wilderness, then take the men,
and I will go alone to Jerusalem and fight with my brothers."

"You are the Maccabee," I said.

And the next day, we joined Jonathan and John at the
Temple and told them of Eleazar's death. . . .

Judas called a council, and Ragesh came, and Samuel ben
Zebulun, and Enoch ben Samuel of Alexandria, and twenty
other Adons and Rabbis, some of them men who had sat
at our first council so long ago, and even as we came together, the elephant troops were entering the city. It was a
grim and worried group of old men who faced the four of
us and listened to Judas's short and bitter account of our
defeat.

"Thus it was," he finished; "and my brother Eleazar is
dead and many other Jews too, so I came back here to defend the Temple. The walls of the Temple are strong, and
if it is your will, I will die here. Or — I will go away to
Ephraim and fight the old war. I do not think that the
elephants are invincible. My brother Eleazar slew one with
a single blow of his hammer. These are beasts that God
made, and man can kill them. We must learn how." He
finished, and below the Temple we could hear the cries of
the mercenaries in the city streets. But the city was empty
and broken, and how much more destruction could they
wreak upon what was already a tomb?

"What does Simon think?" Samuel ben Zebulun asked, and I looked curiously at this proud and angry old man of the South.

"You ask a son of Mattathias?" I said.

"I ask you, Simon."

"I am not the Maccabee," I told them. "I am not an Adon or a Rabbi. I am Simon, the least of the sons of Mattathias, and I judged in Ephraim. This is not the wilderness — this is Jerusalem."

"And what will you do?" Ragesh asked dryly.

"I will follow my brother Judas."

Ragesh shrugged. "And there will be war and more war — and war without end."

"I have never known anything else," I said. "And yet I have not bent my knee."

"You are a proud man," Ragesh said. "Would you put yourself before Israel?"

Jonathan answered him, angrily, almost wildly. "Did my brother Eleazar put himself before Israel? Did my father? Do we walk about in silks, with gold and diamonds?" Judas gripped his arm; tears rolled down the boy's cheeks as he stood there, taut and trembling.

"So I am scolded by children," Ragesh said softly.

"And am I a child?" Jonathan cried. "When I was fourteen I had the bow in my hand, and when I was fifteen I killed my first man. I know you, old man!"

"Enough!" Ragesh roared.

"Enough," Judas said. "Be still, Jonathan, be still."

Enoch of Alexandria rose, a white-bearded, splendid old man of seventy, tall and gentle and soft-eyed. He was one of the old Kohanim who had come back from Egypt, that he might spend the years left to him at the Temple, and now he spread his arms for silence.

"So be it, and peace. I am an old man, Judas Maccabeus, yet I do you honor and there is no man in Israel I put before you. Two things I wanted to see before I died, the holy Temple and the face of the Maccabee. I have seen both, and in neither was I disappointed. Yet I am a Jew — " He paused and sighed. "I am a Jew, my son, and our ways are not the ways of the *nokri*. Shall we kill without end? Then will we not become creatures of death instead of life? When I came through the villages, I saw that the people were at peace, building their houses again, and the grapes were heavy on the vine. What does God ask of man, but that he render justice and keep the covenant? Pride goeth, I tell you. We have driven home to the Greek well enough that the Jew is not a meek and humble creature with whom he can do his will, and now, in Antioch, one party wars against the other for power. I know that, my son, and I am old in the ways of kings and their courts. This Lysias will make peace with us, if we come to him with soft words instead of hard hearts. He would rather fight for power in Antioch and Damascus than here in Jerusalem — and if he asks tribute, we will ask peace and the right to our own ways and our own law and our own covenant with our own God. That is the best way, my son. We do not reject you. Indeed, we offer you the highest honor in all Israel, the priesthood of the Temple — "

They all looked at Judas, who stood with his arm around Jonathan. He did not answer at first, nor was there any sign of his emotions on that handsome, auburn-bearded face of his. Tall, tired, stained with the blood and dirt of the battle he had just come from, his striped cloak hanging from his great shoulders, the sword of Apollonius slung from his side, he was less and more than human. How many memories I evoke of Judas! Yet how little I can recapture him or find him or know him! The Jew was the essence of him — the making of him and the death of him; only a Jew could have listened to the old men as he listened, thinking of Eleazar, loving Eleazar as he must have loved him, remembering the hundred and more times Eleazar had fought beside him — as he said to me once, "How shall I come to harm, Simon, with that hammer on one side of me and your sword on the other?" Only a Jew could have listened, and asked finally, in a voice low with anguish:

"And all we have fought — all our battles, all our suffering and striving — all this you will place at the mercy of a Greek's word?"

Even Ragesh pitied him then, and said insinuatingly, "Not the mercy of a Greek's word, Judas, my son. There is a political balance of power now that did not exist five years ago, and this small defeat by the elephant troops does not change it. We have arms and thousands of trained men, and we have taught the Greek that the Jew is not something to be laughed at. Therefore, we are in a position to bargain, to take full advantage of the delicate situation that the death of Antiochus left, and to turn it to our advantage. This is not a quick or hasty decision, Judas."

"And if I had turned back the elephants," Judas pleaded, "would you have spoken this way? You call me the Maccabee — is this the first battle I have fought? When no one could see hope, when we faced only death and destruction — when this very Temple was a desecration, did I not go out then with my father and my brothers and wage war for the freedom of Israel? And did I not triumph? Does one defeat wipe out every victory we have won? Why do you turn on me? Why do you turn on me? You offer me the high priesthood — did I want it? Did I fight for rewards? Look at me as I stand here — and this is all that I own in the world, the cloak on my back and the sword by my side! Is there any man who can say that he saw a son of Mattathias loot the dead? Do you think me ambitious? Go ask my brother Eleazar whose body lies back there, crushed by the feet of a hundred beasts! I want no rewards — I want only freedom for my land, and you tell me you will sell our freedom and bargain and pledge our lives to the word of a Greek!"

"Judas, Judas ben Mattathias," Ragesh said patiently. "It is not one victory or one defeat. Even before the battle, we had met and discussed those terms we would ask from Lysias — "

"Before the battle," Judas said. "And while I and my brothers fought, you palavered with them here, behind our backs! Ragesh, God have mercy on you, for you have sold me and you have sold my people!"

Now, indeed, I expected Ragesh to fly into a rage, but the whip of my brother's words struck him like a lash across the face, and the proud little man bent his head while his lips moved in silence.

"Do what you will," Judas said; "do what you will, old man. When you called me the Maccabee first, I said that I would put away my sword when you commanded me to. I put it away now." And he turned to us, to John, to Jonathan and to me, and said, softly and gently, "Come, my brothers, and we will go away from here. There is no more for us to do here."

Thus we walked from the council chamber, and more than one of the old men whom we left there, the Adons and the Rabbis, put their faces in their hands and wept . . .

So it was that the Assembly of Elders made their peace

with Lysias the Greek. The tribute was a small one, ten talents of gold a year, compared to the hundreds that had been wrung from Judea in the old days. In return, the Jews were granted full religious freedom and the right to maintain the Temple against the Hellenists who still held the citadel and who refused to bend, either to Lysias or to the council of old men. Lysias also pledged that, apart from Beth Zur, no mercenaries would be maintained in Judea; and that Jewish volunteers would have the right to patrol the roads and the borders.

Thus it was; and in two days, Lysias and his elephant troops left Jerusalem for Antioch. By another gate of the ruined city, Judas and Jonathan and John and I also left, and in all the world, we had only our battle-stained clothes, our swords, our bows, and our knives. We went to Modin, where John's wife and his two children already were living, and that same night, Judas and Jonathan and I slept in the grassy pasture on the hillside behind the house of Mattathias.

The next morning, we went to work on the house, clearing away the fire-blackened timbers, molding new bricks of mud and setting them out to dry in the hot summer sun. And so much is life the living of men, the simple, matter-of-fact, day-to-day living, that it did not take too long for the townsfolk to grow used to the fact of the Maccabee working there on the rooftree, arms and face blackened with the mud and dirt and sweat of toil. How quickly Modin had come to life again! Once more, Lebel, the schoolmaster, taught his classes behind the cool stone walls of the synagogue, pacing back and forth beside his students, rod in hand, bending a quick and critical ear to the slightest imperfection of pronunciation or enunciation. Once more, Ruben's forge glowed red and furious, sending its shower of wonderful sparks over the open-mouthed children who watched, and once more the cisterns filled with olive oil, the wheat grew heavy on the terraces, and the grapes on the vines burst through their sun-laden skins. Again, the chickens ran through the dust of the village street, and again the mothers nursed their babes on their doorsteps, gossiping in the cool, dim evening.

And in the same evenings, Jonathan walked under the olive trees with Rachel, the daughter of Jacob ben Gideon, the tanner, and they climbed to the high pastures and terraces, that they might see the sun set in the west over the Mediterranean — and all the glory of life and living that is given to a man and a maid. . . .

In those days, Judas and I lived very simply and quietly. When it was light, we worked — and we worked with the driving intensity of men who have no further object than the work itself. A little bread and wine, an onion and a radish, and now and then a piece of meat sufficed to feed us. We slept early and we rose early — and we tended ourselves to the few needs we had. Although almost every man in the village was an old comrade in arms, something kept them from the Maccabee. They could not presume upon him. The Maccabee he was; the Maccabee he would always be, and though he worked at the same tasks as they did, he was something apart from them. So it was with Jews from other villages who came through Modin. They went to the Maccabee, saluted him, and sometimes kissed his hand or his cheek. For them, nothing could ever change Judas, nothing could demean him, nothing could lessen him.

And, himself, he changed too. Gentle, he was before, yet he became gentler now; it was almost as if a purity enrobed him, a purity that no other man could have worn with the same unconscious and selfless dignity. We were much together, the more so since Jonathan was like as not to be at the house of Jacob ben Gideon. We talked little, and when we did, it was of the past, not of the future.

There was one evening when Ruben came to the house. We were sitting there at our bread and wine when he entered, uncertainly, hesitantly, looking at us from under his black and shaggy eyebrows, coming step by step on his toes, incongruous, so huge and unwieldy was his short, powerful body — and then standing like an erring child, running his hands through his wiry black beard while he licked his lips nervously.

"Peace," Judas said. "Peace unto you, Ruben, our friend."

"*Alaichem shalom*. And unto thee, peace," Ruben apologized.

"Come in," Judas smiled, and, rising, he took Ruben's hands and led him to the table. I broke bread for him and poured him wine, and then he ate with us, alternately laughing and weeping throughout the meal. All that evening we sat there and talked — of old days, old glories, old fights, until the blood which had grown so cold and tired in my veins ran hot and proud again. . . .

It was the day after that a deputation of Levites, led by Enoch, the old man, the Rabbi of Alexandria, came barefooted to our house and told Judas that the Assembly, convened at the Temple under Ragesh, had chosen him as high priest of all Israel.

Very quietly, he received the news, pausing to thank them and then going on with his work. They stood around uncomfortably until, after a while, Judas said, "I will live here at Modin, even as my father did, and plant my land. When you need me, I will come . . ."

It was the very same day, strangely enough, that we heard the news from the North. Demetrius, pretender to the throne of the King of Kings, brother of Antiochus, had ambushed Lysias, slain him, and hung his flayed body over the gates of Antioch — and the party of Lysias was smashed and dispersed.

That night, Judas said to me, "What was it that the old man, the Adon, would say — that only in blood is the price of freedom reckoned?" "Yes — in that way, something." "So much for pacts," Judas shrugged, "whereby freedom is calculated in shekels."

So it was, as I told before, that Demetrius, the new King of Kings, sent his chief captain and warden, Nicanor, to seek out my brother, the Maccabee. Antiochus had been mad, perverted and cruel and mad, and Antiochus, his son, had been an idiot; but this Demetrius, brother to Antiochus, had been educated in the West, reared in Rome, and he had learned in Rome that it is not necessary to destroy a people to enslave them. His wardens were a new breed, too, straightforward with a veneer of honesty — yet in the end, in the full play of fact, Nicanor was no different from Pericles, or Apelles, or Apollonius; and in the end Judas slew him, with his own hand. But I will come to that.

In any case, Nicanor understood us better than the others had. Without slaves, he came, and on foot rather than in a litter, and only his armor-bearer was with him. Judas and I were working in one of the higher terraces, an ass dragging the plow to break land that had lain fallow these five years, when Nicanor and his armor-bearer came, led by Lebel, the schoolmaster, with Ruben and Adam ben Ebenezer and Jonathan and John following, and half a dozen other men, out of curiosity — and fear too, for we were unarmed and who knew but that the Greeks would send a man to kill the Maccabee as he worked in the fields?

And with them were the Judean children, the wonderfully wise, wonderfully untouched children who had come through war, exile and privation, and still laughed more than they wept. Like a procession, they mounted to our terrace, and Nicanor bowed low to Judas, giving his greeting to the high priest, the Maccabee, the leader whose fame had penetrated to the very borders of civilization. And Judas, who had never been more than a dozen miles past the borders of our little land, returned the greeting with courtly grace. Work-stained, the sweat beading his brow, his long hair tied in a knot at the back of his head, barefoot and ankle-deep in the newly broken soil, he was yet the Maccabee, towering over the rest of them, his great height and great breadth of shoulder as simply borne as his gentle, winning manner. In a thousand places at a thousand times, I remember him, yet I like best to think of him as he was then, standing in the summer sunshine on that high terrace, his close-clipped beard glowing like red gold, his skin burned brown and yet a deeper brown where it was mottled with freckles, his long-fingered hands breaking and kneading a lump of soil. Still less than thirty years old — a good deal less — he was in the full flower of his young manhood, so tall and straight and beautiful that Nicanor, the Greek, could not help but give him that deference that all men paid him.

Afterwards, many of the folk of Modin talked of that day. Like me, they remembered Judas best as he was then — and when they talked, the tears in their eyes would not deny the pride they felt in being of the same people as this man who was like no other man.

Nicanor himself was a well-knit, middle-sized and worldly professional soldier. He was neither the degenerate Apelles was nor the sadistic beast Apollonius was, but rather

a shrewd and calculating court climber who desired money
and power and would stop at nothing to obtain them. Both
he and his master Demetrius knew well enough that the
thousands of mercenaries whose bones lay in our Judean
valleys represented a fortune that would grace the coffers
of any king — and they also knew that there would be no
secure domination of Israel so long as the Maccabee was
against them. Whereupon, Nicanor proceeded not too well,
observing that under the King of Kings there were other
kings, quite naturally; and why should not a son of
Mattathias sit on the throne of Israel?

Judas smiled a little, studying the dirt that he crumpled
in his hands, and shrugged his shoulders. "Why should I be
king?" he asked, and all of it was in that simple question.
I think Nicanor would have liked to talk to him alone, yet
the Greek knew instinctively that Judas would not — that
it was now or never, for all that so many folk from Modin
crowded around.

"All men want glory," Nicanor said.

"And haven't I had glory enough?" Judas murmured.

"And power — and wealth." The Greek stood with his
feet spread, one hand rubbing his chin, staring quizzically
at this tall Jew, deeply puzzled, I think, at how to approach
him and where to approach him — as if here was a pattern
of being and thinking that defied all he knew.

"What would I do with power and wealth?" Judas asked.

"Much, Judas," Nicanor answered sincerely. "You are a
stubborn people, but there is more to life than a plow and a
bit of land. You make a religion of hating Greeks and all
that is Greek — but who has equaled the beauty and wisdom
we gave the world? To have that — to taste it — "

"As we have tasted it in Judea?"

"From these Syrian swine. The very dream of freedom

you fight for, Judas, was a dream born in Greece three centuries ago. You cannot deny that."

"And how long did such dreams last when you knew power, wealth and conquest?" Judas said thoughtfully. "Were you like us then — without slaves, without mercenaries? Then I salute the dead glory of Greece; I see no glory today and I want none of the gifts. I would not know how to use them."

The Greek was growing angry. "I did not come here to be made a fool of," he said.

"I don't understand," Judas said — and the Greek realized that he was telling the truth, that he did not understand. I watched Nicanor, and in his eyes there was a fleeting vision of what Judas was, a shadow of regret, a struggle to grasp what could not be grasped; and then his eyes went past my brother, over the lovely, tumbled Judean hills, the greening pattern of the terraces and the blue, cloud-mottled sky beyond.

"Are you married?" he asked suddenly.

Smiling, Judas shook his head.

"You should be," the Greek said slowly. "Otherwise, when you die, there will be no more like you."

Judas shook his head. He was, I think, puzzled and disturbed.

"I did not know what you would be," Nicanor went on. "Perhaps it would be better if you were king, perhaps it would not. I don't think it would be any use for me to argue with you."

"We don't have kings in Judea," Judas said. "Once we had kings, and they brought suffering to us, and that was a time of sorrow we still weep for in our synagogues."

For a while then, Nicanor was silent; when he spoke, it was almost offhand. "And they say, in Antioch and in

Damascus too, that if the Maccabee were dead, there would
be peace."

"They don't understand," Judas answered softly. "The
Maccabee is nothing. He comes out of the people, and what
he does, he does because the people desire it. And when
there is no more need for him, he is no different from any
other man." Rubbing the dirt from his hands, Judas added
thoughtfully, "Because we were slaves in Egypt, I think, it
is held among us that resistance to tyrants is the first obedience to God. When you go back through Modin, if you look
at the cornerstone of our synagogue, you will see it graven
there, if you read the old Hebrew, and the synagogue is a
very ancient place. I was obedient," he said. "That is all.
If I am slain, the people will find a new Maccabee for
themselves. It will make no difference."

"I think it will make a great difference," Nicanor said.
"I think too that we will meet again."

"It may be," Judas agreed.

And then the Greek left, and Judas and I went on with
our plowing.

Bit by bit, a few people were settling in the ruined city
of Jerusalem. They went into the empty, fire-blackened
shells of houses, and tried to make homes of them, and
many of them were folk who had lived their lives in one
or another of the cities in near-by lands, and had been
driven from their homes by the insane decrees of Antiochus,
the mad King of Kings. Moses ben Daniel was one of them,
and with his daughter, the last surviving relative he had,
he made a home in the Upper City. Still lovely, Deborah
lived in the shadow of Eleazar's death, and her grief was a
lasting, consuming thing. Once, Jonathan and I had visited
them there, but now weeks had gone by since we saw them.

The high holy days were approaching, the Day of Atonement, when Judas would go to the Temple and stand first in the ceremonies, so we put off going to Jerusalem; the more so our surprise when Moses ben Daniel turned up one day at Modin, hot and dusty with hurried travel. As ever, we were glad to see him, for there was a quality in his worldly wisdom and his gentle wit that was all too rare in our little village; but there was little wit in his manner now and less joy. "Call all your brothers," he said to me; and I put him off with, "But first wine and bread — and let me wash your feet, Moses, my good comrade, and fresh linen, so that while we eat we can remember the old days."

"There is no time! Call them now!"

So haggard and worried was his face, so agonized his tone of voice, that I did as he told me to; and a little while later John and Jonathan and Judas sat with me in the house of Mattathias, while the words poured unhappily from the merchant's lips. He started by begging us to believe him . . .

"Should I doubt you, Moses?" Judas asked comfortingly. "Be at peace, my good friend, for this is the ancient home of Mattathias and here there is nothing to fear. Or is it Deborah?"

"She is well, thank God," the merchant said.

"And you see all your kin here," Judas smiled. "We are your children, are we not? For what Eleazar was, we are, only less. Drink your wine and be at peace."

"There is no peace," he said unhappily, "for what I have to tell is like the bitter, poisonous herbs that grow by Arabah, the sea of sorrows. Let me tell you then, and God forgive me and others. A Greek called Nicanor, who is chief warden now for Demetrius, the new King of Kings — "

"We met this Nicanor," I said.

"Then you know him," the merchant went on, "and you know that he is no Apollonius, but a clever and unscrupulous man who will stop at nothing to obtain what he wants. He came to Jerusalem, not with an army, not with mercenaries, but with just his armor-bearer, a well-knit temperate man, and he spoke that way, simply and directly and to the point, modest in his bearing and in his clothes too. Yes, Demetrius is not Antiochus; they go at things differently — but I tell you, my children, the things they go at are the same, the same. His mouth was as filled with peace as a hive is with honey, but when it was necessary, he let the sting that was there show — he let it show. He came before the Assembly of Elders, of which I am one, Judas, my child, my Maccabee — of which I am one, because I was like an Adon in Damascus once, yes I was there and Ragesh too and others, and thus he spoke: There must be peace. Jews will till their land in peace and in peace they will worship in the synagogues and at the Temple; but they must acknowledge that full overlordship of Demetrius; they must increase the tribute to fifty talents of gold and ten of silver each year; they must allow the Hellenists to leave the citadel and take up their residence once more in their great homes in Jerusalem; they must resign themselves to five thousand mercenaries being in garrison at Jerusalem and at Beth Zur — and last of all, may my tongue rot inside of me, they must hand over to Demetrius the Maccabee."

Then there was silence, Moses ben Daniel looking from face to face. Anticipating what had brought him in such haste, rage and anger burned inside of me, and in Jonathan too, but Judas appeared unmoved. His face did not change. Pouring another glass of wine, he said to the merchant:

"Drink, father, and then tell us the rest. No word you say

will be doubted, for there is a bond between us and the bond is greater now."

"So Ragesh spoke, and he asked of Nicanor, What do you want with the Maccabee? There is no war in Israel now, and he tills his land in peace at Modin. Thus spoke Ragesh, and Nicanor answered him smoothly. It was true that the Maccabee tilled his land in peace, but how long would peace prevail so long as the banner of Judas Maccabeus could still be raised? Suppose this same Maccabee desired to make himself king — were there not thousands of Jews who would rally to his standard? Was ambition so strange a characteristic of men? Did they say that Judas was not ambitious? Yet throughout the long war, was it not Judas and always Judas who extended the combat? Was it not Judas who would accept no peace and no compromise? Was it not Judas who demanded leadership for himself and his brothers, demanding that even when the army was divided, a son of Mattathias should lead each part of it? Could they deny this?

"Then Enoch of Alexandria pointed out that Judas was high priest, to which Nicanor countered, Was this not ambition? My children, don't harden your hearts against them. They are old men. They've seen too much war and suffering. They want peace."

"Peace!" Jonathan cried. "God's curse on them for the shame of it!"

"Go on, Moses," Judas whispered. "Tell me what Ragesh said."

"Ragesh — Ragesh — " The merchant shook his head tiredly. "Ragesh held out more than the others — more, yes more. He would die himself, he said, before he sent the Maccabee to his death, but this Nicanor indignantly denied. It was no part of Demetrius's plan to slay the Maccabee. In

Antioch, he would be given a palace and treated as an honored guest — or he could live in Damascus, if he would, with a palace and slaves and all his heart desired, only so long as he left Judea forever. And what bond? Ragesh demanded. What bond? Then Nicanor gave his sacred word — "

"The word of Greeks," I smiled. "The sacred word of the *nokri*."

"But they accepted it," Judas sighed, his face suddenly old and worn. "Word of a Greek or word of a *nokri*, they accepted it, and they bought their peace with Nicanor — and after all, I suppose, the price was cheap. It was I who told Nicanor that when the struggle is done, the Maccabee is no different from anyone else — "

"It's not done, Judas," I said.

"For me, it's done, Simon, my brother."

I rose, wholly dominated by rage now, crashing my fists down on the table. "No! By the Lord God of Israel, what are you thinking, Judas — to give yourself up?"

He nodded.

"Then over my dead body!" I cried.

"And mine!" Jonathan said.

Gripping my brother's arm, I said to him: "Judas — Judas, listen to me! For years now, I have followed you, obeyed you, because you were the Maccabee — because you were right! Now you are wrong! They have not betrayed you — they cannot, those frightened old men! Adons, they style themselves! I knew only one Adon in Israel, my father Mattathias, may he rest in peace, but there will be no peace for him, Judas, if you betray yourself and your brothers and your people! How did he say when he died, the old man? Do you remember, Judas? In battle, you would be first — but it was to me that he gave the burden, telling me: 'Simon, thou art thy brother's keeper, thou and no other.' Do you hear me, Judas?"

"I hear you," he said miserably. "But what can we do? What can we do?"

"What we did before — go into the wilderness. Do you take the word of a Greek?"

"Alone?"

"Alone — just you and I, until this thing comes to a head! Have you ever known a warden to be satisfied? Have you ever known their lust to be satisfied?"

"I go with you," Jonathan said.

"No — go to Jerusalem, Jonathan. Go to Ragesh, and tell him the Maccabee is in Ephraim, the Maccabee and his brother Simon — tell him two men are in Ephraim and that so long as two men walk free on Judean soil, the fight goes on. Tell him it goes on until all the world knows that in Judea there is a people who will not bend their knee to man or God! We were slaves in Egypt, and we will not be slaves again. Tell Ragesh that!"

John wanted to come with us, gentle, scholarly John who had neither the will to hate nor the strength to strike, yet whose loyalty had never wavered and whose courage had never faltered. A trick of birth had made him one of five strange brothers who were knit as never before brothers in Israel had been knit; an indomitable spirit had made him learn to fight, to lead, to do all things foreign to him; and now too, when we were alone, when there were only the four of us against the whole world, his heart was with us; and had Judas and I said only one word, he would have left his wife and children, his home and his synagogue, his precious scrolls — to come with us, to be an outlaw, a fugitive, a man without hope or future.

This, at least, we did not do; and after thanking Moses ben Daniel, kissing him as we would kiss a father, we took our weapons, as much bread and meal as we could carry, and left Modin. We left in the night, saying farewell to no one, for those who did not know would not have to search their hearts for answers, and started our journey to Ephraim. By night we traveled, avoiding the villages, and going across the mountains by the old paths we knew so well, almost every foot of which was marked in our memories by some shade of glory.

Without incident, we came to Ephraim, and there Judas and I took up life in a cave that once had sheltered many Jewish families. Both Jonathan and John knew the place well, and when the time came, one of them would find us there. What or when that time would be, we did not know; but until then we would tarry here — and indeed, it was nothing to gladden our hearts. Much we had been through and there would be more to come, yet nothing burns in my memory so awful and heartbreaking as that lonely exile in Ephraim. Never had our spirits been lower, never had the future seemed so bleak and hopeless — so much so that often enough I felt what Judas had put into words, that this was truly the end.

But what took its greatest toll of me was to watch my brother, to watch that glorious spirit and flame die out of him, to watch the gray streaks in his auburn hair widen, to watch the lines in his young face deepen. I knew well enough that inside of him, the betrayal of Ragesh was eating the life out of him — the simple fact that it should have been Ragesh, Ragesh who had been with him in the very beginning, Ragesh who knew fear so little and esteemed death so lightly that he was almost ready to embrace it out of an intellectual curiosity, Ragesh whose wit triumphed over any adversity, Ragesh who, for all of us, had become like a father — not only for the sons of Mattathias, but for thousands of other Jews. Yet, of this Judas never spoke, and never by word or action did he give any indication of the misery he suffered.

How shall I understand by brother, Judas, and how shall I know the people who birthed me and gave me sustenance? The two are one, and the spirit of Judas was like the essence of life, the fragrance and all the mighty power of life.

And like life, he endured, and the strength in him was more, far more than any strength in me . . .

We did not do much in that time of exile. We hunted a little for small game, that we might stretch out our store of meal; for we considered it best not to enter even those few villages that had taken root in Ephraim. We talked little enough. We slept early and rose with the dawn. We prayed, as Jews pray, because we were Jews and because we could no more abandon our God than we could abandon life itself — and we became very close. How shall I signify that closeness, which is given to brothers and to no others? It is almost like the existence of a single soul in several bodies, like the promise of a time when all men, the Jew and the *nokri*, will lie down together and rise up together, even as the sweet prophet of the Exile said.

And can I say more or know more? Once, without lust, without pain, we talked of Ruth and what she had been. Yet the dead lie easily, easily. . . .

We were thirty-two days in the wilderness before Jonathan came to us, early one morning as we sat at the mouth of our cave. And we kissed him and embraced him, and Judas held him by both arms, looking him up and down, smiling for the first time in a long while to see this slim and supple lad who, like Benjamin, was our youth and our treasure.

"And what has been?" I asked him. "But eat first, and rest first."

"Much has been," Jonathan said. He had been a child, and now he was a man. "I come from Jerusalem," he nodded, "and I have seen awful things. Ragesh is dead, and Moses ben Daniel is dead, and also dead are Samuel ben Zebulun and the Patriarch Enoch of Alexandria and others, and others — " He was very tired; we had not noticed at first, in our joy at seeing him: but now his head nodded as he spoke and pain twisted his face. "So many others," he whispered. "They bought their peace so cheaply, so cheaply, but they sold it at a price." The tears ran down his cheeks. "At a price — "

"Jonathan!" Judas said sharply. "Jonathan!"

"I'm all right," the boy said. "I am here with the Maccabee, so I am all right. But in Judea, they say the Maccabee is dead. I'm all right, only I'm hungry and haven't slept."

Judas gave him food, and I washed his feet and rubbed them with balm. "Tell us everything," Judas said.

"There isn't much to tell. I went to Ragesh, as you told me to, Simon, and I spoke your words to him. Simon, Simon, God keep me from suffering what Ragesh suffered! And then came Nicanor to him and said, Deliver me Judas. And Ragesh told him, Judas is gone — Judas is in the wilderness. No man knows where the Maccabee dwells. Thus Ragesh spoke, and Nicanor was in a rage. Can Jew hide from Jew? he wanted to know, calling the old men perfidious and evil, and swearing by all of his gods that unless they gave him Judas, they would suffer all the consequences of it. Then Ragesh came to me and this he described to me. 'Do you know where your brother is?' he asked me, and I told him

I knew. 'Will you go to him?' Ragesh asked me, and I said, 'Yes, I will go to him when the time comes.' Then Ragesh said, weeping as he spoke, 'Make yourself my messenger, Jonathan, my son, make yourself my messenger and go to Judas Maccabeus, wherever he is, and take his hands and kiss them with my lips, and beg his forgiveness in my words, in my words, and these are the words of Ragesh' — "

Jonathan paused. "Judas," he said, "Judas — these are his words. 'Tell him,' he said, 'that I ask only his forgiveness, not God's. Damned I am and damned I will be, but the heart of Judas Maccabeus must be large enough to offer me some little sustenance.' Those were his words, Judas — "

Through his tears, Judas whispered, "What then?"

"And then Ragesh drank poison and died, and when Nicanor heard of it, he went mad — stark, raving mad, and then he let his mercenaries run amok and they slew the old men and ravaged the city. They killed Moses ben Daniel and they raped his daughter and left her dying in the streets. I went by night with two Levites, and we took her into the Temple, which they had not yet raided, and there she died in my arms, thinking somehow that I was Eleazar come back to her — and then I came here. And that is all, Judas, that is all; and now I am with the Maccabee and I am tired and I want to sleep. . . ."

And the next morning, in the gray and early dawn, the three of us left Ephraim, and now we traveled not by the mountain paths but by the roads. To Lebonah we went first, and then to Shiloh and then to Gilgal, and then to Dan, to Levein, to Horal, to Goumad — to village after village down the valley to Modin. And now we traveled by daylight, not by night, and wherever we went we raised up the standard of Judas Maccabeus.

And wherever we went, men flocked to us, men embraced Judas, tears streaming down their faces, men took out their spears and their bows and their knives and joined our ranks. In both Shiloh and Gilgal, there were mercenaries, and we slew them in a cold and terrible fury, but in the other villages word traveled ahead and the mercenaries fled.

It was early dawn when we started, and by midnight we were in Modin with nine hundred men, and still they came, all through the night as word went out to the countryside that the Maccabee lived.

There was no sleep for any of us that first night. Plunged into despair, first at the disappearance of Judas, and then again at the terrible news from Jerusalem, Modin suddenly became the most wildly joyous and chaotic place in all Israel. Every house, every barn, even the old synagogue itself was turned into a barracks, and still there was not enough room and men bivouacked on the hillsides and the terraces. Ruben, the smith, a totally, volubly, insanely happy Ruben, alternately laughing and weeping, set up an arms shop in the village square. Every grindstone was requisitioned, and all night long the square glowed under the sparks of whirling stone and keen metal, while our captains of tens and twenties and hundreds sought for their old veterans, broke the night with their shouts and orders, and piled confusion upon confusion as they sought to bring an army into being.

There was little enough time, for just across the hills lay Jerusalem, and there was Nicanor and his mercenaries. Surely, by now, he had word of the uprising, and unless he was a complete fool, he would attempt to crush it before it gained any real strength. This we surmised, and our surmise was correct; the thing that saved us and gave us the precious twenty-four hours we needed was the unwillingness of Nicanor — a wise enough unwillingness, for already Judas was sending out bands of archers — to march his heavily armored mercenaries through the Judean defiles by night.

Under the ancient rooftree of Mattathias, we set up our headquarters, and there Judas and I labored by lamplight all night long, creating in a matter of hours a new army. Constantly, John and Jonathan and Adam ben Lazar, who had joined us immediately the word came, brought us information, and, on a great sheet of parchment, we laid out a table of command and organization. As soon as a twenty was formed and officered, we gave the tabulation to Lebel, the schoolmaster, who went through the houses and barns, calling out the names, to turn the organized unit over to Ruben to check on arms, equipment and supply. To further complicate the situation, the children of Modin — and Goumad as well, for that town had virtually depopulated itself — raced all over the place, imitating every action of their elders, and making the night hideous with their screeching. . . .

But the wonder of it was the change in Judas. He lived again. He was the old Judas, patient, gentle, fiery — as the need was — indulgent, hard; he was the Maccabee now, and so they termed him, and so it sounded to mark the night, "Where is the Maccabee?" "I have news for the Maccabee." "I come from Shmoal with a twenty for the Maccabee." "I fought with the Maccabee five years — he needs me."

We needed them; we welcomed them. How many times that night was the blessing for wine spoken, as captain after captain came, dog-weary with travel, to enter the house of Mattathias and pledge his allegiance. And with dawn, only the second dawning since Jonathan had come with the news to Ephraim, we had an army in Modin and

two hundred additional archers on the hills to greet Nicanor
if he should have begun his march by night. And our army
in Modin numbered two thousand three hundred men, hard,
battle-scarred veterans of a hundred encounters. . . .

I made Judas sleep, and I closed the door of the house
and set two men to guard it and see that he lay undisturbed.
Now the first, sweet rosy tint of dawn was in the air, a band
of pink light in the east, where our holy city was, and an
answer to the pink on our high and fertile terraces. Through
the night-wet grass, I walked up to the little olive grove
where once Ruth and I lay in each other's arms, and I
spread my cloak there and let my weary body feel the earth
under me.

I was happy then — I, Simon, Simon of the iron hand and
the iron heart; I, the least, the most unworthy of all my
glorious brothers, the single, stolid, plodding and colorless
son of Mattathias — and yet I was happy in a way that I
never dreamed I might be happy again. For the first time in
many years, my heart was at peace and the bitter venom
had cleansed itself from my soul. My memories were good
memories, and as I lay there, both the living and the dead
were close, and they comforted me. No devils plagued me
and no hates corroded me; the masterful and angry old man,
the Adon, slept gently, and gently too slept the tall and
lissom woman who had held my heart as no other woman
ever held it, or would, who had kissed my lips and given
her soul to me. Perhaps I dozed there a little as the cool
morning wind played over me, for it seemed that I dreamed
as well as remembered, taking the matter of my dreams out
of this ancient, ancient soil of Israel that had reared up so
strange a people as we Jews were. Like a benediction, the
words of the morning prayers were in my mind, *How*

goodly are thy tents, O Jacob, thy dwelling places, O Israel! And those words came to me over and over again — until I dozed more deeply, or slept perhaps, and wakened with the hot morning sun in my eyes.

Straight through the valley passed toward Modin, Nicanor came, with nine thousand men in heavy armor, marching them along the same way we took as children, going to the Temple with the Adon. They had set out from Jerusalem in the early morning, and though our twenties harried them in every pass and defile, they came on under their raised, locked shields. From Jerusalem to Gibeon to Beth Horon, they marched under a rain of the slim and deadly cedar arrows, so that Nicanor learned once and for all what is meant when a Greek speaks of the deadly, snake-like "Judean rain," and all that distance they left their dead in the sun. And yet Nicanor would not be diverted, but marched on, burning the empty villages they passed. At Beth Horon, they camped for the night, but all night long our arrows pattered and whispered upon their tents, and though they camped they did not sleep; and in the morning, with taut nerves and deep hatred, they came down the valley toward Modin. And three miles from Modin, where a peaceful brook ran through the valley bottom, alongside the road, where the hills and terraces sloped up almost vertically, bare of anything but twisted brush, we built our barricade and blocked their way.

Our tactics were no longer new, yet Nicanor was new to them. Because every defile in Judea was a deathtrap, a whole generation of mercenaries lay buried in Judean soil, yet Nicanor came on into the pass, into the trap — because there was nothing else for him to do. We stood in his path, and either he must sweep us aside or retreat to Jerusalem, considering that he would get there. He chose to sweep us aside.

Behind the barricade, we put eight hundred of our best men, armed with spear, sword, and hammer. The rest we deployed on the hills with their bows and their knives and with bundles of thousands of the short, straight, needle-sharp arrows. The barricade was rock and dirt and brush, eight feet high and twenty feet thick, not the shelter of a wall, but an impediment to a phalanx. Our men manned it, and a few yards in front, Ruben, Judas, and I stood, watching the great, metallic mass of the mercenaries creep down the road behind their locked shields and their bristling front of long, unwieldy spears. They filled the full eighty foot width of the valley; they walked in the brook; they crowded the mountainside with their shoulders; and ever and again one of them would pitch forward, held for a moment by the very mass of the phalanx, cheek or eye or brain transfixed by one of our arrows, and then falling to the ground under the metal-shod feet of the others.

They were close enough now for us to see their angry, dirty, sweat-glistening faces; close enough for us to feel what it meant to walk for hours in the burning Judean sun, carrying eighty pounds of hot metal; close enough almost for us to smell, on the morning wind, the hot, sickening stink of their unwashed bodies, and of the leather in their harness. The clangor of their metal filled the pass, mingling with the wild shouting of our archers, with the deeper thud of rocks flung from above, with the screams of the wounded and the sobs of the dying, with the short-breathing, corrupt Aramaic filth that spewed from the mercenaries' lips.

And then, no more than fifty yards from us, they paused. Five men led them, one of whom was Nicanor, and he came toward us with his arm raised — and the noise and shouting fell away, and the rain of arrows halted.

"Will you talk, Maccabee?" Nicanor cried.

"There is nothing to say," Judas replied, his voice cold and piercing.

"You killed Apollonius, Maccabee, and he was my friend — with all your rotten Jewish tricks and traps, you slew him! Do you deny that, Maccabee?"

"I killed him," Judas said.

"Then I make you a pledge, Jew — I pledge that today I will kill you with my own hand and open this pass and clear that Jewish scum from it! And from every olive tree in Judea, a Jew will hang! And in every synagogue, a pig will be slaughtered!"

While he spoke, he came on, and Judas walked toward him. Nicanor carried a shield, but his sword was in his scabbard, and Judas wore neither shield nor armor, only the long sword of Apollonius, slung over his neck and before him. Like a tiger Judas walked, clad only in white linen pants and sandals, bare to the waist, the long, supple muscles rippling as he moved, and like a tiger he crouched and sprang. Few men knew his strength as I knew it. Nicanor tried to fend him off with his shield while he dragged his sword from the scabbard, but Judas wrenched the shield aside and, through the sudden roar of sound, we heard the bone in Nicanor's arm snap. With his bare hands, Judas killed the Greek, with two terrible blows to the head, and then lifted the body, swung it above his head and hurled it onto the spears of the driving phalanx.

The roar of sound obliterated all else. Judas ran back, and a hundred hands reached down to lift us to the barricade. The phalanx drove toward us, met us, scrambled at the barricade, when I saw that like men gone mad our

Jewish archers were pouring down the hillsides into the valley, fighting with rocks and knives and with their bare hands too, filled with a mad, wild, terrible hate, filled with the accumulated agony of a decade of senseless, cruel invasions, filled with memory of countless murders, innumerable rapes and tortures, endless burning and destruction, filled with the rage of free men who had never asked more than their freedom, filled with the memory of desecration and insult and woe.

Then, if the mercenaries had had a leader, if they had held, if they had not been packed so tightly at the valley bottom, they could have done what they had come to do; but the death of Nicanor and then the wild willfulness of the charge broke their morale. The front ranks tried to give back from the barricade, and the rear ranks drove up against the front ranks to overwhelm the barricade — and from the barricade our spearmen caught the fever and hurled themselves down. . . .

There were nine thousand of them and less than three thousand Jews, and for five long, awful hours we fought there in that valley bottom, Judas and Jonathan beside me in a frightful hellish slaughterhouse. Much of that fight I have forgotten; much of it the mind could not retain and exist — for never was there a fight like that before and never again, not even when the end came — yet some things I remember. I remember a pause once, as men must pause and rest when they fight, and I stood in the brook and it ran red against my legs, thick and sluggish, the blood overwhelming the water. I remember walking on dead men five deep, and I remember being caught in a press of bodies where no man could raise an arm, mercenaries and Jews, face to face, shoulder to shoulder. And I remember when, for a long moment, we stood clear with the dead around us piled five feet high, but no living thing within ten yards of us. . . .

And finally, it finished; it was done; we had triumphed; fighting hand to hand and face to face, we had wiped out a great army of mercenaries — yet at what a cost! In that terrible valley of death, less than a thousand Jews stood on their feet, and every one of them was covered from head to foot with blood, naked from the battle, a blood-soaked rag hanging from shoulder or hip; and every one of them was cut and bleeding, so that blood dripped from their bodies and joined the spongy, blood-soaked earth at their feet.

I sought for my brothers, but in that nightmarish place all men looked alike. Sobbing, weeping with exhaustion and fear, I called them and they came to me, Judas and Jonathan and John, too — but John wounded so deeply that he had to crawl over the dead, yet struggled to his feet that he might stand and be among us. . . .

Thus we won a victory; and as Judas said, as we dragged our aching bodies and our moaning wounded to Jerusalem, a victory without triumph, without joy. The night before in Modin was the last time of joyous anticipation, for how many were there now in Modin or in Goumad or in Shiloh who were not fatherless, or brotherless, or widowed? More men there were in Israel, but in that valley of hate there fell the cream of our army, the loyal veterans of our very beginnings. Out of the men of Goumad, only twenty-two were left alive after that great battle, and of the men of Modin, aside from myself and my brothers, only twelve lived. What consolation to us that the mercenaries had perished to the last man, that even those who had doffed their armor and fought their way from the valley were slain by archers, and children too, in the villages of

Gibeon and Gezer near by? Thus it was in the beginning, and again and again and again, for there was no end to the mercenaries with all the world to supply them, and it would be again — and was all of life to be like that, a nightmarish, endless, countless succession of invaders into our little land? Was there no end, no finish, no respite? What consolation when Lebel the schoolmaster had died in that valley, when Nathan ben Borach, who had been with us at the age of thirteen in our first fight, left his bones there, and when Melek, Daniel, Ezra, Samuel, David, Gideon, Ahab, men I had known all my life, children I had played with and fathers of the children too, left their bones to rot with the bones of the mercenaries? What consolation — and when would it end, and how would it end?

We went to Jerusalem, and there we rested for three days before the Jews and Greeks in the Acra learned what losses we had taken. They waited too long, for at the end of the three days two hundred of the dark, fierce Jews of the South had joined us, and when the rich Jews led their mercenaries out of the citadel, we fought them in the streets, hurt them cruelly, and drove them back into their warren. But again we took losses; for myself, the devouring edge of fatigue never left me, and it seemed that my wounds could not heal. Ruben ben Tubel had lost half the fingers on one hand, and for all the bandaging, they festered and bled, and my brother John lay in bed back in Modin, burning with fever, his cuts running pus and poison. As for Jonathan, the spark, the wonderful, buoyant youth had gone out of him, never to return. He was too young and he had seen too much; silent he became, and his new beard grew in all streaked with gray.

Only Judas was beyond defeat and beyond despair. Once, despair had claimed him and owned him, but it would not own him again, and he said to me, not once but over and over, "Simon, a free people cannot be conquered, they cannot be slain — for us it is always the beginning, always the beginning."

Then, in Jerusalem, it was Judas who was fully and wholly the Maccabee. It was he who gathered together the bodies of the old men and gave them burial. It was he who cleansed the Temple once more and put on the spotless white robes of the high priest and led the prayers. It was he who comforted the widows and gave of his endless courage to anyone who asked, demanded, or pleaded. And it was he who drove home the fact that we must fight when we learned, with our wounds still unhealed, that a new army of mercenaries approached the borders of Judea.

Never before had it happened so quickly, and now we had no friends, such as Moses ben Daniel, may he rest in peace, to come ahead and tell us what had transpired at the court of the King of Kings. Once it would have taken the mad Antiochus a year or two years to replace the loss of nine thousand men, but now with the awful noise of that valley of horror still ringing in our ears, we learned the news from Jews who fled before the approaching mercenaries. It made Demetrius, the new King of Kings, appear a veritable demon; no one in our ranks had ever seen him, but tales about him there were in plenty. Could he conjure mercenaries out of the air? Thus it was said, and other things were said too — and what use was it to resist if the hordes of the enemy were numberless? There was a chill wind blowing in Israel then.

And from outside of Judea, from the Jews in other lands, there was only silence, as if they had tired of this restlessness in Palestine, this bloodletting that made only for more bloodletting. And in a way, it was even understandable, for we pursued a mirage of freedom which they had surrendered generations in the past, and yet they survived. In the beginning there had been a strange and splendid and singular glory in the tall, auburn-haired young man who took his weapons from the enemy and his soldiers from the simple, peace-loving farmers who tilled the land. But glory palls.

"Perhaps now," I said to Judas, when we heard that a new army was driving down on us under a new warden called Bacchides — "perhaps now we should wait, go to our homes."

"And what will Bacchides do?" Judas inquired gently, smiling just a little. "Will he also wait until we are tired no longer and until our wounds heal? Nicanor was a friend of Apollonius, and as I hear it, this Bacchides was a friend of Nicanor. Perhaps he will go to the valley where the bodies of Nicanor and his nine thousand mercenaries lie, and will that make him like us better? No, Simon, believe me, we must fight, and only so long as we fight will we survive; and when we turn our backs to them, then it is over and finished. We will not turn our backs to them — "

It was John, lying sick in Modin, who sent us a message pleading for us not to go up against Bacchides, but to defend the Temple behind the Temple walls and try and wring terms from the Greek — terms that would give us at least enough time to raise a new army and to gather our strength, and with this Ruben and I and Adam ben Lazar agreed, and we argued long and hotly with Judas; but he was firm and even angry, crying:

"No — no! I will not listen! What have we to do with walls? Walls are a trap for anyone who is fool enough to trust them!"

"And where will we find men?" Adam demanded. "Can we raise up the dead?"

"We can raise the living," Judas said.

"Judas—Judas," I pleaded, "what are you saying? Bacchides is a day's march from Jerusalem, and here in the city we have eleven hundred men, no more. Where will you find men in a day—in two days? Will you go to Modin? There are no men left there. Or to Goumad? Or to Shiloh?"

"No!" Judas cried. "I will not be caught here, trapped here! Once I would have gone to the Assembly of Elders, as I went to them. And they are dead, because they bought their freedom cheaply. I make no bargains with men who fight for hire, for gold, for loot—with the *nokri* who come down on us like wolves! So long as men fight with me, I'll fight, and I will fight as I know how to fight, in the open, in the hills and the passes, as a Jew fights!"

"Judas, listen to me—"

"No! Now heed me, Simon, for as the old man said, it was you in peace and me in war! What were the words you gave to Jonathan to tell Ragesh—that so long as two men walk free on Judean soil, the fight goes on? Were those the words?"

"Those were the words," I murmured.

"Then if you will go your way, and Ruben too, and Adam ben Lazar and his two hundred from the South, and any others who make cheap victory the price of freedom, then go—go if you will! Jonathan will be with me." And he turned to Jonathan searchingly, and the boy smiled, a sad, lonely smile, nodding.

"To the end, Judas, I am a Jew."

"Then come and leave them to deliberate," and putting his arm around Jonathan's shoulder, he walked with him from the room.

The three of us looked at each other in a long and desperate silence, and then, one by one, we nodded. . . .

That evening, Judas assembled the men in the Temple courtyard. He spoke as he had never spoken, making neither much nor little of what we faced, but presenting the facts as they were, as he saw them, and I do not know but that he saw them well and truly.

"We must fight again," he said, "and I do not know that it is the last time, for I think they will come down on us again and still again. But we must fight, and one day we will be free. If there were time, we could go through the land, and the people would come to us, as they came before, and we would arm them and train them; but there is not time, and we cannot hide ourselves in the wilderness, as we did once, and leave the land all open and ripe for the mercenaries. Then we had a smaller debt to the people, but because they trusted us, they went back to their homes and their fields, and we cannot let this Bacchides go through the land like a wolf in the flock. As few as we are, we must fight, not here behind the Temple walls, but in our hills, as we have always fought." He stopped and waited, but there was no sound from the men. These were the old ones, the handful that were left from Ephraim, the few from Modin, from Goumad, from Hadid and Beth Horon; most of them had fought first under the old man, the Adon, and now they fought under the young man, the Maccabee. They had only to look at Judas as he stood there with his back to the Temple wall, the high, white stone, still lit by the last rays of the sun, framing him, the light glowing in his hair and on his brown, beautiful features, to know the answer to the question he asked. And as always, he said to them gently:

"I want no one with a debt unpaid, with a new wife, a new house, a new field, a new child. Such may go, and there will be no shame in their going. They will fight again. We are Jews among Jews, and there should be no shame in our hearts — "

Men left, weeping as they went; the ranks thinned, but closed, and those who remained stood sure and silent, eight hundred of them. Then Judas went among them, calling each by name, embracing some, kissing some, and they touched him and spoke to him with such love as I have never known to be given to a man. He was theirs, the Maccabee, and they were his. The bond would be sealed, signed in blood — yet I think that even if they knew it then, they would have had it no different.

Then, as darkness fell, they covered their heads with their cloaks, and in a soft yet reaching voice Judas said, in the old Hebrew:

Why do the heathen rage, and the people imagine a vain thing? The kings of the earth set themselves, and the rulers take counsel together, against the Lord, and against his anointed, saying, Let us break their bands asunder, and cast away their cords from us. He that sitteth in the heavens shall laugh; the Lord shall have them in derision. Then shall he speak unto them in his wrath, and vex them in his sore displeasure.

And the close-ranked men answered, "Amen — so be it."

That same night, we left Jerusalem and traveled due west, for we knew that the Greek was coming down from the northwest, and it was Judas's plan to get behind him and strike at him either from the rear or from somewhere on the flank. We had too little force to meet him head on in some valley, bar his path and harry him from the hillsides, but Judas felt that with a little good fortune we might cut off a section of his army and so hurt it that the whole advance might be stopped or even turned into a retreat. Therefore, we marched quickly until well after midnight, covering al-

most twenty miles, and then, secure in the feeling that we
were well behind Bacchides, we set out our sentries and
bivouacked in a broad pasture on the outskirts of Beth
Shemesh. We slept like dead men that night, woke refreshed
with the dawn, and continued westward.

For one reason and another, the spirits of the men were
high. Part of it was the glorious day, the blue sky, the clean
wind from the Mediterranean, and the lovely green of the
terraced foothills; part of it was the fact that they marched
again with the Maccabee, and the deep-seated confidence
that under him they could come to no abiding ill. As we
swung north at the edge of the coastal plain, to return again
to the hills in the rear of the Greek, they lifted their voices
in an old Judean battle song — and broke it as suddenly,
for there, in the broad coastal valley, were the mercenaries,
thousands upon thousands of them, a broad mass in front
— and then a long, extended flank that cut off our retreat
to the hills. . . .

I think I knew it was the end — I think perhaps we all
knew it, even Judas, yet his voice rang out in high spirit
as he called us to follow him and then set out at a run,
driving all our strength against that extended flank.

We turned the surprise into something else; somehow —
whether through traitors or spies we never knew, but
somehow — Bacchides had anticipated our tactic, and for
once the Greek had laid a trap for the Jew; yet we sprung
the jaws. Desperate we were, and desperately we smashed
the phalanx at its weakest point, driving our unarmored
bodies against the massed spears, separating them, making
first a small hole and then a larger one through which we
poured, closing with the mercenaries and driving them
into flight by the fierce, unfettered violence of our attack.
For the moment, it seemed like a victory, and we shouted

triumphantly as we cut them down, pulled them down from behind; but then, over the din, we heard the voice of Judas calling us to stand, and as we broke off the pursuit, we saw that both ends of the long flank had reformed themselves and were moving in upon us, and behind them the serried ranks of the main army.

We fell back into an area of high boulders and narrow ravines, where the phalanx could not be used against us, but Judas dared not order a retreat for fear it would turn into a rout, for fear they would pull us down even as we had pulled them down a moment ago. Already, we were outflanked; already they were closing in on us from every side. Judas did the only thing he could do; he pulled us together in among the boulders and rocks in a rough circle, and there we fought.

Never will I forget that wild, bestial roar that went up from the mercenaries when they saw that at last they had a Jewish army in a position from which it could not retreat, could not escape. They had waited many years for this. They had carpeted our Judean soil with their dead for this. They had planned for this, dreamed of it — and here, at last, it was.

Yet we stung them. We were no sheep to be pulled down in the fold, but rather the oldest, hardest and best fighting men in all the land of Judea, and we did not leave them that day without a little glory. No, Judas — you left your mark, you left your mark.

First, as they closed in upon us, we shot away our arrows, not as we were wont to shoot in the defiles, filling the air with them until they fell like rain, but slowly and carefully, seeking a mark for every sliver of cedar, knowing that when the twoscore arrows each of us carried were shot away, there would be no more. We feathered the crevices of their armor; we buried our shafts in their eyes, in their brows, in their arms, and they paid dearly for that first attack. They shouted less; they came more slowly — and yet they came.

Until midday, we fought with our spears, and when they were broken, with our swords and our knives and our hammers, and in that time we beat back charge after charge, how many I don't know, but many, many — so many that the memory itself is unbearable with pain and weariness. And then they drew back to rest, to regroup their forces, to count their dead who lay around us like a wall.

They paid a price, but so had we, and out of our eight hundred, less than half remained. Old wounds had opened and new wounds had seared them. When I dropped my sword, I felt that to lift it again would be an effort beyond any mortal will of mine. My mouth was dry as parched leather, and when I tried to speak, only hoarse croakings came forth. All about us the wounded lay, pleading for water, and all among us were the dead who would plead no more. I looked for Judas and Jonathan, and my heart beat less wildly when I saw that they still lived and stood — as Ruben did and Adam ben Lazar too; but Judas bled from a long cut across his breast, and the face of that fierce and vengeful man from the South was smashed in, so that his mouth was a raw and gaping wound.

Judas came to me, stepping across the bodies of the dead, and he held out a flask of water.

"Give it to the wounded," I managed to croak.

"No, Simon, better that the sound should drink — otherwise there will be no wounded tonight."

I wet my lips; I could not do more than that. Ruben came to me and kissed me. "My friend, Simon, good-by." I shook my head. "No — good-by," he repeated, "and peace unto thee. I am happy. This way I would want it. It has been a good thing to live with you; it will not be hard to die with the sons of Mattathias."

I could not think of the dead, or the end, or the past or the future; I could only think of each blessed moment of rest, and I could only desire that there should be a moment more, a moment more before they returned to the attack.

They came again. Our circle was smaller. They came again and again, and now I was only a few yards from my brothers — they who had been on the other side of the circle before. We beat them off, and they came again, and now we were a half circle against a mighty boulder, and here we would stay and here we would die.

Every motion became unendurable agony. Now I felt no pain from my wounds; now I felt nothing and heard nothing, but knew only one thing, the terrible, awful weight of my sword, and yet somehow I lifted it again and again and thrust and hacked, even as my brothers were thrusting and hacking, even as Judas fought with the long, keen weapon that he had taken from dead Apollonius so long ago. And still they came — and I knew that they would come forever, until I died, until every Jew died. Time stopped; all things stopped, except the movement of the mercenaries crawling over the piles of dead to get at us. Sometimes, there would be a pause, but always the sublime sweetness of it would go almost instantly and they would be back at us.

And then there was a pause that did not come to an end, and suddenly I was conscious of night, not twilight, not the slow change from day to evening, but night enfolding us and a driving, beating rain on my face. For a moment, I was certain I stood alone in that ghastly place of death, and I wet my mouth with rain and cried out — not words but frantic, sobbing sounds, and I kept that up until I felt hands on my face, and then I knew I lay on the ground and there was a voice in my ear, the voice of my brother Jonathan, asking me, asking me, my brother's keeper, "Simon, Simon, where is Judas?"

"I don't know — I don't know."

Together, we crawled from body to body; there were no other living, no other living. From body to body, we crawled, and we found Judas. Black as pitch was the night, yet when he was under our hands, we knew him, and somehow we found the strength to raise him in our arms and to carry him from that hellish place.

Very slowly we moved, very slowly, and every step was pain. Sometimes we were so close to the mercenaries that we could hear their voices plainly, and then later we heard them no more — and still we went on. How long I don't know; that night had no beginning and it had no end, but sometime we found a narrow cleft in the rocks, and there we lay down with our brother and for all of the driving rain, we fell immediately into the deep sleep of utter exhaustion.

I don't know what time it was the next day when we woke. Rain still poured out of the gray skies, and neither the mercenaries nor the place where we had fought were in sight.

We had no words to speak; we had no tears to shed. It was done, and Judas, our brother Judas, the Maccabee who was without peer and without reproach, was dead. Tenderly, Jonathan and I bore his body in our arms. All things were over, all things were done, yet still we walked and still we went inland in the direction of Modin and the old rooftree of Mattathias.

There are no words for me to say what I felt then, or what

I thought — just as there were no words that could pass between Jonathan and me. Judas was dead. . . .

So I write it, an old man, an old Jew searching in the past, in that strange and troubled land of memories. So I wrote, and now I can write no more, for it seems now that there is little purpose and less knowing in the telling of this tale.

Now night is a somber time, and though all the land lies in peace, I, Simon, the least of my glorious brothers, know no peace.

PART FIVE

The Report of
the Legate Lentulus Silanus

MAY IT PLEASE THE NOBLE SEN-
ate that my mission is done; as instructed, I proceeded to
the land of the Jews — or *Yehudim*, as they title themselves — and remained there three months in pursuance of
my duties. During that time, I held several conversations
with their chieftain, the Maccabee, as they call him, and
also styled Simon the Ethnarch; and these conversations
touched on many matters, including future relations between Judea and Rome. This I will deal with in the course
of my report, and again in the few recommendations I
humbly submit. The rest of the time was spent in a study
of their land and customs and in the preparation of this
report.

As ordered, I went by ship to Tyre, and there disem-
barked. Having no knowledge whatsoever of Jews, having
neither met nor seen one prior to my arrival at Tyre, I determined to spend a few days in that city and facilitate my
journey to Judea. Thereupon, I proceeded to the Jewish
quarter, which is fairly large in Tyre, and made myself ac-
quainted with these strange people for the first time.

Fortunately, I encountered no language difficulties.
Aramaic is the common tongue of almost all peoples dwelling in this part of the world, and it is so close to the dialect
spoken by the inhabitants of Carthage — which I mastered

during the Punic Wars — that I found myself very soon speaking it as well as a native. I would recommend that all legates and ambassadors dispatched to this area be versed in the Aramaic, both to glorify the long arm of Rome and to facilitate exchange of ideas.

Aramaic is the common tongue of the Jews, as well as of the Phoenicians, the Samarians, the Syrians, the Philistines and the many other people who inhabit this area — and also the Greeks; but among the Jews, on certain occasions, they will use Hebrew, the ancient language of what they call their "holy scriptures," a speech related to the Aramaic but hardly intelligible to me. Even children appear to be versed in both tongues, but for matters of everyday usage, I found the Aramaic to be sufficient.

With the Jews in Tyre, I had less trouble than with the local overlords. The latter were at first inclined to circumscribe my coming and going, whereupon I went to Malthus, the prince, and let him know in no uncertain terms that whatsoever my treatment was, the details would be included in my official report to the Senate. After that, the interference ceased.

The Jews, on the other hand, have a clearly defined code of conduct toward strangers, and though most of them had only heard of Rome and hardly seen a citizen before, I was received with great courtesy, nor was I barred from any part of their little community, even their holy places which they call "synagogues." This amazed me all the more since I had already learned — during my few hours in Tyre — with what hatred and suspicion and contempt they are regarded by all the other inhabitants of the city. Nor is this hatred unique to Tyre; I found it a constant quality during the whole of my overland trip to Judea, even slaves, whose condition defies description, finding time and venom with which to hate the Jews. So consistent a manifestation as this intrigued me highly, and I think I have discovered many of the factors which contribute toward it; some of these I will enumerate and elaborate upon in the course of my report.

Of the Jews in Tyre, I will say little, since I consider it more useful to describe my first impressions of them in their native land, Judea; yet I must mention that in all ways, they keep themselves apart from all other inhabitants, neither eating the same food nor drinking the same wine. Also there is about them something shared by the Judeans, but far more noticeable in a non-Jewish land — that is a fierce and unbending pride and superiority, which is some-how mixed with incredible humility, a quality which both attracts and enrages, so that from the very first, in spite of their courtesy, I found myself repressing a desire to evidence hostility toward them.

Among them, I found and hired an old Jewish man, one Aaron ben Levi, or, in our terms, Aaron the son of Levi; and I might mention here that these people have no sur-names, yet the humblest of them will trace their genealogy carefully and specifically over five or ten or even fifteen gen-erations. That they are a very ancient people, no one can gainsay, perhaps the most ancient in all this area, and they also possess a sense of the past which is both astonishing and disturbing.

This Aaron ben Levi proved most useful as a guide and as an informant; for he had been a camel driver and caravan man all his life, except for those years when he left his call-ing to fight under the banner of the Maccabee; and he not only knew every road and bypath in Palestine, but proved most valuable in his memories of the Jewish wars. I also purchased a horse and saddle for seventeen shekels, both of which are noted and attested in the general accounting, as well as an ass for the old man; whereupon we journeyed southward along the main coastal highway toward Judea.

A word or two about this camel guide of mine, since many of his characteristics are typical of the Jews and will thereby prove valuable in estimating the potential of these people — as well as the necessarily great menace of them. His age was somewhere in the late sixties, but he was dry and hard and brown as a nut; he had a high, thin nose, most of his teeth, and a pair of sparkling and insolent gray eyes. Unlike most of these people, who are generally taller than any others in this part of the world, or even in Rome, he was small and bent, but his whole attitude and bearing was outrageously patrician. Though before I took him for hire he had been without work for more than a year, and thereby a charge of the community, literally a beggar, he gave every impression of doing me a great favor by accepting my food and money. Though never by word or look could he be accused of actually offending me, he somehow mixed every word and every movement with a pitying sort of contempt that indicated clearly enough that even though I was less than dirt, it was an accident of birth that made me so, and therefore I was not wholly to blame.

I recognize that these are strange impressions for a citizen of Rome and a legate of the Senate to record; but in all truth, they are so characteristic of this whole people — although varying in subtlety according to the individual — that I cannot refuse to note them.

At first, it was my intention to force him to keep his place, and to treat him as I would any chance guide, but I soon realized the futility of this and began to understand a maxim fairly common in these parts, to wit: take a Jew for a slave, and he will soon be your master. The Senate will acknowledge that I am not without experience in these matters, and as a centurian I learned to lead men and maintain their respect, but with these people, that is impossible. This Aaron ben Levi never failed to advise me upon any and all subjects under the sun; his advice was always patronizing and brooked no argument, and he consistently gave forth with that stark, somewhat sickening, proud and humble Jewish philosophy, which is compounded out of their history and their barbaric and somewhat vile religious beliefs, and embodied in what they call their "holy scrolls," or, in their tongue, their Torah. For example, I asked him once why he, like all his people, insisted on burdening himself with his long woolen cloak, a garment that falls from head to feet and is striped all over in black and white, and instead of answering, he asked me:

"And why, Roman, do you wear a breastplate that gets so hot under our sun that it probably burns your skin?"

"It has nothing to do with your cloak."

"On the other hand, it has everything to do with my cloak."

"How?"

He sighed and said, "A false balance is an abomination to the Lord, but a just weight is his delight."

"And what, precisely, has that to do with it?" I asked.

"All or nothing, as you will," he said rather sadly, and that was the end of it. I could either kill him or send him packing, but neither would further my purpose, which was to get to Judea and open negotiations with the Maccabee. So I swallowed my anger and took refuge in silence, a thing one is forced to do with these people. Another time I asked him about the Maccabee, the first Maccabee, who was called Judas the son of Mattathias and who was slain early in their recent wars against the Greeks.

"What sort of a man was he?" I asked.

And this old, miserable, wretched camel driver looked at me with pitying commiseration and said, "You would not understand, even if I told you in the greatest details."

"Suppose you try to tell me."

"Life is short and death is forever," he smiled. "Shall a man try to do what is futile?"

It was then that I first used an expression which sooner or later, in one form or another, comes to the lips of everyone who has to do with these people, saying, "You filthy Jew!"

The reaction was quite different from what I expected, for the old man straightened up; his eyes flashed such hatred and anger as I had not seen before, and he said very softly, "The Lord God is one, Roman, and I am an old man, but I led a twenty under the Maccabee, and I have my knife and you have your sword, so let us see what a man of the Maccabee is like, even if I cannot tell you what he himself was."

I resolved the difference without having to slay him, for I did not see that the purpose of Rome would be served in my killing an aged and rather feeble camel driver; yet it was a lesson to me in what these people are and how they must be approached. Difference is enshrined with them, and what we consider holy, they consider profane, and what we consider fine, they consider despicable. All things desirable to us are considered hateful to them, and all the tolerance we have toward the customs and the Gods of others is turned by them into a fierce intolerance. Even as they decry our pleasures, so do they blaspheme against our Gods and against the Gods of all people. Without a morality, they are also without a God, for they worship nonexistence, and their synagogues and their holy Temple in Jerusalem have no images or presence within them. Their God — if it is a God that they worship — is nowhere, and even its name, which is written, is forbidden to be spoken by any inhabitant of the land. This name is "Yahvah," but never is it even whispered; instead they address this mysterious personage as *Adonai*, which means "my lord," or as *Melech Haolom*, which means "king of all lands," or in any one of a dozen similar fashions.

At the root of this is a thing they call the *b'rit*, which may be freely translated as a covenant or agreement between themselves and their Yahvah. In a fashion, it is more this covenant they worship than the God himself, and to implement it they have a code of seventy-seven rules which they call "the Law," though it is not judicial law as we know it, but rather the basis of this *b'rit* of theirs. Many of these are horrible and disgusting in the extreme, as for instance the law which forces the circumcision of all male children; others are senseless, such as the law which forces them to rest on the seventh day, to let the land lie fallow on the seventh year, and to free all slaves after seven years of servitude. Other laws make a fetish of washing, so that they are cleansing themselves eternally, and their law forbids them to shave, so that all the men of the land wear long hair and close-cropped beards.

This I did not learn at once, nor the other similar matters which I will go into during the course of this report, but I feel it best to state them here in relation to this camel driver and his actions; for, as I pointed out, his actions could be taken almost as an exaggerated outline of the people I was to meet. I might also say that his dress was the dress of the Judean men, sandals, white linen trousers, a short coat, a sash, and over it the long, heavy woolen cloak, which they draw up over their heads when they enter the synagogue or the Temple. Nakedness is abhorred among them, although they are shapely enough, the men of great bodily strength, the women of surprising attractiveness and appeal. These women insert themselves into the life of the community in a way that is quite alien to us; they seem to show no particular respect or obedience to the men, but rather share that objectionable Jewish haughtiness in an even greater degree. The dress of the women consists of a single long, short-sleeved garment that falls almost to the ankles and is belted by a bright-colored sash at the waist. Like the men, they frequently wear a long woolen cloak, but in their case it is never striped, and their hair they wear long and usually in two heavy braids.

I go into these and other matters in such detail for two reasons: first, because I feel that this, as the first official report to the Senate concerning these people, bears a special responsibility in specifics as well as in general terms, and second because I see in the Jews a grave matter which Rome must surely face. For that reason too I shall attempt to be as objective as possible and to overcome the deep dislike for these people that I gradually assumed.

The trip from Tyre to Judea was uneventful, for the entire coastal road is under the iron hand of Simon the Ethnarch, and he will tolerate neither banditry nor interference. On the Plain of Sharon, just opposite Apollonia, I saw my first Jewish military patrol, ten men on foot — which is their usual mode of travel, since their country is very small and mountainous throughout — and it served as good example of the Jewish custom of armament and war. Their soldiers, who unlike those of all civilized people are neither professionals nor mercenaries but volunteer peasants, wear no armor. For this they have, as with most matters, two explanations; one that it would be an affront to their Yahvah to put their trust in metal rather than in what they term, in their consistently contradictory fashion, his awful goodness, and secondly that it would so impede their movements in the mountains as to outweigh any benefit that might be derived from it.

Instead of a sword, they carry long, heavy-bladed, slightly curved knives which they use with terrible effect in close combat, although their officers tend to wear Greek swords, both as a mark of victory over the invaders and in imitation of the first Maccabee, Judas ben Mattathias, who from the very beginning of his struggle used the sword as his only weapon. Their principal weapon, however, is the Jewish bow, a short, deadly weapon made of laminated ram's horn. They have a secret process for softening the horn; it is then cut into thin strips which are glued together in the desired shape. Their arrows, which are twenty-seven inches long, are made of cedar, slender and iron-tipped; and with these arrows they are most prodigal, filling the air with them, shooting one after another in such quick succession that they come down like rain, and in their narrow mountain defiles there is apparently no protection against such attack.

Their table of organization consists of tens and twenties and hundreds and thousands, but there seems to be no perceptible difference in leadership since the captain of any group, whatever its size, is always known as the *shalish*. Also, there is no military discipline that would be understandable in Roman terms. Every action is discussed with all the men, and they make no move either offensive or defensive without unanimous consent of all the troops; anyone who disagrees with any particular tactic is permitted to leave the ranks and go home, and it seems that there is no particular onus upon him for so doing. Under these conditions, it seems incredible that any sort of military action could be maintained; yet it is a matter of record that they only recently emerged from twenty-seven years of continuous and bitter warfare.

The fact that all their methods appear so unwarlike and that they are a people who literally worship peace should not lead the Senate to underestimate them; for it will emerge from this report that in all the world there is no people so dangerous and so deceitful as these same Jews.

The patrol halted us and questioned us. There was no hostility whatsoever in their actions, yet my guide, Aaron ben Levi, took the very act of halting us to be a personal affront. When they asked where we were bound, he replied:

"And am I a slave that I cannot walk where I will?"

"With one of the *nokri?*" a word they use for all who are not Jews.

"With ten of the *nokri,* you young fool who was sucking his mother's pap when I already fought alongside the Maccabee."

And so it went with that peculiar insolence that Jews cannot refrain from using even against each other. Finally, it was ironed out and the patrol escorted us to the border of Judea, and all that distance they never ceased to ply me with questions about Rome, all of the questions subtly barbed and so construed to evoke points of their own superiority.

Of Judea, of the land itself, I cannot speak too highly. To come on it out of the Phoenician lowlands is like coming from a desert into a garden. You enter the hills and on every hand the terraces rise, like enchanted hanging wonderlands. Even in the North, which is the least cultivated part, the country has the aspect of a carefully tended garden. In the whole land, there is only one city, Jerusalem. The mass of the population live in small villages, which cluster in the bottom lands or cling to the hillsides, and the population of the villages varies from twenty to one hundred families. The houses, which are usually set in two lines on either side a single street, are made of sun-baked mud bricks, coated with lime on the front, and in this temperate and gentle climate, the brick endures for generations. Very often, there is one stone building in the village, a sort of meetinghouse, which is called the "synagogue" and serves both as a school and as a place of prayer. Almost above all other things, these people esteem literacy, and I have never met a Jew who could not read and write. In all probabilities, this serves to increase their arrogance, and without question it feeds their contempt for the outside world where so few are scholars.

Olive groves abound, and here and there on the mountains are carefully tended forests of cedar and hemlock. The terraces have been constructed over a period of a thousand years, and they are filled with soil carried by basket from the rich bottoms, where the humus lies thirty and forty feet deep. Everywhere on the hills are cisterns, with stone aprons to catch the rainfall, and one is constantly amazed by the prodigious amount of human labor that has gone into the making of this land — the more so when one learns this, of all places on earth, is the one with the least slaves. Whereas, in our last census, we numbered twenty-three slaves to each free citizen, here in Judea it would be the reverse, with perhaps one slave to twenty or thirty citizens. This in itself is a danger that must not be ignored, for these people free all slaves by law after a period, and among them it is a crime to strike a slave or to keep a slave in ignorance. And when one considers that free slaveholding is the very basis of Western civilization, the firm rock upon which the Roman republic so securely rests, one can see that the question of the Jew is not merely a local annoyance.

We proceeded inland by way of a poor road — none of

their roads are of any worth compared to ours — that paralleled a pleasant little stream, which dashed and tumbled through the hills until we came to the town of Modin. I was particularly interested in this village, for it is the ancestral home of the Maccabeans, and throughout their rebellion it was used as a rallying point for their forces. For this place, the Jews have a peculiar veneration; my guide spoke of it with awe; and any man who was born in Modin — few are left, so many having perished in the wars — is entitled to the honors of an *Adon,* their name for local people of dignity and respect. When we came to Modin, he went into the synagogue to pray and I wandered through the town by myself for over an hour. Aside from the fact that it was an unusually pretty and well-kept village, ideally situated in the rolling foothills, I could not see that it was too different from countless other Judean villages. The people there seemed healthy and well-formed, and they were very pleasant. All of Judea is wine country, but this village lies in the center of their best vineyards; and I was constantly offered goblets of the local wine, of which they are very proud. Though never, during all of my stay in Judea, have I seen a case of drunkenness, these people drink wine as readily as water; they have endless variety of white and red wine, and they are all well versed in a peculiar lore of the grape. Wine drinking, as other things, they surround with endless ceremony and prayer, and they expressed great pleasure when I spoke highly of their brew.

From Modin, we continued along the road to Jerusalem, going through the thickly populated heart of their land. In the day's journey between Modin and Jerusalem, I counted twenty-one villages. Every inch of the land was terraced and planted. The cribs were filled with corn; sheep and goats nibbled on the reaped fields; cheese hung over every doorway, and cisterns filled with olive oil abounded. Baking is done in common, and in many villages, we were greeted by the fragrant odor of mountains of newly baked bread. Chickens, a basic food and the standard meat dish of the land, were at home everywhere, in the roads, the fields, and in and out of the houses too, for these are a people who rarely close their doors, and that curse of Rome, thievery, is practically absent here. The children, who appear to be numberless in Judea, are round-cheeked and happy; the whole aspect of this land under Simon the Ethnarch is one of such health, richness, and satisfaction that though I have traveled in three continents and seen at least a hundred great cities, I have never encountered elsewhere the same fruitful life. Nor is this land plagued, as we are, with the scum of free men who do no work and have no means, but bleed their betters, the plebeian curse. As a matter of fact, differences in wealth and station, which were great at the outbreak of the war, disappeared almost entirely as the whole people suffered. The very rich sided with the invaders, and were either slain or exiled, and so many died during the wars that in the end there was a shortage of men rather than land.

I enumerate these virtues that the picture may be fulfilled; yet I must add that you cannot like a Jew for what you would admire in others, for they are too conscious of their achievement. They take nothing for granted, not courtesy, not good manners, not virtue, but must always underline and underline again that these things are the result of their being Jews. They worship peace, yet never allow you to forget at what cost they achieved it; their family is like a stone arch over their heads, but this they know, and always they despise the *nokri* for his lack of the same virtue. Power and those who wield it, they hate;

all other Gods than theirs they malign; and all other culture than theirs is offensive to them. So that even while you admire so much that which they have, you build a seething hatred for them. This combines with the fact that they possess so little of the grace and delicate knowledge that makes for noble human beings.

It was toward evening that we reached Jerusalem, a noble and beautiful city, crowned with the holy building of all the Jews, their Temple. Half of the city is given to the Temple, its many buildings, its courts and walks and the massive walls that surround it — as massive as the walls that surround the city itself. It is not size or architectural splendor that gives the city its beauty, but rather its location and style, so that it almost breathes the fanatical love which their people bestow upon it. With my guide, I approached it toward sunset, when all the walls and buildings and the Temple too were bathed in the rosy glow of twilight. We passed through the gates, and even as we did, we could hear the deep, sonorous chanting of the priests and Levites from the Temple courts. In spite of myself, in spite of the resistance to the people that had already rooted itself within me, I could not but be moved and impressed by the beauty of the music and the strange gentleness that overcame the people while it was in progress. So childlike and simple was their air toward each other, and toward me as well, that I was moved to ask Aaron ben Levi the reason. He answered enigmatically:

"We were slaves once, in the land of Egypt."

It was the first time I heard that phrase, which is never far from the thoughts of these people, and afterwards I discussed it in some detail with Simon the Maccabee.

As we entered the city, a handful of the soldiers who kept a rather loose and easy guard at the gates went with us, nor did they interfere with us as we climbed through the city toward the Temple. It was fairly dark now; the singing died away; and through the open doors of the houses, we could see families sitting down to their evening meal. The streets were clean and new, as were most of the houses built either of stone or mud brick and always painted or lime-coated white. Compared to one of our Western cities, Jerusalem is amazingly clean, but except for the Temple, it is more like a group of villages than what we know as a city. The inhabitants live in an easy and free companionship; their doors are never closed; and both their laughter and their tears are common property.

We got as far as the outer entrance to the Temple before we were stopped, though we had to stable our beasts a hundred yards below.

Courteously, but firmly, two white-robed Temple servants, who are called Levites and pride themselves on being descended from the ancient tribe of Levi, barred our path and, ignoring me, informed my guide that the stranger could go no further.

"Naturally," Aaron ben Levi agreed, with that disgusting note of muted contempt, "since he is a Roman. Yet he comes as an ambassador to speak with the Maccabee — and where shall he go if the Maccabee will not see him here?"

They took us then to the palace of Simon, which would hardly be called a palace in our land, a clean, spacious stone house, newly built on the hillside near the Temple, overlooking a deep ravine which separated it from the Temple. The few furnishings in the house were simple affairs of cedarwood, and the hangings were of heavy, brightly dyed wool, and there I was greeted by a middle-aged, rather handsome woman, the wife of the Ethnarch. Dark-eyed, dark-haired, reserved always in my presence, she was hardly typical of Jewish women — and it was only later, through the reading of a manuscript which I shall enclose with this report, that I was able to surmise her relationship to her husband; for though there was deep respect, there appeared to be little enough of love between them. The Ethnarch has four sons, tall, well-formed boys, and the life they live is so simple as to be almost rigorous. His daughter had married some years before.

One of the sons, Judas by name, took me to my chambers, and shortly thereafter a slave brought a bath of hot, salty water. I removed the dirt of my journey and lay down gratefully to rest, and while I lay there, wine and fresh fruit was brought and set down on a low table beside me. Then, for about an hour, I was left to myself, a rest for which I was very grateful.

These matters I detail to point out again how curiously virtue mixed with evil in these incredible people. It is hardly possible that any stranger in Rome — or Alexandria or Antioch — could so easily reach the first citizen, nor would the welcome be so forthright or pleasant. No one questioned what I did there, what I wanted of the Maccabee or even what my name was. No one asked to see my documents, passes, or warrants. They simply accepted me as a tired stranger, and treated me with that codified formality which entitles all strangers to certain things.

When the hour was passed, the Maccabee or Ethnarch himself appeared. This was my first sight of that almost legendary man, who is the sole surviving one of the five Maccabean brothers, Simon the son of Mattathias, and since I do not doubt but that any action the Senate decides to pursue will be through him, I shall attempt to describe both his appearance and his personality in full.

He is a very tall man, at least six feet three inches in

height, and built proportionately — of immense physical strength and bearing. His age is somewhere less than sixty years. Almost bald, his hair and beard retain a trace of that red which is a family characteristic, and also characteristic of many of those who call themselves Kohanim, a *gen* of the tribe of Levi. His features are large and strong, his nose high-bridged, reminding one of a hawk's beak. Under shaggy, overhanging brows are a pair of keen and pale blue eyes, and his mouth is full and strong, almost heavy-lipped. His beard is quite gray, and unlike most of the people, who clip their beards to within an inch or two of the skin, he wears his in its natural growth across his breast, a massive, fanlike thing that strangely enough only adds to his majesty and dignity. His hands also draw the eye, for they are well-formed and large, and he has a breadth of shoulder that is overwhelming. Altogether, he is one of the most striking and impressive men I have ever encountered — and just to see him is to understand the incredible devotion and respect in which the Jews hold him.

When I saw him first that evening, he wore a simple white robe and sandals and a small blue cap upon his head. He had drawn aside the woolen drape that closed off my chamber from the rest of the house; unannounced, unescorted, he stepped into the room hesitantly and apologetically — as if to disturb me in my rest were a mortally deplorable act upon his part. In that moment, seeing him, taking in both the political circumstances of this man and his physical appearance, I had to decide immediately upon a course of action that would best fulfill my mission and advance the interests of Rome. By and large, these people have very little knowledge of Rome. Among them one cannot, as one would in Syria or Egypt, simply mention the name of the august Senate and obtain in response both respect and obedience. Also, I had come alone, without servants or defenders; this of course was my choice, and I adhere to the belief that nothing so advances the prestige of Rome among the cities as the manner in which her legates go from place to place, surrounding themselves not with soldiers and spears but with the long, mighty and inexorable arm of the Senate. Nevertheless, I had to establish this fact with one who most likely was unaware of it — and acting upon an understanding of that necessity, I bearded this mighty man, challenging him coldly and dryly.

I informed him that the Senate had dispatched me to Judea to meet the Maccabee and to extend to him my hand — which became the hand of Rome, and of the Senate too — if he so desired. I was not pleasant, but rather let a hard note of power creep into my voice, and I pointed out to him that Carthage and Greece and certain other nations had come to realize that peace with Rome is preferable to war.

Without question, this was the proper attitude to take toward him, yet I must report, in all honesty, that he did not seem particularly disturbed. If anything, he showed more interest in how I had been treated during my time in Judea than he did in relations between our two countries, and when I went into the insolence of my camel guide, he smiled and nodded.

"I know that man, that Aaron ben Levi," he said, "and he has a long tongue. I trust you will forgive him, for he is an old man, and his past is more glorious than his present. He was a great bowmen in his time."

"And yet you reward him with poverty and obscurity?" I inquired.

The Maccabee raised his brows, as if I had said some-

thing totally unintelligible and he was too good-mannered
to let me see that I was speaking gibberish.

"Reward him? Why should I reward him?"

"Because he was a great soldier."

"But why should I reward him? He didn't fight for me.
He fought for the covenant, for Judea, as all Jews fought.
What is to set him apart?"

By now I was used to the dead end of unreason that one
came to always in any matter of dispute or discussion with
these people. Also, I was very tired, and noticing this, the
Maccabee bade me good night, inviting me to come the next
day to his public chamber and witness his judging of the
people, since in that fashion I would learn more quickly the
customs and problems of the land.

At this point, I think it would prove valuable to say a
word or two concerning the title and position of this Simon
ben Mattathias, since that will make more understandable
an incident that took place the following day in the judgment chamber. Full clarity I cannot provide, for there is
something in both the political and personal relations these
people practice with each other that is totally alien to our
way of thought and life; but I can present certain aspects of
the matter.

Simon is the Maccabee, that is, he is heir to a strange
and curious title that was first bestowed on his younger
brother, Judas, and which today has somehow fallen upon
the whole family, so that the father, Mattathias and all of
the five brothers are known familiarly as "the Maccabeans."
Precisely what this title means is most obscure, though
Simon himself contends that it is a title given to a leader
who comes out of the people and remains faithful to them;
that is, faithful from a Jewish point of view, from the point
of view of a people who abhor order and despise authority.

However, other Jews I have discussed this with disagree. And thus the word itself is allied to so many explanations that it is near meaningless. That is not to say it doesn't command respect; there is only one Maccabee, and he is Simon the Ethnarch, but the lowliest beggar in the street can halt him, dispute with him and talk to him as an equal. This I have seen with my own eyes, so I can attest to it. In this land, where all men read, prate, and philosophize, there can be no emergence of a cultured and superior strata of human beings, such a group as is the wealth and glory of Rome; yet so persistent and diabolical is this strange and flagrant Jewish democracy that one must look upon it as a disease from which no land is immune.

As to the government which Simon heads, it is so loose as to be almost nonexistent. He appears to be the highest authority, since cases in dispute, both large and small, are brought before him, that he may judge them. Yet he is humbly and abjectly responsible to a body of old men, Adons and Rabbis as they are called, who constitute the Great Assembly. Unlike your own august personages, this Assembly cannot legislate, since the Law is considered a contract between men and Yahvah, and neither can it declare war; indeed, war is made by gathering together thousands of the people and placing the question directly before them. As unreasonable as this procedure sounds, it is nevertheless frequently used.

It was the next day that Simon sat in judgment, and I observed, sitting at one side of the room, keeping my peace, but carefully noting what befell. This I consider the duty of a legate, for a picture of any people valuable enough for the Senate to act upon must be composed in detail out of many contradictory factors — and the more so when one deals with a race so sly and complicated as these Jews. During this day's judgment, one incident occurred that was of such interest that I feel I should repeat it. A tanner came before the Maccabee, and he had with him a frightened Bedouin boy, a waif of one of the many barbarian tribes that roam the desert to the South. Five times this boy had run away, and each time the tanner had regained possession of his lawful property, several times at considerable expense. Quite naturally, he was aggrieved; yet the law forbade him what would have been a normal act in the public weal in Rome — that is, to flay the boy and hang his skin in a public place as a lesson and a warning to other property.

Instead, the tanner came before the Ethnarch asking permission to brand the boy, so that even when his term of servitude was over, he would carry the sign of a slave with him through life. To me, this appeared both a mild and just request, and I expected Simon to grant it out of hand. But the Maccabee appeared unable to make so simple a decision, and he demeaned himself by entering into conversation with the slave, asking him why he had run away.

"To be free," the boy answered.

The Maccabee was silent for quite a while then, as if those obvious words contained some deep and mysterious significance. When he finally spoke, rendering his decision, his deep voice was filled with the most awful melancholy I had ever heard. These words he spoke, which I noted down:

"He will go free in two years, even as the law says. Don't brand him."

Whereupon the tanner demanded indignantly, in that insolent tone any Jew feels free to use to any other, regardless of birth or station, "And the money I paid the caravan?"

"Charge it to your own freedom, tanner," the Maccabee said coldly.

The tanner began to protest, addressing the Maccabee

by his own name, Simon ben Mattathias; but Simon suddenly leaped to his feet, one great hand out, breaking in on the other, shouting at him:

"I've judged you, tanner! How long ago was it that *you* slept in a lousy goatskin tent? How short is your memory? Is freedom a thing you can put on or take off, as you would a coat?"

That was the only time I saw the Ethnarch angry — the only time I saw the deep and corroding bitterness within him emerge, yet it gave me the best clue to what the real Simon ben Mattathias is.

We dined together that evening, and at the table I couldn't help smiling at the curious and primitive scene I had witnessed earlier.

"Did you find it amusing?" the Maccabee asked me. There was something burning within him, and I chatted easily for a while, to take the edge away, asking him various questions about slavery and concerning their curious religion. When his mood had become a little more amiable, when only we two sat together, the sons having gone to their beds and his wife to take the air on the balcony for a while, complaining that her head ached, I said to him:

"What did you mean, Simon the Maccabee, when you asked that tanner whether freedom is a thing you can put on or take off, as you would a coat?"

The old man was handling a bunch of the wonderful, sweet Judean grapes; now he put them down and stared at me for a moment or two as if I had awakened him from sleep.

"Why do you ask?" he finally said.

"My function is to ask, to know, to understand, Simon ben Mattathias. Otherwise, I fail Rome and I fail myself."

"And what is freedom to you, Roman?" the Maccabee wondered.

"How is it that you cannot ask a Jew a question without him questioning you in turn?"

"Perhaps because a Jew's doubts match your own, Roman," he answered, smiling rather sadly.

"Jews have no doubts. You told me yourself that they were the chosen people."

"Chosen? Yes — but for what? In our holy scrolls, which I am certain you despise, Roman, it says, *And I will give thee for a light unto the Gentiles —* "

I couldn't help saying, "What amazing, incredible egotism!"

"Perhaps. You asked me about freedom, Roman, and with us, that is somehow different than with others, for once we were slaves in Egypt."

"You said that before," I reminded him, "like a spell. Is it a spell — or an incantation?"

"We don't deal in spells or incantations," the old man said contemptuously. "What I said I meant. We were slaves in Egypt once, a long time ago, a long, long time ago in terms of the *nokri*, but with us the past lives; we don't destroy it. Then we were slaves and we labored morning, noon and night under the lash of the overseer — and we were given bricks to make without straw, and our young were torn from us and man was separated from his wife, so the whole people wept and cried out to the Lord God in our agony. Thus it was burned into us that freedom is a good thing and deeply connected with life itself. All things have their price, but only in the blood of brave men can freedom be measured."

"That is very moving," I answered, rather dryly, I am

afraid, "yet it doesn't reply to what I asked you. Is freedom your god?"

Simon shook his head resignedly, and now indeed he was the Jew, completely the Jew and one with my dry and despicable camel guide; for this rude highland chieftain was pitying me even while his patience extended itself.

"All things are our god," he mused, "for God is all and one and indivisible — and I do not see how I can explain it better, Roman."

"And other gods?" I smiled.

"Are there other gods, Roman?"

"What is your opinion, Jew?" I asked him, forging the insult and allowing it to penetrate, for I was sick to death of his humility-ridden insolence.

"I know only the God of Israel — the God of my fathers," the Maccabee said imperturbably.

"Whom you have spoken to?"

"I never spoke to Him," the old man answered patiently.

"Or seen?"

"No."

"Or had witness of?"

"Only in the hills and fields of my native land."

"Where he walks?"

"Where, among other places, He abides," the old man smiled.

"Yet you know there are no other gods?"

"That I know," the Maccabee said.

"I would think," I said, "that a decent respect for the gods of others, would prevent such a bland and broad elimination — or at least for the feelings of others."

"The truth is the truth," he replied, genuinely puzzled.

"And do you know the truth so well, Jew? Can you answer all things, all questions, all doubts, all hesitations, all bewilderment? Did God give you the truth when he chose you, a handful of mountain peasants, out of the whole great and boundless and civilized world?"

I expected him to be angry, but there was no sign of anger in his pale and puzzled eyes. For a long while, he looked at me, searched my face, as if he were seeking to find something there that would quiet his own bewilderment. Then he rose and said:

"You will excuse me, for I am weary," and he left me alone.

After he had gone, I sat for a time by myself, and then I went out onto the balcony, the finest feature of this house of his, a wide and spacious veranda, fitted with couches and overlooking a deep and narrow gorge. Below it are the city and the tumbled Judean hills, and in situation it makes up for what it lacks in architecture.

There, on this terrace, his wife still sat. I would have retired when I noticed her, but she called, "Don't go, Roman, unless talking with the Ethnarch has tired you too much to talk further."

"I was admiring this place. Yet I shouldn't be here with you alone."

"Why? Would it be wrong in Rome?"

"Quite wrong."

"But we do things differently in Judea. My name is Esther, and in any case, I am an old woman, so sit yourself down here, Lentulus Silanus, and no one will think the worse of it. And you can tell me something of Rome — if it will not bore you to entertain an old woman — or perhaps I will tell you something of Judea."

"Or — "

"Or of Simon the Maccabee?"

I nodded.

"Simon Maccabeus — yet it may be that I know less of him than you do, Roman, for as you may have gathered, he is a strange and willful man, and unless it was his brother Judas, I do not know that there was ever a man like him before in all this world. Simon of the iron hand, they call him, but underneath there is little enough iron in him."

I sat silent and waited. By now, I knew enough of Jews to doubt my ability to make any appropriate comment. What pleases others offends them, and what offends others pleases them. So long as I am in Judea, I am Rome; and Rome is always interested, always curious, always inquiring. This woman needed to talk and wanted to talk, and since there was some curious satisfaction in talking to a Roman, I lay back on the couch, watching her and listening.

"He is my husband, Lentulus Silanus, and there is no man like him in all of Israel today — is that strange? Or is this so tiny a land, so unimportant and uncivilized that what I say amuses you? I know — many things amuse you, or perhaps they don't, and part of the legate's uniform is that cynical, supercilious smile of yours. I've been watching it. Or it may be that I do you an injustice and you are genuinely amused at these queer and uncouth Jews. Why are you here? Why did they send you? Don't bother to answer a garrulous old woman, and in any case I was talking about Simon Maccabeus. He had four brothers, you know, so there were five we call the Maccabeans, but they are dead now, and something is dead inside of him. All he could love, all he ever knew how to love were those brothers of his — and one whose name was Judas. It was after Judas died that he married me. Not because he loved me. Oh, I grew up in Modin with him, and he had seen me every day since I was a child — but he couldn't love me, not any woman, not even one whose name was Ruth and who was the most beautiful that ever walked in Modin. But I bore you with this gossip, for it is of him you would hear and not of me."

"Surely of you," I ventured, "for you are a part of him."

"Now those are pretty words indeed," she said, smiling for the first time, "but hardly true, Lentulus Silanus. No one is a part of the Maccabee — no woman that ever lived. He is a lonely and sorrowful man, and thus it has ever been, and the sorrow is for the life he lost, the life that all other men have but was never for the Maccabeans. Think, Roman, of what it is to live without a soul, without yourself, but only for something outside of you. Consider these five brothers — and go through Jerusalem and Judea and ask of them, and you will find no word against them, no sin to stain them — only that they were without peer and without reproach — "

She stopped suddenly, looking out over the lovely, moonlit valley, and then said:

"But at what cost! What a price they paid!"

"Yet they were victorious."

She turned those deep, brooding dark eyes on me, and there was in them a trace of anger, but mixed with and submerged to such a pool of regret, sorrow, and hopelessness as I have never seen in the eyes of another. Then it passed and only the sorrow remained.

"They were victorious," she nodded. "By all means, Roman, they were victorious. For thirty years my husband knew only warfare and death. What do you fight for, Roman? For land? For loot? For women? Yet you want me to explain to you a man who fought for the holy covenant between God and mankind, which says only that each human being should walk erect and clean in freedom — "

I watched her, knowing there was nothing to say, trying

to understand the amazing way of these folk, who, reject-
ing all that is worthy and substantial, make an altar of
nothingness.

" — without glory. Where was the glory for Simon ben
Mattathias? For his brothers — yes. For the least of his
brothers. Speak a word against Judas, Lentulus Silanus, and
for all the sacred laws of hospitality, he will strike you
down with his own hand. Or Jonathan, or John, or Eleazar.
For in his love for Judas, there was something else that tore
out his heart — I don't understand it — but it tore at him
always, always, and only them could he love, he who is like
no other man in all the world . . ."

Rigid, I lay, watching the tears stream down her cheeks,
and I was almost grateful when she rose, excused herself
hurriedly, and left me.

After that, for three weeks, I saw nothing of the Ethnarch
and almost nothing of his wife. During that time, I employed myself with the taking of notes and a study of the
land and its people. Three trips I made under the acid
guidance of Aaron ben Levi, one to the Dead Sea, a deep
and caustic pit of motionless water that might have been
created by demons for demons, one to the beautiful mountains of Ephraim, and one to the South. On two of these
trips I was accompanied by the boy Judas, an amiable and
handsome son of the Maccabee.

Also, I attended a session of the Great Assembly of
Elders, but I do not think it would be profitable to include
the tedious and meticulous legal-religious discussions I
heard. During these journeys, I stayed at numerous villages
and saw much of the life of the Jews as they live from day
to day; the more difficult then for me to explain to you, the
noble Senate, how without being able to detail a specific
act of antagonism I came to hate them so — and came to

accept, if not to fully understand, how and why they are hated by other people.

At the end of this period, Simon suddenly appeared at dinner, offering no explanation of the weeks during which he had avoided me. In that time, he gave the impression of having aged, of having gone through some trying ordeal, but he said nothing of it until after the meal, until he had recited the prayer with which all meals end, and dipped his hands ceremoniously into a bowl of water. Then he invited me to sit on the balcony and chat with him — which I was most pleased and eager to do, since I now considered the time ripe to enter into political discussions concerning the future of both our countries. I must also admit that the personality of the man exercised a certain spell over me. The necessity I had built in myself to despise him always melted in his presence — yet always returned afterwards.

When we were on the balcony, lounging on the deep couch with the clear, star-sprinkled Judean sky overhead, he made a curious observation, saying:

"The guilt I must bear to live in this palace is compensated only by this ledge. Here, somehow, I find a degree of peace. Is that strange, Lentulus Silanus?"

"Strange? I think your guilt is stranger."

"How so? Is it a good thing for a man to exalt himself over others and build him a palace?"

"If he is the Maccabee."

Simon shook his head. "Least so, if he is the Maccabee. Yet let that rest. You stay in Judea — do you like our land?"

"It is not a question of liking or disliking the land. I shall have to make a comprehensive report to the Senate concerning Judea, and how shall I do so if I come one day and go the next? Also, they will ask me, what of the Maccabee?"

"And what will you answer?" Simon smiled.

"I don't know. I see so little of you. I felt you deliberately avoided me these past weeks."

"No more you than anyone else," Simon said. "I was troubled by the past, so I went to my memories to write them down and find understanding there."

"And did you?"

The old man regarded me thoughtfully, his pale eyes probing like knives, but with curiosity and not with anger and resentment, and once again I had that strange and disturbing sensation of unexpressed and pitying superiority woven through with humility, as if I were a dog and he not my master but of the same race as my master. Then it was gone, and he shook his head.

"You have many memories," I said.

"Too many. But that's the price of living, isn't it?"

"Yes and no," I shrugged. "In Rome we would not consider it in that fashion. Pleasure is a good thing to remember, and love, too, I suppose, and a job of work well done or a mission accomplished — and, above all those, strength, power."

"From all I have heard," he mused, "Rome is very strong."

"The queen of all nations — and master of half the world."

"Soon to be master of the rest?" the Ethnarch asked softly.

"That is not for me to decide. I am a legate, a courier between nations, one of the many men who quietly and — I trust — uncomplainingly do the work of the Republic and contribute in some small measure to the extension of civilization and peace."

"Even as the Greeks did before you," the Ethnarch reflected.

"I trust better. But tell me, Simon, what you wrote."

"The story of my brothers."

"One of my lasting regrets," I said, "is that I was never able to know them. They were great men."

"How do you know?" Simon asked.

"Can one spend a month in Judea and not know?"

He smiled, "And already, Roman, you are learning a Jewish turn of phrase. Yet I don't think one should waste time regretting the dead. Life belongs to the living."

"Which is strange coming from you. I know of no people so obsessed by their past as you Jews."

"Because our covenant is of the past. We were slaves once in Egypt. Can we forget that?"

"I don't imagine you want to forget. But about what you wrote, Simon, could I read it?"

"If you read the Aramaic," he answered carelessly.

"You set no store by it?"

"None," he shrugged. "What I wanted to do, I could not do, and when I was finished it seemed to me that what I put down was the rheumy searching of an old man for his dead and lost youth. If you wish to read it, however, you are welcome to. I wrote it for others more than for myself."

We talked on of one thing and another, and then, before he left me for the night, he brought me the long scroll of parchment upon which he had set down the story of his glorious brothers. That night, I didn't sleep, but lay awake, the smoking lamp drawn close, reading what this lonely and masterful Jew had written.

This manuscript I enclose with my report, for I consider that better than any personal observations of mine, it probes the Jewish mind and what they so confidently term their Jewish soul, or *n'shamah*, as they have it — the spirit that abides within them and joins them with the rest of life. This is the original manuscript which Simon, the Maccabee, gave to me, saying, "If you wish, Lentulus Silanus, you may have it — if it will mean anything to your Senate. It is of no value, and I set no worth upon it."

There, however, I consider him wrong, and I judge it well worth the trouble of the noble senators to have this rendered into Latin by competent translators, that it may be perused by everyone who has anything to do with Judea or Jews. Not only does it deal with military tactics in detail, but it specifies those subjective elements which make these people so dangerous, so deceitful, and so consistent a menace to Western ideals and civilization.

Even the flamboyant and emotional style of presentation is worth remarking, for it is an indication of many qualities in this seemingly cold and hard man whom they call Simon of the iron hand. Also contained in it are many clues to the religious ritual of the Jews.

I did not see the Ethnarch on the following day, although I spent some time with his wife, but the day after that, he and I were alone at the morning meal, a simple repast of fruit, bread and wine, which he usually took on the terrace. He did not refer to the manuscript, but instead directed a series of questions at me, concerning Rome, its size, its wealth, the nature and condition of its armies, its navies — and particularly, the military tactics which brought about the downfall of Hannibal and his Carthaginians. His questions were extremely clever, pointed, and always focused on the fact that Hannibal had maintained his Carthaginian army in Italy for sixteen years against all Roman pressure.

"What I cannot comprehend," he said thoughtfully, "is the position and condition of the people of your land — the Italians."

"Why?" I asked him. "The people are a rabble of earth-bound, ignorant slaves. Should it matter to them who rules, Carthage or Rome?"

"I can't say what would matter to them," Simon reflected, "for I am an old man, and in my whole life I have never been more than a few score miles beyond the Judean border. Yet in the end, Carthage fell."

"Because of the strength and consistency of Rome," I answered proudly. "Because it became a maxim in our city that Carthage must be destroyed — as it was."

"Yet it was a maxim with the Greeks that Judea must be destroyed, and we were not."

"Antioch is not Rome," I smiled. "And in any case, Simon, you have a debt to pay. You cost me a night's sleep with your writing, but in the end I found only questions and not answers. With the death of Judas Maccabeus, you leave off — as if that were all that mattered — yet that was more than twenty years ago, and today Judea is free, and even in far-off Rome, honor is done to the Maccabee."

"Still — it was all that mattered," the old man sighed. "Perhaps all of my writing was pointless, yet when I finished telling of the death of my brother, I could write no more."

"Still, there was more? Much more?"

"Yes."

"Even I have heard of how, after Judas's death, you and your two brothers gathered together what men of high heart there were and fought again — and then were driven into the desert beyond the River Jordan, and how for so long you maintained yourself there."

"That is so," the old man nodded. "We went into the desert because all hope and all future seemed lost, yet it was the covenant of the sons of Mattathias that we would

fight, even if we alone of all Israel fought. To the banks of
the Jordan, we never turned our backs, but then there were
none left but the dead, and we three swam the Jordan and
went into the desert, even as our forefathers did so long ago,
going into the wilderness but not bending their knees to
any man. And then, living in the desert, without rooftree or
shelter, we stayed alive — somehow we stayed alive, and we
sent our brother John back to Judea on a mission, and the
wild Bedouins fell upon him and slew him. He was gentle,
gentle and loving, and in all his life he hated no man and
never did he do an unkind thing or raise his voice in anger.
Yet because he was a son of Mattathias, he turned his face
away from the holy scrolls he loved, from the sweet quiet of
the synagogue and the home, from his wife and his children,
and he took a long sword in his hand. We are not mercenaries, Roman, and with us the whole fabric of life is the
face and the manifestation of God, and all of life is sacred.
There is no sin like the shedding of blood, and to take a
man's life away is an act of awful evil. So you may not
understand what it meant for John — who was so much a
Jew — to become a creature of battle and bloodshed. Yet
he did it. Willingly, he did it, and in all the years he was
by my side, I never heard from his lips a word of complaint,
never a word of regret, never a word of fear. Unlike the
rest of us, he was thin and always frail, but such a spirit
burned in him as I never knew. Even when he was so
sorely wounded, and lay day and night, week in and week
out in burning fever, he never complained, never regretted.
And the wild Bedouins slew him, and he died alone in the
desert — and then only Jonathan and I remained. Once I dispatched my brother Jonathan to Rabbi Ragesh — he was
called the father of Israel then — and I told my brother to
say to Ragesh that so long as two free men walked on

Judean soil, our land would not be enslaved, and thus it was, Jonathan and I in the lonely desert."

He paused, his eyes fixed on something across the ravine, across the blue Judean hills. His great hands clenched and unclenched, and the lines on his face became deeper etched. He was not telling me these things; he was expelling them from himself.

"Yes," he went on, "there were two free men, but we did not awaken Israel from the dark pit of despair and defeat. The spirit of Judas did that — of the Maccabee, like whom there was no other, ever, or will be again. And bit by bit, the land roused itself. Men who loved freedom crossed the Jordan and came to us, and embraced us and kissed us for the sons of Mattathias who had died for their people and for the dignity of all men. So our strength grew and our numbers grew — and one day we crossed the river and came back to our country. Then it was as before — wherever we went, the people rose up and joined us. Once again, we taught the Greeks that a Jew can fight. It didn't happen at once. You don't buy your freedom as you buy a cow or a bit of land. Year after year, we paid the price — but in the end we won, and there is no overlord in Judea now, only a free people who live in peace. . . ."

"And thus is twenty years accounted," I said.

"If you read what I wrote, you read the accounting," the Jew reminded me. "We reaped what Judas sowed, for he taught us what we never fully knew before, that no man ever dies uselessly or futilely in the struggle for the freedom of man. That he taught us — and what more would you have me say? War is evil and killing is evil, and he who takes up the sword must perish by it. Thus is it written in our holy scrolls. We fought for our freedom and — God willing — we will never fight for any other cause. We were not chosen to teach the ways of war, but the ways of peace and of love. Let the dead rest, and if you would know what we fought for and how we fought, go through the land, Lentulus Silanus, and watch how the people live. I have troubled my memories enough."

"Yet you trouble it strangely, Simon Maccabeus, for you never see the whole, but only a part. Do you truthfully think that your tiny state could smash the Syrian Empire single-handed?"

"Yet we did — "

He was less certain now. "But did you?" I demanded. "Was it not Rome that smashed the power of Greece and barred the further advance of Syria? Was it not a Roman legate who stood on the Egyptian border and said to a Syrian army, Go this far and no farther? You knew nothing of Rome, but Rome knew of Judea. Can you survive against the whole world, Simon? That is a dream; a dream, Simon. You say you fought for your freedom and you will never fight for any other cause. That is a bold statement, Simon — for I will not believe that a Jew is so different from all others. Your country stands here at the crossroads of the world, and those crossroads must be kept open, Simon. Whether you knew it or not, Rome fought on your side, Simon. And where will Rome fight tomorrow? Consider that, Simon Maccabeus."

The Jew stared at me, his pale eyes puzzled and sad. He was disturbed, not with fear, but with a deep uncertainty. Then, he made as to dismiss me.

"One more question," I insisted, "if the Maccabee will allow me?"

"Ask it, Lentulus Silanus."

"What of Jonathan?"

"Why? Does it matter? They are all dead, my glorious

brothers, can they not rest in peace?" Then he reached out
a hand and touched my shoulder. "Forgive me, Lentulus
Silanus, for you are a guest in my house, and may my
tongue rot if I say a word that offends you. Only some
things are more easily said than others."

"Let it pass," I assured him.

"No, for as you said, you are a courier, and what you hear
will pass your lips. There is not much to tell of Jonathan,
for as he grew without our mother, he was our child, our
beloved, and in the first years, it was as a child he fought. He
never had what we had, the sweet and generous years when
we were children at Modin, for as a child he took the bow
in his hand, and all he knew was war and the only memories
he had were memories of war and exile and struggle. Yet he
lived through it, through the awful slaughter when Judas
died, through the time of exile in the desert. Just as I
mourned my brothers, so did he mourn them, and year after
year, we fought together for Judea and for Israel, and then,
almost at the end, almost at the moment when we had won,
the Greeks took him . . ." His voice died away, and he sat
bent over and staring across the valley.

"They took him?" I prodded softly.

"They took him," the Maccabee repeated, a hard note of
bitterness in his voice. "They captured him and held him
for ransom, and I emptied my coffers to pay them what
they asked and the people gave up what little gold and
jewels they had. Every bit of gold and silver in the land
the people gathered together, willingly, so that they could
buy back the life of a son of Mattathias, and this we handed
over to the Greek, and then he slew my brother . . ."

This foregoing, as well as I can recall, is the conversation
I held with Simon Maccabeus. Certain details should be

added, as for example the fact that in the course of their twenty-year war for freedom subsequent to the death of Judas Maccabeus, they fought, as near as I can learn, twelve major battles and three hundred and forty minor engagements. This I consider of extreme importance, for therein lies the clue to their victory. This tiny and seemingly defenseless land — which has only one walled city of any consequence, no standing army, and only the loosest type of administration — literally bled the Syrian Empire of the Greeks to death. If one merely goes through their archives and computes the price of the thousands of mercenaries they have slain in their valleys and defiles, one emerges with a figure calculated to stagger the imagination. Then one begins to comprehend why, for the past three decades, the Syrian kings have engaged themselves in a seemingly insane and lustful search for wealth, sacking their own cities within their own empire, selling their own free citizens into slavery, so that they might find money to prosecute their wars against the Jews. Therefore, one is forced to deal with a natural and obvious question — why they did not give up this enterprise and allow the Jews to live in peace? To that, there is a complex of answers, some of which I presume will interest the Senate sufficiently for me to go into them.

For one thing, the antipathy toward these people must be reckoned with. Their notions of freedom, their whole concept of what one may best call the rights of individuals, are a threat to free men everywhere and to our entire slave structure. As with us, the peoples hereabout recognize slavery as the basis of freedom, since it is only in those societies which rest upon the firm foundation of slavery that free citizens are able to advance civilization. The Jewish notion of freedom as applying to all men, even slaves, is, when once understood, a menacing factor. Taken in conjunction with the fact that they exalt disobedience and rebellion, making a prime virtue out of a stubborn and senseless unwillingness to bend a knee to man or Yahvah, their God, they become even more dangerous. Without question, they were once a slave people who were led from their slavery by one Moses, and this has instilled in them so deep and unwavering a hatred of natural obedience and subjugation that it is quite impossible to regard them as civilized human beings — even though one must confess that they possess certain salutory virtues. Yet even these virtues, as I remarked before, are distilled by the peculiar Jewish method of application. One must also note, in connection with the antipathy of others toward them, their exaltation of peace. They are almost servile in their desire for peace and love. They wholly refuse to recognize that war is a part of the pattern of civilization, and they instantly condemn any act of manliness or strength as brutality. Unlike all other people, they do not hire mercenaries but demean their own free citizenry in war that contradicts everything they profess to believe; but to my observation, this regular method of contradiction is a basic part of Jewishness. In all the world, there exists no record of a war so bloody and terrible in its toll of life as these thirty years of Jewish resistance; and the very unreasonableness of that resistance could not but contribute to increasing the hatred and determination of the Greeks. I once brought this up with the Ethnarch, saying to him:

"Would it not have been better, at any one of several points, for you and your brothers to have made peace, for the sake of law, order, and well-being in general?"

"At the price of our freedom?" he wanted to know.

"Yet you set up freedom as an abstract," I pointed out to

him. "If it is, as you seem to indicate, a virtue in itself, then what can we say to slaves?"

He was clearly troubled by this. "I don't know," he answered.

"You will admit," I persisted, "that slavery is the basis of freedom?"

"How can I admit such a thing?"

"Still, you have slaves."

"That is true, yet in the course of the war, the slaves disappeared."

"How was that?"

"We gave them their freedom, so that they could fight beside us."

"And did they?"

"They did — and they died beside us too."

So it is clear to the noble Senate what manner of threat the very way of life and thought of these people contain. Without doubt, this was an important contributing factor in the attacks of the Greeks, but other factors must be noted. In the very first years of the Maccabean uprising, the losses sustained by the Syrian Empire were of such staggering size that the only manner in which they could ever be recouped would be by a final conquest and rape of Judea. Tied up in this was the question of the wealthy Jews, a rather small group of cultured people whose residences were, for the most part, in the city of Jerusalem. They were an anathema to the other Jews, who resented bitterly the fact that these cultured Jews had shed the miserable and barbarian mark of their Jewishness, adopting Greek ways and Greek dress, and speaking Greek instead of the Hebrew or the Aramaic. At the very outset of the rebellion, these Jews wisely made a pact with the Greeks, employed their own mercenaries, and shut themselves up in a great stone citadel within the city of Jerusalem — in which citadel they maintained themselves for two decades and more — until Simon laid siege to the place, took it, and leveled it to the ground.

Whenever the ardor of the Greeks cooled and they considered withdrawing completely from Judea, these Hellenized Jews employed every effort and every strategy to prevent such withdrawal and to fan anew the flames of war. Little wonder then that the hatred between these few Hellenized Jews and the village Jews cut deeper than any hatred between Greek and Jew; only through complete destruction of the Maccabeans could the Jews in the citadel regain their position and property — and one can readily sympathize with their predicament. It should be noted that when the citadel finally fell, Simon did not slay these Jews, but permitted them to remove from Judea to Antioch and Damascus. I earnestly recommend that the Senate make contact with them in those cities and cultivate them for a time when their services may prove valuable for the advancement and betterment of Rome.

A third factor responsible for the extent of the war is revenge, Judas Maccabeus having slain with his own hand two of the most popular and valued Greek commanders, Apollonius and Nicanor. There were others, but these three, antipathy, the need for money, and revenge, are the principal reasons for the prolongation of the struggle — in the course of which the Syrian Greek Empire was bled dry.

That so small a land as Judea with so inconsiderable a population as these Jews could sustain this long war is difficult to believe; and, indeed, if Jews lived as other people do, in cities, with a civilized way of life based upon slavery, then they surely must have come to defeat.

But being the agrarian people they are, rooted as they are to a soil they cultivate with their own hands, it is possible for them to display remarkable tenacity of purpose. When this is combined with their barbarian methods of war, with their absolute reluctance to engage in a forthright struggle or test of strength, with their tactic of trap and countertrap, and lastly with the favorable terrain they occupy, it is difficult to conceive of any method of conquest except from within.

Thus my recommendations, with which I intend to finish this report. In the making of it, in the details of its preparation, I have attempted to be wholly objective, seeing in such objectivity the highest duty of a legate to the Senate. I have given myself a liberal allowance of time in which to study these people, and I have mixed with and spoken with all parts of their society, the farmers, the vintners, the craftsmen, the priesthood, and even the few merchants they have among them.

I have tried, perhaps unsuccessfully, to deny myself the indulgence of hating Jews. I have tried to look at the world as they do, yet I must confess that for a Roman that is next to impossible.

I have tried to ignore their slurs and insults, conceiving of my mission as one above such mundane practices. I have tried, even, to sympathize with them.

For all of that, I have of necessity come to the foregoing conclusions, most of which have been duly recorded here. In a general sense, they may be stated so:

Jews cannot be trusted, for the Western mind can find no basis of mutual understanding. All our concepts of freedom, dignity, and responsibility are alien to them.

Jews are naturally inferior, since they reject the best of civilization and appear unable to cope with the higher aspects of life.

Jews are the enemies of mankind, since they reject and despise and slander all that is precious to mankind, the gods of men, the beliefs of men and the customs of men.

Jews are a basic threat to Rome itself, since they stand in opposition to the basis of Western culture, free slavery.

Jews are the enemies of all order, since they enshrine disorder and disobedience and worship the very act of resistance.

For all of the foregoing reasons and for others which have appeared throughout this report, I would strongly recommend to the noble Senate that it consider ways and means for the subjugation and subsequent elimination of these people. Small though they be, contained as they are in their little country, they nevertheless must be understood and respected as a threat. Speaking as a humble legate, I would submit that it is highly questionable that Rome and Judea could exist in the same world. Never were two systems more contradictory, more unable to find common ground either for alliance or for submission.

Nevertheless, I would not oppose an alliance between Rome and Judea. When one looks upon the world between Egypt and Persia, one must grant that Judea, lying like a jewel among thirteen emasculated kingdoms and two dying empires, is both a balance of power and a decisive factor. An alliance with Judea, temporary though it is, would place us in a position to wield that balance of power; and thereby we could accomplish at little cost what might otherwise spend countless legions. Also, a war at this moment might not be decisive by any means. I shudder to think of our heavily-armed legions marching through the defiles of Judea. At the height of his power and glory now, the Maccabee could call to him, overnight, fifty to seventy-five thousand armed men, veterans backed by years of warfare, and I do not think that against their firm opposition, any force on earth could penetrate Judea.

Nor, from all I can see, is the Ethnarch opposed to alliance. Only three days ago, I pressed him for a straightforward answer.

"My mission cannot go on forever," I pointed out to him. "Much as I like Judea, I must return to Rome."

"I would not keep you here against your will, Lentulus Silanus, for all that a guest is welcome and for all the good talk we have had — although to you I imagine it has been the tedious rambling of a garrulous old man. What can I do?"

"Send ambassadors to Rome with me to conclude the alliance."

"If it were that simple — "

"It is that simple," I assured him. "These are not Greeks you deal with, but Romans. If I give you my hand, I give you the solemn bond of the Senate, a word that is not broken. And then, where will there be king or petty lord, or King of Kings, or Emperor, that will dare send his mercenaries into a land that has made a solemn pact with Rome?"

"And how does Rome profit from this?"

"We make a firm ally, a strong friend in peace, a keen sword in war. The star of Greece is setting, just as the star of Carthage set, and Egypt and Babylon — and all the mighty empires of old; but there is a new star on the horizon, the young and mighty power of Rome, a power so strong, so certain, so constant that it will endure forever."

"Nothing endures forever," the Maccabee said moodily.

"However that may be, Simon, will you send us the ambassadors?"

"If you wish, I will send two men to talk with your Senate —"

"Or better, go yourself," I told him.

"No — no, Lentulus Silanus. I am an old man, and I know only Jews and Judea. What would I do in Rome where I would be a rustic and foolish curiosity?"

Though I pressed him to go himself, he would not be persuaded; yet he agreed to send ambassadors to represent him.

I cannot do more than report and advise; this I present to the noble Senate, may your lives endure and your fortunes increase. I salute you.

LENTULUS SILANUS, LEGATE

AN EPILOGUE

Wherein I, Simon, Give an Accounting of a Dream

So LENTULUS SILANUS LEFT ME, AND with him went two Judeans to appear before the Senate of Rome, yet I knew no peace, but was troubled in heart as never before. A golden sun shone over the whole land, like a sweet benediction, and when I put on the striped cloak of a Jew and walked down the hills and through the valleys to Modin, the land was like a garden, blessed and peaceful and truly like a scented offering to the Lord God of Hosts. May he endure, may his spirit grow!

Never was Israel like this before in all its time, for the children played without fear, laughing as they ran through the grass and splashed in the streams. On the hillsides, the white lambs bleated for their mothers, and between the rocks pink and white flowers grew. Nowhere was there a break in the terraces; layer upon layer, they climbed the slopes, and the crop was a good thing to see, so rich and verdant. Who could see such things and deny that this was the land of milk and honey, blessed and thrice blessed?

Yet my heart was heavy.

There was the smell of good things, bread baking, cheese curing, and the scent of new wine in the vats. Chickens were plucked and hanging, ready to be stuffed and put into the ovens, and the scent of olive oil was in the air too.

When the wind blew, there came down from the hilltops the lovely fragrance of the pines — for what is so sweet and precious as a place men laid down their lives for, even brother for brother.

Yet I did not rejoice, and my heart was heavy.

I went through the villages, and wherever I went, the people knew me and did me honor, for the sake of my glorious brothers. The best of everything had to be mine, and this and that I had to taste, for the land had been fruitful.

And everywhere, the people said, "*Shalom Alaichem, Simon Maccabeus.*"

To which I answered, "And unto thee, peace." Yet the comfort I sought eluded me. To Modin I walked, where the rooftree of Mattathias stood empty, thinking that in the gentle pain of yesterday, there might be some surcease. I climbed the hillside I had climbed so often so long ago, as a child first and then as a boy with his sheep, and then as a man with a maid — and there I lay down on the soft grass with my face turned up to the sky, the cool blue Judean sky. I watched the woolly clouds that blow in from the Mediterranean, rolling slowly across the heavens, lest they leave all too quickly this small and holy land. To a degree I was comforted, as who will not be comforted in a place where his father and his father's father walked? Yet even there, in that grove of old and sturdy olive trees, my heart was troubled and uneasy, and the pain was deep and penetrating.

How little things change, and in Modin I was Simon ben Mattathias, and when I walked down to the village, nestling there in the valley below, I came home. I joined the people who were going to the synagogue for the evening prayer, and I stood among the congregation, my cloak over my head; for even the Ethnarch and high priest is a man like other men in Israel.

Food I took with Samuel ben Noah who vinted wine and lived in a house I was not unfamiliar with. Four pressings he placed upon the table, and while his children listened open-mouthed, we talked of the lore of the grape, as Jews will. Then the neighbors joined us, and there was more talk, the easy bucolic talk of a place like Modin, for this was my home and here I was not Maccabee or Ethnarch, but the son of Mattathias.

At last, I bid them good night and went to the old house, where I laid down on a pallet; but I could not sleep. . . .

Going back to the city the following day, I fell in with the little old man, Aaron ben Levi, who had been camel guide and escort for the Roman, and for a space the two of us walked together. I asked him how was it that he had returned to Judea.

"I grew tired of the *nokri*, Simon Maccabeus, and of one Roman in particular, I grew tired to death. Wandering is for the young, my old bones ache, and when I lie down to sleep these days, I am not at all certain that the Angel of Death will not wake me before the dawn. I am out of Goumad, as my father was and his father before him, and also through my father, a Levite — " He grinned at me, half challengingly, half apologetically. "So I go to Jerusalem where I may be permitted to act as a Temple porter?"

"Why not?"

"Or a storyteller — I am not at all decided."

"So long as you don't have to work."

"In that statement, Simon Maccabeus, as in everything, there is a little bit of the truth. Yet should I be ashamed of the past? Only a great cut here in my arm — " he stopped to roll back his sleeve and exhibit a cruel scar — "only this cut prevented me from being with you in that last fight on the seacoast, where only you and Jonathan lived, so my time is borrowed, by grace of the Almighty, blessed be his name, and should I use the little left of it to labor in the fields?"

"I should think that the Roman would have paid you well enough for you to do nothing at all for a good while."

"And there you are wrong, Simon Maccabeus, for that Roman is a close and careful man, and he weighed every shekel three times in the palm of his hand."

"You didn't like him?"

"Indeed, I hated him, Simon Maccabeus, and I think I would have slain him, were he not a stranger in Israel."

"Why?" I asked curiously. "Why, Aaron ben Levi?"

"Because he was evil."

I shook my head, smiling. "Three months he lived in my house. His ways are the ways of the *nokri*, that's all. Hard and close he is, but thus he was trained."

"And do you really believe that, Simon Maccabeus?" the guide asked me caustically.

I nodded but said nothing, wondering what was in the mind of the little man as he marched along beside me, rubbing his beard thoughtfully. Several times he swallowed, as if each time there were words on his lips that he had rejected, and at last he said diffidently, "Who am I to advise the Maccabee?"

"And if I remember," I murmured, "you were never backward with advice."

"It is true that I am a poor man," he said reflectively, "but nevertheless a Jew is a Jew."

"Whatever you have to say, Aaron ben Levi, say it."

"Lentulus Silanus hated you, and not as himself but as Rome, and between Jew and Rome, there is no peace and compromise. That comes from an old and foolish man, Simon Maccabeus, so you can take it or throw it into the dirt you walk on."

And after that, we walked on in silence, for the little man was afraid he had offended me, and he kept his peace . . .

I dreamed that night in Jerusalem, and I woke up in an agony of fear. This I dreamed — that the Legions came to Judea. Never have I seen a Legion, but enough I heard of them to picture the long, heavy wooden shields, the heavy iron and wooden spears, the massed metal helmets, the close ranks. Thus I dreamed. I dreamed that the Legions came to Judea and we smashed them in our defiles; and they came again and again, until the whole land stank with the dead of Rome. And still they came, and again and again and again. And always we fought them and slashed them, yet there was no end to them. But to us there was an end, and one by one we died — until in all of Judea there was no Jew, only the empty land. And then I dreamed that a deep and terrible silence pervaded Judea, and from that I woke up, whimpering in fear and sorrow.

Esther woke too, and I felt her warm hand upon me as she said, "Simon, Simon, what troubles you?"

"I dreamed —"

"All men dream, and what are dreams but nothing and the shadow of nothing?"

"I dreamed that the land was empty and lifeless and forlorn."

"And that was a foolish dream, Simon, Simon, for where there is the good earth, there are people, and they will take the crops from it and grind the wheat and make their bread — always, Simon, always."

"No. What I dreamed was true."

"What you dreamed was a dream, Simon, my child, my strange and foolish child, just a dream."

"And there was no Jew. As if I stood on a high rock, overlooking the whole land, and wherever I turned my eyes there was no Jew, only a whisper as if many voices said, *We are rid of them, rid of them —*"

"And when was a time when the *nokri* did not say *We must be rid of them?* Please, Simon."

"Still I hear it."

"Will others decide that, Simon, when we are such an old, old oak, with roots so deep? Men are never without doubt and fear, but a woman knows, Simon."

"And somewhere," I said, "through it all, was the Roman — that smooth, dark, knowing face of his — the way he smiled, lifting that thin lip of his. Evil —"

"Lentulus Silanus was a man like other men, Simon."

"No — no —"

"Be quiet, my husband, and rest and be easy. There is too much of the past; it weighs too heavy. Be easy . . ."

Her hands stroked me, comforted me as I wanted to be comforted, until presently I sank into that land between sleep and waking, thinking of all the good and honor I had known, and how many had loved me even though I had loved so few.

I thought of my brothers, and it was an old oak, truly, that could send out so firm and mighty a limb as Judas Maccabeus, or Eleazar, or John, or Jonathan. Blessed are they and may they rest in peace, rest easily and in peace. Life is a day and no more, but life is also forever. Soon, soon enough, I, Simon, the least of all my glorious brothers, would go the way they went, but not so soon would it be forgotten in Israel — and among the *nokri* too — that there were five sons of the old man, the Adon Mattathias.

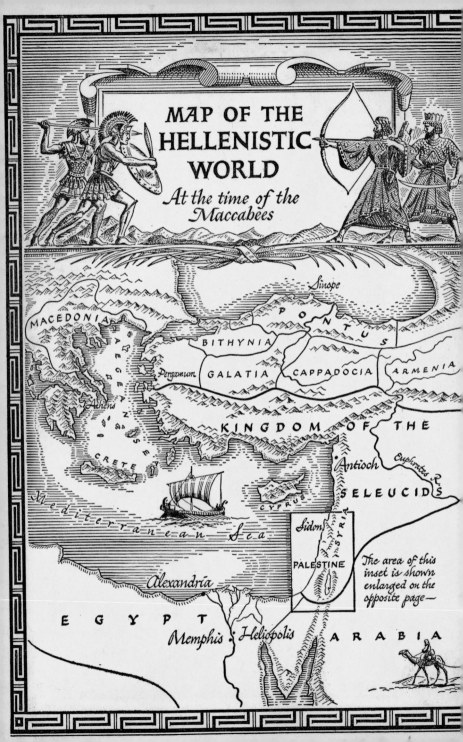